MW01125660

THE THREAT BENEATH

As events unfold in Gothenburg on Sweden's west coast, they prompt national and even regional consequences in faraway Israel and the Gaza Strip

This is the second book in "**The Hart Trilogy**"

Ilya Meyer

Previously by the same author:

Bridges Going Nowhere (2014)

Cover design: Noah Stutzinsky

The Threat Beneath

Text copyright © 2015 Ilya Meyer

All Rights Reserved

This book is dedicated to

Amy

and everyone in your generation.

With my fervent hope that our generation

has given yours a world worth inheriting.

THE THREAT BENEATH

"Literature adds to reality,
it does not simply describe it."
C.S. Lewis

I hope this book succeeds in blurring the
sometimes fine line between reality and fiction
– otherwise I will merely be recording events
and describing reality instead of adding to it.

Ilya Meyer
Modi'in and Gothenburg, spring 2015

Prologue

The nation was in shock.

In the capital, the pre-election findings were absorbed in stunned silence.

The first Islamic Republic outside the Muslim world was well on its way to being born.

Legally.

Democratically.

And surprisingly.

But the emerging trend didn't surprise everyone.

Analysts in Jerusalem had been quietly predicting just this for more than a year now. Not the exact figures, not the full extent of the massive support the vote-counters were set to reveal in the post-election ballot breakdown.

But definitely the trend, certainly the identity of the big winners, the biggest single political party in the nation's political make-up.

And all the indications were that nothing was going to be the same again. Ever.

The government in Jerusalem had been working hard on contingency plans for precisely this eventuality – this virtual certainty. Jerusalem had been so convinced that the political scene would shift, bringing with it massive change not just for Europe but for the rest of the Western world too, that Israeli Prime Minister Tal Nahum had tasked no less than three teams, working in parallel and without any knowledge of each other, to come up with a plan of action.

Unsurprisingly, all three came up with more or less the same plan.

Because as the First Islamic Republic of Sweden was set to emerge on election night Sunday the 20th of September, Jerusalem knew, just knew, that it was going to have a problem with Stockholm.

Rafah, Gaza Strip

Adan Hamati looked out over the ruins of Rafah, the Palestinian Arab city on the southernmost border of the Gaza Strip abutting Egypt's Sinai Desert.

He took in a picture of absolute desolation.

Uprooted trees, bulldozed houses, smashed walls. Nothing but piles of rubble and dead vegetation decaying slowly in the dry sandy heat of the late Gaza summer wherever he looked.

And everywhere a disgusting smell of decomposition, of stomach-heaving, nausea-inducing putrefaction.

"You bastards," he muttered in a low breath, looking carefully around to make sure nobody was within earshot. "You absolute bastards. May your mothers suffer the indignities of whoredom servicing a thousand flea-bitten Jews, may all your sisters be given to our *shahids* in the afterlife. And may your sons all drown in putrid effluent!"

The Zionist Imperialist Entity had waged yet another war on the people of Gaza, with more than 2000 fatalities among the brave martyrs of the Gaza Strip. The 3rd such war in less than 10 years.

In addition to the dead, these latest hostilities had left many families homeless, infrastructure had been damaged, the people were grumbling against their Hamas rulers and even demanding change. Change! The ungrateful wretches. Hamas had staked out the path to glory, leading all the way to the holy city of Al Quds and liberation of the land. The brave warriors of Hamas had succeeded in kidnapping four teenage Zionist settlers and had in fact killed them – there was some justice in this world after all – but unfortunately the Jews had eventually found out the identity of the perpetrators and killed not only them but also some members of their extended families who had tried to prevent the arrest of their loved ones, may the memories of the brave martyrs be a blessing.

"You bastards!" he muttered once again, spitting into the dirt in disgust.

But Adan Hamati's wrath was not directed at the Zionist colonisers, the Jewish occupiers of holy Palestinian land. His animosity was reserved solely for the hated Egyptian enemy who were so near yet so far, just beyond the security fence that cut Rafah in half, one Palestinian and one Egyptian. With a 500 metre broad swathe of levelled land on either side of the security fence to provide an uninterrupted field of vision for the well-armed Egyptian observers. When the damned Jews controlled the territory, even they hadn't done what the accursed Egyptians did: lay waste to homes, orchards and streets and dig deep ditches which they flooded with sewage and excrement. "To keep Palestinian terrorists out of Egypt," according to General Darwishi of the Egyptian Sinai High Command.

There was no longer any easy way in or out of Gaza via Egypt's Sinai Desert. The sewage-filled ditches and flooded smuggling tunnels had already claimed more lives than Adan Hamati cared to remember. They had drowned tunnelers and smugglers in filth and human waste as the underground passageways collapsed under the weight of the flooded ditches criss-crossing the sands above them. So many young Palestinian lives extinguished! Young patriots burning with zeal to carve out an independent state first in Gaza and then in the territory currently occupied by the blaspheming, secular, whisky-slugging and womanising so-called 'leaders' of the corrupt Palestinian Authority of that bastard Mahmud Abbas, who ruled the people from the protection of his Muqata in Ramallah. After Gaza and Ramallah, Allah the Merciful willing, Hamati's plan was to take over Al Quds and the rest of occupied Palestine, currently in the hands of those other sons of pigs and apes, the Jews.

Casting one more look of blazing hatred in the direction of the Egyptian security fence, Adan Hamati turned on his heel and made his way slowly, deliberately toward the nearest outskirts of the still standing parts of Rafah city on the Gaza side of the fence.

Proud Palestinians fenced in like rats. One fence to the east built by the Jews, the other to the south built by the even more hated Egyptians.

Adan Hamati had his plan worked out, and this time there would be no softly-softly approach, no winning of propaganda victories or brownie points in the diplomatic arena.

This time, the world was going to take notice.

Properly.

Because this time, Adan Hamati was not aiming for symbolism but for results. Real, tangible results.

In Al Quds. Which the Jews called Yerushalayim, and the Christians called Jerusalem.

Al Quds. Where the flag of Palestine would fly from atop the Jews' accursed Knesset, Allah willing.

Beer Sheva, Israel

Benny Hart knocked on an unmarked door and opened it without waiting for an answer. "Is this the office of the Human Resources Directorate?" he asked. Pretty pointlessly, since that was precisely what the sign on the door proclaimed in neat white letters on a blue background.

The man sitting behind the wood-and-steel military-issue desk looked up from his computer screen, frowned, stroked his neat moustache with his right hand and gestured, without saying a word, for Benny Hart to sit opposite him.

Benny rolled his eyes in impatience, puckered his lips and sauntered over to the desk, shutting the door quietly – but not quietly enough – behind him. The desk officer looked up, frowned again, and looked back at his screen. Still without saying a word.

'Great!' thought Benny to himself, 'we've gotten off on the wrong foot, and it's not yet nine in the morning. Brilliant, just brilliant. This is going to go really well.'

Benny Hart, a young, blond, blue-eyed, fair-skinned giant of a man, tried valiantly to fold all hundred and ninety-five centimetres of his length into the steel and plastic visitor's chair. Unsuccessfully, as it happened.

As it happened quite often, in fact. The new post-army generation of *sabras*, native-born Israelis in this, the 8th decade following Israel's independence, weren't exactly small of stature. But Benny took size to a whole new level. Literally. People often asked him if the weather differed at his ears and toes. Very funny indeed, the first hundred or so times. A bit boring by the time he'd heard it a thousand times.

'I'd better get my act together if I'm to stand a chance against the crack elite troops of Human Resources,' muttered Benny to himself. 'Looks like I'm in for a second breakfast now – of humble pie.'

He gave up trying to fit neatly into his chair and instead pushed it back to stretch out his legs.

Which was a shame, because the scraping sound of the chair on the tiled stone floor caused his moustachioed nemesis to look up sharply from his computer screen. This time he too sat back in his chair and sized up Benny Hart from his side of the desk.

"You're Officer Hart, Benny? Correct?"

It wasn't really a question, more an order barked out at an underling, awaiting verification.

No point denying the obvious. Benny Hart nodded.

"Is that a 'yes'?" Speak up man!"

Benny looked at the officer behind the neck, wondered fleetingly what it would feel like to kick him in the groin from his seated position at the desk, smiled regretfully at the image of what was not to be and instead answered with a crisp "Yes. That's me."

Moustache Man looked at him. It was clear Benny Hart was not one going to make it into his shortlist of all-time favourite people.

"You're the one who caused all that ruckus in Switzerland a few months ago? Operating outside your remit on foreign soil, where you had no right to be in the first place, and certainly under no orders from Shin Bet to engage in clandestine activity that would embarrass the State of Israel. This," he made a great show of looking down at his computer screen as though to check the name of the man opposite him, "is the Shin Bet, Mr Benny Hart, and we do not, I repeat do NOT, engage in cowboy activities off our own bat. We're a disciplined corps of professionals who follow orders. Your inability to follow orders means I've now got to place you somewhere, and frankly you're a problem I could do without."

Startled at this outburst, Benny Hart blinked at the onslaught for the first few seconds, then sat upright, leaned slowly and deliberately across the desk and looked long and deeply into Mr. Moustache's eyes.

Then he started speaking.

"Sweden, you stupid desk-jockey. I was in Sweden, not Switzerland. Learn to read Hebrew. Or at least learn to read a map. No wonder the Service has problems, it's idiots like you who make dimwits like Yasser Arafat and Jimmy Carter seem like Nobel Prize-winners. Oh wait, they are Nobel Prize-winners…"

Without waiting for a response from his shocked adversary, Benny Hart continued: "And I was perfectly entitled to be in Sweden – I was there on holiday. Not only that, I was not 'engaging in cowboy activities' but assisting the security service of a friendly ally, Sweden, to identify some of the Palestinian Arab terrorists whom you desk-monkeys here should have been monitoring. You failed. Abysmally. That's why they were able to make their way to Sweden and engage in mayhem. The Swedish security service SÄPO were very happy with my assistance. And I provided only advisory and identification assistance, nothing else. Now get off your high horse, give me my new assignment and let's hope it's far from here because you wouldn't want to cross paths with me on a dark night after work hours, you imbecile!"

And with that Benny Hart leaned back in his chair, pulled out his smartphone and started playing a game of online Scrabble with his sister Amira, who was at home in Ashdod, suffering an enforced day off work.

After the sounds of ego-pricked spluttering subsided from across the desk, Benny raised one eyebrow, looked across at Moustachioed Marvel and asked: "Nuuu? Where have I been reassigned? Come on, out with it. Or do I have to reach across the desk and make you talk?"

With his eyes mere pinpoints of black fury, the officer made a show of hitting a number of keys on his keyboard – as though he didn't already have the details at hand! – and pointed to a printer at the other end of the room, from which a number of sheets of paper were emerging.

A nasty little smile was playing across his tight lips.

"Gaza, Boy Wonder. You're going to Gaza. Good luck, hope you have a lovely time. If you like I'll start making the necessary preparations for the return of your body from there – if our Hamas and Islamic Jihad 'partners for peace' actually return your body."

Benny Hart sat still for a moment. Gaza! He hadn't expected to be assigned to Israel's extremely troubled south-western border area. The odds weren't good. Still, he had to admit HR simply had to reassign him away from Judea and Samaria. Following the operation in which he had arrested Palestinian Arab terrorist Haydar Murad and Murad had almost succeeded in killing Benny before being shot by another Shin Bet officer, Benny was now too well known in the area, too blond, too tall, too noticeable, too – well – too Benny.

But seriously, in this day of the Internet, of instant image-sharing and constant access to social media, would reassigning an active Shin Bet officer a few dozen kilometres to the south really make a difference? Whatever the vicious terrorists working for the Palestinian Authority and PLO in Ramallah knew today, their equally vicious Islamist counterparts working for Hamas and Islamic Jihad in Gaza knew tomorrow. He was pretty much being set up to be either killed in action, or resign voluntarily. And all because some jumped-up little Hitler who spent his life sitting behind a desk was bitter at never having made it himself as a field agent but was forced to spend his life in Beer Sheva in the Negev Desert, a hundred kilometres from the nearest civilisation.

Well, that was this idiot's problem, not Benny's. Reverting to type, Benny took stock of the situation and realised that tomorrow would reveal just what was in store for him. Meantime, he had to leave this room before he gave in to the temptation to find out first-hand how much satisfaction was to be had from connecting the hardened toe-cap of his desert boot with the soft squidgy nether regions of his adversary's anatomy.

Benny Hart stood up, grabbed the sheaf of papers, nodded curtly in the direction of the Whiskered Wonder and walked out of the room, taking elaborate care to leave the door wide open as he left.

Benny Hart smiled with serene satisfaction as he heard a snort of exasperation and the sound of a chair scraping across the tiled floor as the HR officer got up to shut the door.

"That's probably more physical action than he's had in a week," muttered Benny to himself as he pulled down his blue-tinted Rudy Project wraparound sunshades from on top of his blond hair, perching them firmly on his nose.

With that he strode through the lobby, past the armed guard at the front door and down the three short stairs out into the blazing sunshine of a typical Beer Sheva late summer morning. In the parking lot outside he got into his white office-issue Hyundai i35 and sped off.

Stockholm, Sweden

Marita Ohlsson sighed, rubbed her temples as unobtrusively as she could and edged her chair away from the conference table.

The world was aflame around them – heavens above, the very streets of Stockholm and Gothenburg and Malmö were aflame around them – but in the corridors of power in Stockholm it was business as usual.

Which meant conferences. Lots of conferences. This was 'the Swedish way'. Confer while Stockholm burns.

For SÄPO, the Swedish Security Service with responsibility for threats both domestic and overseas, the past year had been a hectic one indeed. The more so for Marita Ohlsson whose official position was that of Director General of the Middle East Statistical Analysis Unit, MESAU. Her real job, however, was far less mundane, and it had just one focal point: liaison with the only functioning democracy in the Middle East. And judging by the turn Sweden had taken while everyone was busy looking the other way, soon probably the only democracy in Europe too – Israel.

It had all started off at the end of the previous year, with a low-budget Palestinian Arab terror attack on Gothenburg, Sweden's second-largest city. Low-budget it may have been, but for a few crucial hours a handful of militants had succeeded in shutting down the entire industrial, commercial and traffic infrastructure of the city. It was more luck on the part of the police and error on the part of the terrorists that had saved the day. Well, that and the fact that a couple of Israeli security service agents 'just happened' to be in the area and had lent a crucial and not always very discreet hand in bringing order into the chaos of the Swedish police response.

Marita Ohlsson smiled when she recalled the Israeli agents. Or at least one of them. Benny Hart. They'd worked well together, and after it had all blown over they'd spent some quality time together in Eilat on Israel's Red Sea coast. Some VERY quality time. She smiled again, then quickly straightened her features into a frown of concentration as she peered at the papers in front of her. 'Pull yourself together, girl!' she admonished herself silently. 'You're on the clock now, and this is no time for daydreaming.'

Marita Ohlsson tossed her head to shake away all thoughts of Benny and his charming – and frighteningly capable – sister Amira and dragged her attention back to the droning voice of the presenter, statistical analyst Martin Lindell, who was now pointing to a PowerPoint slide displayed on the huge wall-to-wall screen.

Martin Lindell clicked the remote and a second slide floated onto the screen beside the first one.

"As you can see from the comparative stats and tables, there is a wide – and constantly widening – gap between the claimed countries of origin of many of our asylum-seekers, and their real origins. Three main sources of nationality discrepancy are in particular focus: Syria, Ethiopia and Afghanistan. They are paralleled by Iraq, Somalia and Iran. This means that statistically, there is a surprisingly large percentage of people claiming to come from Syria, Ethiopia and Afghanistan who actually come from Iraq, Somalia and Iran respectively. And our painfully slow process of vetting reveals firstly that we simply do not have the linguistic skills or the financial resources to adequately check them all, and secondly that what we are doing is permitting the establishment a battlefield between Sunni and Shia forces here on our home ground. In Sweden. What we are facing, peeps, is a net increase in infiltration – officially sanctioned. This may all sound a bit academic and bureaucratic, but as you can see here," he played his laser pointer across the screen "the figures, the demographics, the security connotations of inter-Islamist animosities playing out on our home turf right here, are truly frightening."

He paused, and looked around the conference room. "Or at least, they should be. And that's before we even begin to factor in the likely results of the elections this autumn, and the effect they are likely to have on the Islamist portion of our electorate. It's not my job to come up with solutions to the problem, I'm just here to quantify the problem. And as you can all see, it is a massive problem. Any questions?"

There were none. Because nothing of what Martin Lindell had to say came as the least bit of a surprise to the people gathered around the conference table. The meeting was being held at SÄPO headquarters and within these walls at least, if not within Rosenbad, the seat of Swedish government, all this was old news.

SÄPO had been trying for months now to persuade, cajole, convince, even threaten, the well-paid politicians in Rosenbad to deal with the issue decisively, robustly. No luck. In fact, the current Swedish government wouldn't even discuss the issue. Because it was waiting, paralysed, for the next Swedish government to take the reins of state in just a few months. A new Swedish government that was all set to be very unlike anything the nation or indeed Europe had ever seen before.

Which was the second major problem facing SÄPO after the abortive Palestinian Arab attempt to hijack Gothenburg last December: the elections this coming September.

Following several years of unfettered immigration into Sweden from mostly Muslim countries, with several hundred thousand asylum-seekers being given residency in the beautiful Scandinavian country, and despite repeated warnings by SÄPO and indeed the electorate that the Swedish state could not possibly hope to integrate such a large number of people with such totally disparate values in so short a space of time, the Swedish Migration Board finally acknowledged what everyone else already knew: that the

Migration Board had not done its job in the most competent way. In fact, its red-faced Director General admitted in an acutely embarrassing press conference attended by almost a hundred Swedish and overseas reporters, the Board had failed abysmally and must recognise that Sweden was now officially home to many thousands of people whose real identities were totally unverifiable. And they were now officially Swedish citizens, with all the rights that entailed.

But that admission came only a few short weeks before the September national elections. Elections that were set to sweep an Islamist-dominated government into power. The pundits were all in agreement that the coalition of hard-line Islamist parties probably would not be able to muster a full majority in Parliament, but they would definitely be king-makers in the make-up of the next government. They'd side-line traditional coalition partners such as the Conservatives, Social Democrats, Liberals, Christian Democrats and others. Thankfully, fringe fascist parties claiming to support women's rights and environmental issues but in fact merely created to provide a lavish meal-ticket for their well-paid elected representatives, had been kicked into oblivion in the previous election almost four years previously. They were currently balancing precariously around the two percent figure – well below the four percent threshold for entry into parliament.

Sweden now had the rather dubious distinction of being on its way to becoming the first Islamic Republic of Europe.

Democratically.

A democratic process that was being exploited to undermine democracy and dismantle it bit by bit.

Because the expected results were being proudly and openly trumpeted by the Swedish Islamist parties waiting impatiently in the wings.

Accelerated building of mosques and madrassas. The inclusion of Islamic Studies as a compulsory subject in all primary schools. A *blitzkrieg* motion that would be hustled through Riksdagen – the Swedish parliament – requiring churches to show 1000-plus attendance figures or face being converted into mosques. This latter would really hurt, as it was intended to do, because most churches in Sweden simply were not large enough to accommodate 1000 people. But the law was the law, and if these draconian measures became law the Swedish police would be faced with enforcing them in obedience to the nation's new masters in Rosenbad.

The problem facing SÄPO – which of course operated outside the remit of the uniformed branch of law enforcement – was that it was bound to uphold the law, yet felt a burning need to do something substantial before such massive changes could be made to that law.

Changes within the framework of the democracy that was Sweden.

Marita Ohlsson looked at the glum faces around the conference table.

Things were going to get interesting if Sweden was to succeed in throwing off the shackles of Sharia-dominated government control.

She wondered what the nation's chances of success were. Or if indeed there was enough get-up-and-go in the population to bring about a change. Swedes weren't exactly noted for their revolutionary zeal...

Gothenburg, Sweden

They looked at one another, the excitement so tangible they could almost taste it in the air.

Three young men – boys, really – and a girl. Each daring the other to either trash the scheme or give it the thumbs up. And nobody really daring to go first.

It was Aisha Naddi who broke the silence. "Look," she said, "if we keep this to ourselves, if we don't speak to a single other person about it, and I really mean a SINGLE other person, I think it could work. Give me one reason why it wouldn't?" she demanded defiantly.

Zahir Tafesh, Ghalib Ajrour and Amir Assaf all looked at her. None felt able to answer either way.

"Well then, let's go for it. You know it makes sense," said Aisha.

The three young men, all the same age as Aisha and all just out of senior-high school and thus still in their teens – barely – looked at each other and nodded in agreement.

It was Zahir who spoke first. "Look, it's like a gift from Allah. Who'd have thought the Jews would be so stupid as to give us this opportunity, served on a silver platter? Future generations will curse us if we don't seize the chance and make something good come out of it. Forget Mecca, praise be to Facebook, I say!" and they all burst out laughing.

Although Aisha was the outspoken member of the group, and the only girl, it was neither she nor Zahir who set the tone. That honour went to Ghalib Ajrour who, a full head taller than the well-built, constantly muscle-pumping Amir Assaf, was both an imposing sight and a natural leader, with a quick intelligence and an uncanny ability to accurately size up people at first sight.

Like his cousin Amir, Ghalib had a fit physique and was blessed with good looks. Which he had used to good effect on, at last count, at least 25 girls during his school years. Not good Muslim girls like Aisha – they were naturally off-limits. But fair-skinned, blonde and blue-eyed Swedish girls – well, they were always suckers for his dark-eyed, olive-complexioned good looks. Ghalib had left a string of girls with unwanted pregnancies – it was part of his personal *jihad* against the unbelievers, he said, to destroy their honour and then leave them for his male friends to enjoy afterward. The girls would probably go get abortions anyway – no fifteen- or sixteen-year-old girl today would go through with an unwanted pregnancy so for him it was a both a safe and particularly enjoyable way to fight his own personal brand of *jihad*.

Needless to say, Ghalib had a lot of followers among young Arabs of Palestinian descent living in Gothenburg, as well as among many other youngsters from the wider Muslim community. The sexual abuse of young girls was a huge problem in Britain, with the systematic grooming of young white girls by predominantly Muslim men taking on almost epidemic proportions in cities such as Bradford and Rotherham. And true to form the British establishment had reacted by assigning the blame to 'individuals', not their culture, their ethnic background or their religious beliefs. In Sweden, too, the problem was swept under the carpet by a political and media elite uncomfortable with pointing out the common denominator linking the perpetrators. Thus, people like Ghalib could operate in perfect safety in a society unwilling to confront them for fear of being branded 'racists' or 'Islamophobes'.

The phenomenon was so widespread, in fact, that the country's right-wing Sweden Democrats party had gained a huge following among the nation's electorate by training the spotlight on the deliberate grooming of vulnerable young Swedish girls by Muslim men. The problem, however, was that since the age of consent in Sweden was fifteen, among the youngest in the Western world, there was no legal way of tackling the issue unless documented violence was involved, making it a criminal offence. And Ghalib and his compatriots were very careful never to use violence. Why use violence, anyway, when they could rely on good looks and sweet talk for a one-night stand that remarkably often took place not at night but in the morning or afternoon in the communal laundry-room of the block of apartments where the girl lived? And without exception, it was indeed a one-off event, it was a point of honour with Ghalib never to return to the same girl. That, after all, was the whole point – to leave his mark on as many Swedish girls as possible: if he had a say in it, no Swedish man would ever find a girl who hadn't already been 'visited' by a Muslim warrior fighting the good fight in his own way.

The four peered once again at Zahir's smartphone. Yes, the Facebook message was there all right. The President of the Jewish Community of Gothenburg, Anna Berkowitz, was proudly notifying her Facebook friends that the Israeli ambassador to Sweden, Mrs Ronit Gottlieb, would be joining her for dinner at home on the 18th of the month and that she was 'so very excited to be hosting Her Excellency at home'. As before, the immature schoolgirl thrill that was evident in the Jewish Community President's Facebook status brought forth a snort of derision mixed with giggles of incredulity that someone who was apparently important enough to be elected to such an important post by the members of Gothenburg's Jewish community could be so careless about security protocols as to post this in social media. Amir Assaf was one of many Palestinian Arabs who had succeeded in becoming Facebook friends with various Jews and Israelis living in Sweden, not least thanks to the useful expediency of his first and last names. Both were good Muslim Arabic names. But coincidentally, both were also good Jewish Israeli names. Infiltration into Jewish social media sites in Sweden was as easy as, well, as easy as infiltration into Swedish girls, not to put too fine a point on it.

It was Zahir who had studied chemistry at school, and he reckoned he pretty much knew what to do. Only problem was getting the materials.

"That won't be a problem," said Aisha. "You know that Järnia hardware store in the shopping parade near where I live, at Kortedala Torg? During the day all that stuff, fertiliser and what-not, is piled up out back for hours after the morning delivery before they get around to taking it into the fenced-off storage section. If you're quick nobody will even notice it's gone until they do their next inventory."

Nobody disagreed. But it was Amir who suggested having a back-up plan.

"Not so much a back-up plan," he hurriedly explained as Zahir turned slowly to stare at him. He'd ruffled Zahir's feelings, maybe Zahir thought Amir didn't have faith in his abilities with chemicals. "What I mean is, you do your expert scientist bit, but we also set a second device, to catch anyone trying to get out. Or better still, to catch policemen and fire-fighters on their way in."

That brought a round of smiles and Amir breathed a sigh of relief. If this was what it was like to keep together a band of just four revolutionaries, he thought to himself, it must be hell itself to try and bring unity among *shahids*, martyrs, God's warriors, call them what you will, in larger organisations such as Hamas, Islamic jihad, even Hezbollah (may Allah the Righteous strike those accursed Shia dogs with His shoes and burn their moustaches and their wives' moustaches too).

Amir took the floor again. "The problem remains: how do we get into the apartment building? The devil's in the detail. We don't want to attract undue attention getting in."

Ghalib answered for everyone: "We won't attract undue attention. Nobody pays attention to the postman delivering the afternoon mail. Leave it with me."

After a few more minutes of discussion the group of four broke up and each went their separate way. There were no demands on their time now that they had graduated from school this past May, the summer had another six weeks to offer them before the September national elections, and none of the four had been offered a place at a college or university of their choice. A job was out of the question when they could make almost as much money picking up social security and unemployment benefit.

They had enough time to put their plan into action.

Ashdod, Israel

Amira Hart fired off a seven-letter, 83-point word in Scrabble to her brother Benny and sat back, wondering what to do with the rest of her day off. Scrabble with Benny (sounded almost like a *film noir* title, she mused to herself with a little laugh) was about as exciting as watching paint dry, but the poor sap enjoyed locking horns with her over the Internet. He seldom won. At least not when they played in English. When they played in Swedish, however, it was a different matter – Benny's written Swedish was better than his sister's, although not by much. The thing was that he read a lot in Swedish, but didn't have much cause speak the language, whereas she read a lot in English but spoke Swedish almost every day in the course of her work.

Because following last winter's impromptu and highly unofficial Mossad operation in Sweden, Amira Hart's Mossad bosses had moved her from a more or less desk job to a fully active role. Her new sphere of operations was officially titled 'Liaison Officer Northern Europe' but she had just one single task thanks to the fact that she was fluent in Swedish and also had Swedish citizenship and, crucially, a genuine Swedish passport: her job was to monitor the veritable motorway of *jihadis* making their way from Sweden to the rest of Europe, and from both Sweden and the rest of Europe to the borders of – some Israeli security analysts claimed even into – the increasingly beleaguered Jewish State of Israel.

Against that background, what promised to be a new Islamist-flavoured Swedish government, staunchly anti-Israel and increasingly openly anti-Semitic, was going to make Amira Hart's life even more interesting. Norway and Denmark, Sweden's neighbours, were in an uproar over Sweden's open-door policy which allowed anyone claiming to be a Syrian asylum-seeker to get virtually immediate Swedish permanent residency and citizenship. Unvetted...

Amira swiped her forefinger across the tablet and replaced the Scrabble game with the document on which she had been working. "Week off my foot," she snorted to the empty living-room. "I could just as well be at my desk working with a big screen and a proper keyboard." She looked at the wall opposite her, at the framed photograph of herself, her brother Benny, and their parents Sarah and Dov. The corners of her pretty mouth turned down into a wry smile as she recalled the fights she had gotten into on these very streets around their family home when she and her kid brother were growing up. The Crayola Family, the local kids called them. She'd fought them all every time she heard the term, feisty kid that she was, but she had to admit that the local children couldn't have come up with a better, more descriptive name for the Harts. Her mother Sarah was petite, fair, freckled with a fiery shock of unruly red hair framing her face and a pair of piercing green eyes. Born in Scotland of Jewish parents whose ancestors had lived in Scotland for as long as anyone could remember, she had come to Israel for a summer of picking oranges on Kibbutz Yagur before returning to her architectural studies in Edinburgh. At the kibbutz she had met Dov, a Swedish Jew whose parents had originally come from Belarus. Dov was everything his wife was not: huge, once blond but long-since bald, quiet-spoken, but with his skin tanned to a leathery brown complexion from years of conducting seaworthiness tests on the Israel Navy's various cutting-edge surface vessels far out to sea.

After years of failing to conceive, Sarah and Dov had decided to adopt, and the first offer they had was of a little baby girl who had arrived in Israel with her mother after her father perished in the trek from Ethiopia to the Promised Land. The mother died in childbirth, leaving little Amira alone in the world. Not long after adopting the apple of their eye, their beautiful little Amira with her glossy black skin and jet-black hair, Sarah conceived and nine months later gave birth to Benny who, in keeping with the disparate appearances of the other members of his family, looked nothing like any of them: fair-skinned like his mother but with blue eyes and light-blond curls. Amira smiled at the photo once again. Yup, the Harts sure were the Crayola Family, boasting every colour under the sun. For the umpteenth time in her adult life, Amira shrugged away her feeling of guilt over the many fights she had gotten into as a scrappy schoolgirl every time someone had pointed out the obvious. They hadn't meant any harm, after all. As a family the Harts were pretty much rainbow-coloured, it had to be admitted.

But Amira had more pressing problems than regretting her childhood feistiness. Sweden was due for national elections on the 20th of September and the signs weren't good. The Mossad was not concerned with the domestic politics of Sweden or indeed of any other country, except inasmuch as it impacted the lives and security of the State of Israel and its citizens in Israel or overseas. And the signs were that the Swedish elections were going to make waves for Israelis both at home and abroad.

Amira picked up her phone and quick-dialled a number.

She spent the next few minutes pleading with her boss to be allowed to cut short her union-imposed vacation so she could return to work. Something had come up that required urgent attention and she didn't want to wait out the rest of her statutory vacation period to check it out. Yes, it really was urgent. No, she wasn't making it up just so she could get back to work. Yes, it really did require someone with skills in both Swedish and Arabic to examine the electronic chatter. No, she wouldn't make up some other excuse just to stay on at work after that. Yes, she would immediately take the full remainder of her vacation from tomorrow onward.

How wrong she was.

Rafah, Gaza Strip

Adan Hamati no longer saw himself as a political activist trying to fly the Palestinian flag. He had tried the soft approach once before, hoping to inspire the West with the moderation of Palestinian aspirations – just a homeland, *their* homeland without any Jews in it. That's all he wanted. But their careful plan, which had almost worked a year ago in Sweden, had ultimately failed and the world had stayed silent. Even the Swedes, normally such ardent supporters of everything Palestinian and so strongly opposed to everything Israeli and lately even everything Jewish, had failed to show their sympathies. Of course, that was all down to the Swedish Secret Police, who had put a firm lid on his operation and all information about it. What should have been a striking symbolic gesture to focus attention on Palestine had instead been portrayed in the media as a series of technical bridge-construction hitches and slippery road conditions.

It was a debacle, nothing less.

Well, now it was gloves off. Adan Hamati saw himself as a *shahid*, a *jihadist*, a warrior defending his people and re-establishing his homeland at all costs.

The fact was that when he looked at the situation, everything was actually going his way: the world community was siding with the Palestinians, giving them unimaginable sums of money and, even more valuable, giving them unprecedented levels of international diplomatic support. Palestine had even been recognised by several key EU countries, led of course by Palestine's biggest supporter, her biggest per capita financier and her most faithful defender in the media and at UN and EU headquarters: Sweden.

The fly in the ointment was of course Egypt, whose new ruler, that miserable wannabe pharaoh al-Sisi, had declared the Moslem Brotherhood an illegal organisation and had clamped down on the Brotherhood's Gaza comrades, Hamas, declaring them too an illegal terrorist organisation. What a strange state of affairs it was, Hamati mused, that the accursed Shia pigs of Teheran actually supported the Palestinian venture more than the Palestinians' Sunni brothers in Cairo did. But the time for Egypt's punishment would come, he'd make sure of that.

First, however, he had to attend to the Zionist Occupying Force in Palestine. He intended to clear them from the land, from Rosh Hanikra in the north via Tel Aviv in the middle to Eilat in the south. And everything in between.

Hamati has learned his lesson: no more soft tactics; if you wanted results, you created mayhem on an unprecedented scale. Just look at the success of Islamic State in Iraq and Syria. The more brutally the holy Daesh fighters behaved, the more ground they won. Adan Hamati fully understood the reasons for this, even if the West, which was severely impacted by Islamic State, didn't: Firstly, there was the West's craven fear of the bold actions being taken by the holy Islamic State fighters, which the West persisted in terming 'human rights atrocities'. The western world simply didn't have the stomach to tackle such ferocity. And secondly, there was the West's inability to agree on how to tackle the political movement known as Islamism without getting embroiled in an existential war of religions. That was all down to the first five letters of that political movement's name: Islam. Five letters denoting a religion, which shielded its namesake political movement, Islamism, from insight, from criticism, from attack. And all because of those first five letters in the movement's name.

Adan Hamati knew that this weakness of the West was also the strength of the Islamists, among whose ranks he included himself and the entire Palestinian cause – yes, even the ungodly Jew-loving pigs in Ramallah led by Mahmud Abbas. So he intended to fully exploit this weakness and enhance his strength in the holy war that would deliver Al Quds into the hands of Palestine and thus safeguard it for the Palestinian people and for all Islam.

Hamati appreciated that he had come tantalisingly close to success last time. He knew, just knew, that the key to success lay in keeping with a format structured around a tiny band of dedicated Islamists, working off the electronic grid and shielded from both insight and response by working from behind the protection of those five magical first letters of his eight-letter political cause. This time he would succeed. He would provide the plan, Allah would provide the means.

Hamati was ready to show Islamic State that he was not only an able disciple of the strictest interpretation of Islam but also ready to take the reins of leadership in Gaza, ready to join up with his brothers in the *Khalifa* or Islamic Caliphate by way of Al Quds.

Beer Sheva, Israel

Benny Hart shouldered his backpack and closed the door to his now former office behind him.

"Gaza, here I come," he muttered to himself.

He knew this wasn't going to be a pleasant assignment, but it was a vital one. There was no question of him running around the desert in fatigues chasing terrorists, this was more a back-room job monitoring movements, coordinating strategies and responses.

In fact, not even that. Israel's border with the terrorist enclave of Gaza was bristling with electronic surveillance equipment on the ground, underground and up in the air in the form of both unmanned aircraft patrolling the skies and static blimps tethered to the ground.

The task was straightforward enough. If 60-year-old Ahmed in Khan Yunis coughed, Benny had to know about it. If 14-year-old Marwan was late for school on a Tuesday morning, Benny had to know about that too.

Because Israel's border with Gaza was a powder-keg of violence that erupted with predictable regularity whenever Hamas felt the outside world was losing interest in Palestine. It really was as simple as that.

The task of watching every movement in the Strip and of predicting the next Palestinian Arab orgy of shootings, infiltrations, rocket fire, mortar barrages and attempted kidnappings was down to the young men and women – women mostly because of their proven better ability to focus – of the Baz (Hawk) Battalion's ElecOps section.

Benny drove to his new forward base in the dusty town of Ofakim, a mere handful of kilometres east of the Gaza Strip.

It wasn't a bad posting, after all. Ofakim was just sixty-five kilometres from his parents' home in Ashdod. His parents were both in Scotland on holiday, and only his sister Amira would be there. Great, they'd have the place to themselves for the next ten days until Sarah and Dov returned, which meant nine days of doing as they wanted until the morning of their parents' arrival heralded a frantic clean-up campaign. Great, a clean bed at home every night, air-conditioned comfort, decent food, and a drive of fifty minutes to and from work morning and evening.

Life could be worse, he smiled to himself.

Benny would soon find out that he had grossly underestimated what life could throw his way. Or, at least, what Adan Hamati was capable of throwing his way.

Gothenburg, Sweden

Nishtiman Halabjaee had just completed her three-year training course at Solna Police Academy and was now finally a patrol officer in Gothenburg. Born in Sweden of Kurdish parents who had fled Saddam Hussein's brutality back in the 1980s, she was inordinately proud of her Kurdish background and Muslim roots yet firmly acclimatised in the Sweden that she and her parents and three siblings had made their home. Sweden was the country that had rescued her parents from an Iraq that to this day was being torn asunder by religious, sectarian and political strife, conflict inspired by forces well beyond the borders of the nascent Kurdistan. Sweden had given the Halabjaees a safe haven and the Halabjaees in turn had given Sweden four children brought up on an ethos of dedication to education, hard work, a proud refusal to accept social services hand-outs and a determination to only own what they could themselves afford to pay for – no loans, no social security cheques.

Above all, the Halabjaees were immensely proud that Nishtiman, their eldest child and only daughter, had chosen to become a police officer. Although they still held out hope that after she got that out of her system she would follow her parents' advice and go into law. The way they saw it, having served as a policewoman would stand her in good stead when the day dawned that she finally saw reason and left the rough and tumble of street policing to go into the more rarefied, the more academic and, quite frankly, the more respectable, world of law. Still representing the forces of law and order, but in a less hands-on way. Was that too much for a parent to ask?

And there was something else that bothered them: Nishtiman's insistence on her use of the Muslim headscarf. Nishtiman had been brought up to be proud of her religion but was actively discouraged by her parents from attending any of the radicalised mosques that were popping up all over the city and indeed throughout the country. Sweden's Kurds were by and large staunch supporters of an independent Kurdistan and could not understand why the world community would not grant them official recognition, but they were also equally proud of their hard-earned place in Swedish society and of their moderate interpretation of the Muslim faith.

Nishtiman did not burn with religious zeal, but she cast herself as a role model for the country's all too easily disaffected young Muslims. Which is why she wore a traditional Muslim headscarf as part of her police uniform. A signal to Sweden's young generation that Muslim girls should have independent lives of their own and that Muslim boys should uphold the law and work within it.

Nishtiman had encountered more than her fair share of animosity from the public she was sworn to serve. Firstly from died-in-the-wool male Muslim conservatives – seldom Kurds but more often Arabs and Somalis – who felt she was selling out to 'the Swedes' by turning her back on Muslim society and harassing Muslim youngsters. There was nothing Nishtiman could do to get through to them that becoming a police officer did not involve selling out or targeting Muslim youngsters – unless these youngsters were breaking the law. In which case it made absolutely no difference if they were Muslim, Buddhist, Christian, Hindu, Jew or whatever – law-breakers received the attention of the law. End of story.

More trouble, however, came from a strong undercurrent of ultra-conservative native-born Swedes, people to whom the very sight of a veiled Muslim woman brought out all the hatred they had stored up for a religion and a community that they felt steadfastly refused to integrate into Sweden. A police officer was supposed to look like – well, a police officer. Not like someone draped in a curtain that hid her hair and half her face and got in the way when she was supposed to carry out her police duties.

Nishtiman was a dedicated officer whose diligence and calm professionalism had caught the eye of her superiors. With the Swedish police fully embracing the national policy of ethnic diversity in the workplace, Nishtiman was slated to rocket ahead in the ranks of the police force – carried on and up by virtue of her minority ethnicity, minority religion, foreign-sounding name, olive complexion, and female gender. She quite simply ticked all the right boxes in a Sweden fully committed to the biggest social upheaval in modern times: the deliberate exchange of populations in the political echelon's steadfast refusal to back down from its experiment involving mass immigration but zero integration.

It was a good job, then, that Nishtiman Halabjaee fully deserved every encouragement, every support, she received along the way. Because more by happy coincidence than through actual intent and planning, she genuinely was the right person in the right place at the right time.

Nishtiman Halabjaee's usual partner on patrol was Per-Olle Pettersson. Only nobody called him any of that – he was called Pop for short by everyone who knew him – including his wife Linda.

"Right!" said Pop as he and Nishtiman approached their patrol car, a Volvo XC70 D5 AWD in full blue-and-yellow-on-white war-paint. "Shall we toss for it or are you going to claim women's privileges and take the wheel? Again..."

Nishtiman smiled and dangled the car keys in front of Pop. Despite the banter, she and Per-Olle got on really well, both on the job and occasionally even out of uniform. He was married and had three painfully active young children, whereas Nishtiman, eight years his junior at twenty-four, was single and still living at home with her parents in their five-room apartment in Tynnered, western Gothenburg. Until Mr Right came along. She wanted to pick Mr Right herself. Her father concurred but never missed an opportunity to present his daughter with a veritable smorgasbord of what he considered eligible young men. Her mother maintained a strategic silence but gave her daughter quiet encouragement to stake out her own path in life – including in her personal relationships.

Whenever discussions at home got a bit too intense on the future-partner front, Nishtiman took temporary refuge with Pop and Linda. Not overnight stays but long, relaxed dinners at the weekend when the three could just kick back and chat about utterly irrelevant things after the kids were in bed. Bedtime usually meant that Nishtiman had to read two stories each to the two oldest girls with the baby dozing comfortably in her lap while their parents – the slackers! – claimed to be tidying up in the kitchen and living room. The adults' topics of conversation were inspiring quite simply because they were eclectic and unimportant and succeeded so well in taking Nishtiman's mind off the often dark reality she faced when in uniform. The three discussed football (boring), the likely name of the newest young addition to the Royal Family (barely borderline interesting), the likely outcome of the upcoming elections (very interesting indeed), the relative pros and cons of the Volvo XC70 D5 AWD as an urban police car versus the BMW 525d Touring xDrive (REALLY boring).

Linda and Pop were Nishtiman's oasis, it's where she fled to recharge her batteries and get some much-needed grounding in real life and the small everyday triumphs and tribulations of real people making a living and bringing up young children.

Nishtiman tucked a stray hair back under her police-issue head-covering, clutched the car keys even more tightly and said smugly: "If you spent less time in front of the mirror dolling yourself up to meet the public, you'd be at the desk earlier to get the keys. Sucks to be you, doesn't it?"

And with that she blipped the remote, opened the driver's door and got behind the wheel.

Rolling his eyes in mock exasperation Pop opened the front passenger door and got in. This suited him fine. Nishtiman was a way smoother driver than he was, she stood out from most of her colleagues, male and female alike, in that she genuinely seemed to know what the turn indicator was for and actually used it. Every time, no less. He was content to sit up front and watch the world go by.

After booting the on-board videocam, number plate recognition system and other electronic monitoring equipment in the car and briefly testing the lights and siren, Nishtiman set off. Today they would be patrolling Biskopsgården, a high-density residential estate built in the 1960s and set amid beautiful woodlands and granite outcrops. Beautiful landscape back then and today too, but socially the area was woefully depressed. There was constant argument among those in the know about whether this was because there was such a high concentration of foreigners, mostly Muslims, living here, or conversely that there was such a high concentration of mostly Muslims living here because there was nowhere else for them to live – because ethnic Swedes simply tended not to mix very well with new immigrants. The age-old chicken-and-egg question.

Nishtiman guided the patrol car out of the station and headed up Hjalmar Brantingsgatan and out to Biskopsgården.

She looked sideways at Pop. "So, what d'you reckon? Will things quieten down there once school restarts and most of the youngsters are back within a regular timetable, off the streets? I mean, I'm getting fed up having to call for back-up to look after my car so it isn't torched when we respond to a call-out. What a ridiculous waste of police resources – a second car and two officers just to make sure the first car isn't destroyed by bored punks."

Pop looked at her with quiet amusement. "No point getting your hair in a twist! There's nothing you – or I – can do about it, so what's the point of getting all upset? We turn up, we do our job best we can, we get out. The rest is up to the politicians to sort out." And with that he looked out the window as they cruised past row upon row of well-built, well-equipped but boring-looking apartment blocks. Swedes with what they fashionably called a 'social conscience' referred to this area as a 'ghetto'. Per-Olle Pettersson snorted in disdain. Ghetto my foot. In his youth, after his nine-month stint in the military, he had travelled the world. Seen the appalling ghettoes of Calcutta, Rio, Mexico City. Places where life was cheap and untimely death stalked everyone. This was no ghetto! This was just an area where unemployment was rife, where prospects were low, where there was a high proportion of immigrants – most from Muslim countries. It was quite simply an area that native-born Swedes tended neither to visit nor talk about.

This 'ghetto' talk was sheer idiocy, Pop reflected to himself, not for the first time. His own parents had raised him here, on Godvädersgatan just over there on the left, back in the day when he was a toddler in short pants. It was a lovely area, lots of woods where you could climb trees, ponds where you could catch tadpoles in the summer and go ice-skating in the winter, rocky outcrops behind which you could try your first – and his last! – illicit cigarette at the tender age of fourteen. Fair enough, the area had not worn well over the decades but still – this was no ghetto. A ghetto was more a matter of mind-set, of allowing an area to become physically dilapidated and fall into disrepute. That wasn't the case here. Biskopsgården was disadvantaged owing to high immigration, non-existent social integration, and massive unemployment. It was populated by people who in any other circumstances should and would have been bilingual but, owing to the peculiar circumstances that threw them together here in a melting-pot that didn't encourage them to mix together, in fact were merely semi-lingual: the youngsters had a grounding in their mother-tongue from Syria, Iraq, Somalia, Afghanistan, Iran, wherever, and they also got by in the Swedish of their adopted country. But they weren't really entirely proficient in either language. And they weren't entirely at home in either culture.

And that gave rise to frustration. Immense frustration. Not just linguistic but cultural too since language was also the bearer of culture and opened the door to social integration. Only there was precious little social integration going on.

Ah well, not his problem, reflected Pop as he gazed out the car window.

Nishtiman slowed down as they hit the big high-rise estates and they settled into their routine of measured, regular patrols up and down the local roads. 'Showing a presence' is what the top brass called it. 'Sitting aloof and arrogant inside a tin box instead of actually talking to people' is what front-line officers like Nishtiman Halabjaee and Per-Olle Pettersson called it.

It was the regular routine of 'We're here but don't really want to be' of police patrols in an area where the police were regarded with suspicion at the best of times, and where the police actually got in the way when bigger plans were afoot.

Elsewhere in Gothenburg, more specifically in her fourth-floor apartment in the newly fashionable Haga area, Anna Berkowitz, President of the Jewish Community of Gothenburg, smiled contentedly at her reflection as she passed by her hallway mirror.

"Two more days," she smirked to her husband Isaac. "Just imagine! The day after tomorrow we'll be hosting the Israeli ambassador and her husband! What's the correct title for addressing her, I wonder," she twittered on contentedly as she busied herself with preparations for her big day.

Isaac Berkowitz looked at his wife, shook his head in despair and glanced back at his laptop screen. His wife had never given him an easy life during their twenty-three childless years of marriage, renowned as she was for having strong opinions but very little common sense. But this really, truly, took the cream cookie.

The message stared him straight in the face. He was, after all, one of her Facebook 'friends'. Sometimes – increasingly often, in fact – he wondered if indeed he was friends with his wife Anna on any level at all.

Especially now. This wasn't just embarrassing, it wasn't just school-girlishly immature. All that sort of thing he'd grown accustomed to over the years. Her self-centredness, her wheedling until she got what she wanted, her utter disregard for anyone who didn't see things her way. She never felt that she owed anyone an explanation – she reckoned she knew what was right and acted accordingly. Irrespective of how badly the results turned out. She'd succeeded in losing them a lot of friends over the years, she'd alienated a sizable portion of the Gothenburg Jewish Community's membership. But she got her name in the papers and on TV. And that was what mattered. To Anna Berkowitz.

That was her to a 'T'. Saying whatever put her squarely in the media spotlight was what she did best.

But this: this wasn't just regrettable. This was potentially dangerous.

And Isaac Berkowitz didn't know whether to risk yet another unpleasant and ultimately pointless blow-up with his wife – because she just wouldn't listen no matter he said – or whether to hold his tongue and hope that with the grace of God his unease would prove unfounded and that the next two days would pass by uneventfully.

After all, there was nobody to whom he could turn with his concerns. I mean, how could you say you were worried just because your wife had publicised on Facebook that she was throwing a dinner party? Albeit a dinner party that specified the exact date, time and location of the Israeli ambassador's whereabouts in a private apartment that was the very epitome of a soft target for potential terrorists.

Stockholm, Sweden

As the 20th of September approached, all the polls indicated that most votes would go to a coalition of softly-softly and hard-line Islamist parties that had come together under the banner of 'Islamist Republic of Sweden', IROS for short. The Swedish Church, led by an Archbishop who saw herself as more social worker and aspiring politician than leader of her ever-dwindling Christian flock, was outspoken in favour of this new trend. "There's nothing wrong with progress," she sermonised to her steadily diminishing congregants. "If many, perhaps even most, Swedes feel warmly embraced by Islam then there is no reason for the Church to maintain its imaginary monopoly on the souls of the Swedish population. When the people speak via the ballot-box on the 20th of September, they will find that the Church – their Church – wholly backs whoever wins the election. Churches come and go, the importance of one religion over another is a manmade construct and we want no part of such divisiveness. Islam is a welcome contributor to the new Sweden."

Multinational corporations with operations in Sweden reacted by selling off facilities, Swedish banks started moving their assets offshore, and the more well-off Swedes – including a remarkably high percentage of politicians – responded by snapping up second homes in Britain, Spain, Portugal, Israel, Cyprus, Crete, Australia and Canada. The Vatican, meanwhile, avoided addressing the issue, and the

Archbishop of Canterbury mumbled something about how right it is to respect other faiths and that it was important to respect Islam specifically so that Muslims would respect Christians when they came to power in Europe.

And in the meantime, the often internally bickering but largely united IROS in Sweden went from strength to strength.

IROS was made up of three smaller parties that had banded together to surge jointly into the Riksdag or Swedish parliament and on into Rosenbad, the seat of government. There was the relatively moderate, Sunni-dominated Sunnasweden party, the Shia-controlled Democratic Islam and the IS-affiliated and therefore Sunni-controlled Mansur.

Nominally in close competition with each other – and in various parts of the Middle East actually engaging in all-out war to annihilate each other – this unlikely conglomerate had banded together for the 'greater good', putting aside all their differences to deliver Sweden into the fast-expanding *Khalifa* or Islamic Caliphate. Sweden would be the first European and Western country to fall, with the far smaller populations of Norway and Denmark, located to the south and west of Sweden, ripe for picking later, once the Swedish Islamist wedge was driven between them.

The first item on the agenda, the very first policy statement by the government-in-waiting of the new Islamic Republic of

Sweden once it formally took the reins of power, related to the 'liberation of Jerusalem from the unbelievers'.

One election previously – just four years ago but it seemed like ages ago – the Social Democrat-led coalition government of Sweden had taken the bold step of recognising Palestine as a sovereign state. Albeit a state without borders, without a currency (it used the Israeli shekel), no foreign policy (apart from the destruction of Israel), no capital (except the one it wanted to take from the Jews, Jerusalem).

Still, that move had opened the floodgates. Additional European Union and other Western countries followed suit, recognising Palestine despite Israel's protests that no peace had been achieved or indeed ever been discussed.

While the EU shed crocodile tears over the peace talks it had deliberately torpedoed, while the UN scheduled debates and issued condemnations of the Jewish state (and only the Jewish state – the UN apparently regarded this as a conflict involving just one party), while the new über-Democratic US administration chided Israel over the kitchen extensions of some Jerusalemites and at the same time ignored the increasing mayhem on Jerusalem's streets as Arab citizens used their cars and trucks to mow down innocent Jewish passers-by, the people of Israel finally, after decades of harsh political infighting, began to see the writing on the wall: that there was no time, place or effort to waste on party-political bickering, because the Jewish state was facing a two-pronged existential threat.

The first was from within the EU as a bloc, because the EU was Israel's largest single trading partner, and the second was in the form of the ever more strident military posturing by Sweden and other belligerent Western states increasingly falling under the Islamist sway.

All this before Jerusalem even began to contend with the creation of the other new Sunni Islamic entities being established right on Israel's borders: in Gaza, in Judea & Samaria, in Syria and increasingly in Jordan. Inspired by Boko Haram, al Shabab, Islamic State, al Qaeda and others.

And as though this were not enough, all this still didn't take into account that other massive existential threat to the state of Israel: the Shia Islamic Iranian proxy, Hezbollah, which had taken over an entire country, the once-beautiful, now thrice-destroyed state of Lebanon, and was now strengthening its hold on various parts of the fast-crumbling Syria.

The stage was set for a summer of turbulence. Mostly focused on Israel, but much of it originating from Sweden.

Gothenburg, Sweden

Aisha Naddi, Zahir Tafesh, Ghalib Ajrour and Amir Assaf surveyed their little home-made armoury.

Zahir Tafesh explained how it would work.

"I've been inside the building. We ignore the lift shaft because once there is a fire or explosion nobody will use the lift – that's the ABC of emergency evacuation procedures and everyone knows that. The secondary device is these three canisters of camping gas and the old oil-soaked clothes in those plastic sacks there. I've doused them in petrol so they'll burn well, but I've also soaked them in plenty of used cooking oil from my grandmother's kitchen and thrown in some old plastic-sheathed electric cables – that mixture will produce a lot of thick, black, acrid smoke to make the stairwell seem dangerous and impenetrable to anyone who doesn't know this is only a smokescreen – until the gas canisters explode when it really will become dangerous to be in the stairwell. Any police attempting to come to the rescue will see the fire and smell the black smoke belching upwards and be trapped in the stairwell below the target apartment. The ambassador and his SÄPO gorillas, meanwhile, will be trapped above it."

Zahir sat back, smiling broadly. "What? No questions? You know it's your job to position this properly so we can light this up Aisha, right?"

Aisha Naddi nodded. "Yup. I've got two disposable cigarette lighters and also a couple of matchboxes as backup. I'll leave them all beside the sacks for your use on my way out. No problems. We're in the second-floor apartment, keeping that old couple gagged and tied up until we're ready. Once the ambassador is inside the building I take the lift down to the first floor, position it all as agreed and then walk downstairs and exit from the front door, leaving the chain and lock on the floor just inside the main door for you. Then I go to the van and wait."

Zahir nodded. "Right. Ghalib, you've got the job of getting us into the building in the first place. You got the code from the mailman?"

"Chill out," replied Ghalib Ajrour. "Of course I've got it. And she's a mailwoman, not a mailman. A hottie too, I got her phone number."

Aisha snorted derisively but said nothing, staring pointedly out the window.

Ghalib continued. "We walk into the building, all four of us together. We wait for the ambassador bitch to arrive, give her and her bodyguards half an hour to settle down and drink some Christian blood or whatever the bastard Jews do when we're not looking, then we get to work. Aisha first and then us."

Amir Assaf looked at the other three and recited from memory: "As soon as we enter the apartment of the oldies we pack the four 20-litre sacks and their chemical primer around the main bearing wall that encloses the fridge and freezer units. Then when Aisha goes down and we see her walking to the van, Zahir sets off the fuse. Meantime I check once again that the two pensioners are secure and can't get out to raise the alarm." He winced. "I mean, do we really have to …"

Ghalib cut him short. "Look you numbskull, we've been through this a hundred times before. You can't make an omelette without breaking eggs. These two are our eggs. If only they had the sense to be somewhere else on that day their lives wouldn't be in danger, but if they're at home this is the only way to do it. It's a small sacrifice for *jihad*. Even non-Muslims can be *shahids*. I appoint them honorary *shahids* in our cause. Not sure if the old boy will manage his 72 virgins, however." He grinned widely at his own joke.

Aisha's mouth turned down in distaste.

Amir took over. "We get their front door keys and lock them into their apartment, walking down the stairs. We turn on the gas canisters and set fire to the sacks Aisha has left in place, make sure it's all burning well, then walk quickly – but without running – to the front door. Zahir and I walk out, chatting and laughing like we're sharing a joke as we go past the SÄPO bodyguard in the car outside. We go to the van, get in and drive off. That's us done."

Ghalib, his eyes glistening in anticipation, took up the narrative, one they had rehearsed countless times over the past few days. "As soon as you're out of sight on the way to the van, I also exit the main door, picking up the chain and looping and padlocking it between the grab-handles on the outside to prevent anyone from opening the door from inside or out. Then I walk to the van and off we go. We don't stay to watch, we'll see it all on TV in the evening. I drive home so I can get the van back to my uncle's grocery store, dropping you lot off near home so you can walk home singly. Any questions?"

There were none. Each knew their role by heart.

The plan was so simple, with so few components, it couldn't possibly go wrong. And it was going to succeed because they were just four youngsters on nobody's radar – not uniformed police, not SÄPO, heck they weren't even old enough to have gotten their first parking ticket. And they hadn't made any use of mobile phones or email or Facebook messages to contact each other while all this was in the planning. They were quite simply electronically invisible.

They were going to create history. A Zionist imperialist ambassador would be taken out of circulation. And they would lie low until after the Swedish elections on September 20th. After that, when IROS took over control of the country, they would come out into the open and receive the adulation of a new Sweden that had an all-new agenda.

It all came down to Ghalib Ajrour making his way past the SÄPO car as nonchalantly as he could and getting to the van without drawing the bodyguard's attention.

Stockholm, Sweden

In the heart of Stockholm's diplomat quarter, Israeli ambassador to Sweden Mrs Ronit Gottlieb and her husband Dan picked up their packed luggage and walked to the door of the Israeli ambassador's official residence. There they were greeted by two Swedish bodyguards, SÄPO close-protection experts belonging to the Special Diplomatic Protection Unit or SDPU.

Isabella Kronlind had served in the Unit for three years now. Tall at one metre eighty-two and with a strong yet not overly muscular physique, she wore her auburn hair in a tightly drawn-back ponytail and was dressed in her usual informal uniform of black trousers, white T-shirt and lightweight Kevlar navy-blue bulletproof vest tailored to look at first glance like a casual sweater, with a black blazer to round off the ensemble. As usual she was wearing a pair of stout yet soft Danish-made black Ecco casual shoes. Great for grip, very lightweight, superbly comfortable heels, perfect for standing around all day. And for running. Nobody apart from her husband Paul knew that she actually had four pairs of identical Ecco footwear – she couldn't possibly wear the same shoes day in and day out while on the job.

Her partner on today's protection detail was one of her favourite workmates at the SDPU. Henrik Winqvist, whom she called "Shorty" because he was almost a whole centimetre shorter than she was, was good-humoured, calm under fire, sharp-eyed and in their down-time always full of spicy stories about his latest conquests. Not girls – his girlfriend Marie, herself a black belt in Brazilian jiu-jitsu, would have made mincemeat of him if he dared fool around. No, his tales of conquest were always about how he had succeeded in acquiring some unbelievably boring postage stamp from some unheard-of country, beating other collectors to the prize. Every time he launched into his stories of the secrecy and cloak-and-dagger tactics he had employed to keep his rivals out of the loop while he closed in for the kill on a tiny piece of paper most people wouldn't look at twice, Isabella shook her head in wonder that someone so handsome, so vital, so full of life and always on the lookout for a good time together with Marie and their friends, could have such an unbelievably boring hobby.

Ah well, it took all types.

Right now there was thankfully no time for tales of derring-do about the philatelic underworld. Today Isabella Kronlind and Henrik Winqvist were going to escort Israeli ambassador Mrs Ronit Gottlieb and her husband Dan from Stockholm to Gothenburg, a journey of 550 kilometres door to door. The ambassador was going to attend a major fund-raising event at the Radisson Blu Hotel in the heart of Gothenburg on the Saturday night, with a few private social engagements thrown in on Thursday and Friday evenings, including a visit to Gothenburg's beautiful old synagogue on Östra Larmgatan. Ronit Gottlieb was not a particularly religious woman, although her husband Dan came from what was once a traditionally religious Jewish family, but she always enjoyed the quiet, the peace of the short Friday night service in particular, wherever in the world she happened to be. It was balm for the soul, drawing to a close yet another hectic week and heralding what the sages always said should be a night and a day – the Sabbath – given over to introspection, celebration and study for mankind's better future.

"Hi Bella," Ronit Gottlieb smiled at Isabella Kronlind. "Looking great as usual. One day you're going to have to give me the secret to managing your weight and still eating all you want. I'm going to worm your secret out of you yet before we leave Sweden!"

Isabella Kronlind smiled back. It was their usual banter. The ambassador was herself a fine specimen of a human being bearing in mind she was nearing retirement age and this was set to be her last overseas appointment before returning to Jerusalem and taking her obligatory pension at age 65.

"Mrs Ambassador, it's no secret. Just get out of bed at 5.30 am, work out in the gym for 40 minutes, go for a 10 kilometre run and give yourself 10 minutes of quality time in the sauna before starting your workday. Easy as eating cake. Only, avoid the cake…"

"Bella, you've still got me wrong. I want the flat stomach and the abs, but without all the effort. Get back to me when you've got something sensible to say to me. Right," she looked round at her husband Dan, who was being regaled with the lowdown on Henrik Winqvist's latest acquisition, a triangular stamp from Nepal dating back to the 1940s and which was a 'real steal' at just 3000 kronor plus two duplicate Georgian stamps dating from 2001. Dan already had a glazed look in his eyes. And it was just 9 o'clock in the morning.

Isabella Kronlind spoke quietly into her cuff mike, put her hand on the door knob and opened the door, walking out onto the landing and punching the elevator call button. Nodding the all-clear to Henrik Winqvist who brought up the rear, the four of them waited by the elevator, smiling a quick hello to the security guard stationed outside the apartment's front door.

After the elevator deposited them on the ground floor, Isabella led the way outside, waited for the other three to catch up, spoke once more into her cuff mike and then pulled the door smartly open. She stepped out quickly and shut the door behind her. Scanning first one way and then the other, she looked down at the bottom of the five granite steps leading from the building to the road, where a black Volvo S80 was parked, its engine idling lazily. Behind it was a second, identical, black Volvo S80 and in front of the two was a marked police car, a Volkswagen Passat Station Wagon. Now that Sweden's second automaker Saab no longer existed, the nation's fleet of ageing police Saabs was being gradually phased out, those wonderful police workhorses replaced by a variety of German brands. Volkswagen because of their lower price, but BMW too because of their greater power. And of course the police drivers simply loved the good old-fashioned rear-drive BMWs rather than the boringly safe front-drive Passats. Boys will be boys, even when they were adults and in uniform. But the Police Purchasing Board had gone one better: all police vehicles would from now on be four-wheel drive, for their greater versatility. Many tears were shed by the boys in blue, who felt their favourite toy was being snatched away from them.

The driver of the lead Volvo got out of the car, walked around to the passenger side and opened the rear door. Ronit and Dan Gottlieb were hustled quickly into the armoured cocoon of the lead S80 and its driver went to the front passenger door of the second Volvo, whose driver had kept its engine running all the while. Henrik Winqvist took the wheel of the ambassador's car and Isabella Kronlind took the front passenger seat.

The three-car convoy set off for the train station. Driving 550 kilometres was tedious and involved an unnecessary number of personnel. The high-speed train was secure, comfortable and quick, taking less than three hours to cover the distance.

Ofakim, Israel

"Not again, surely!" Benny Hart looked up from the data streaming across his computer screen. It surely couldn't be. This looked like a repeat of the last time around.

Or was it?

Ofakim was a small town in Israel's northern Negev Desert. It was surrounded by a number of scattered small towns and villages as well as dozens of *kibbutzim* and *moshavim* – the former communal farms where everything, from clothing to footwear to the members' houses, was owned by the collective, and the latter where everything was owned privately apart from major capital items such as tractors, combine harvesters and so on.

Kibbutzim as a phenomenon had been in decline over the past decade or two. Not that they were closing down or being abandoned, they were simply metamorphosing into something new, something more akin to a cross between a *moshav* and a gated community or country club. Everyone still lived in their same homes and did the same jobs as before, but now private ownership was not only allowed, it was actually required. Today people got a salary for the job they did, instead of as before just working and drawing an allowance from the public kitty, an allowance that was the same for everyone. Those days were gone. Today, the more you worked, the more you earned. But you still got to live in your lovely house in clean, quiet, rural surroundings.

It was a good change because the nation's all-important agricultural and industrial work continued unabated in these somewhat more remote parts of the country.

What was not so good was that with the increasing personal affluence of kibbutz members, there was a corresponding increase in the rate of theft of their belongings.

And right now, it seemed, vehicles were in vogue. Not agricultural implements such as tractors and motorised ploughs, but cars, vans and light pick-up trucks.

Benny Hart chewed his lower lip in concentration and peered at the screen again.

Fact was fact. Thefts had occurred. But did this constitute a trend?

Something like this had happened before. About a year ago. Back then it was a desk constable in the northern coastal city of Netanya who had made the connection. Back then it wasn't vehicles but wallets. Yet not even wallets, not all their contents in the form of credit cards and debit cards. Just cash. That nationwide spate of thefts had fuelled a major terrorist operation overseas, in Sweden.

But there were no reports of unusual numbers of such thefts this time around. Just vehicles.

Or was Benny Hart imagining things?

It was not unknown for bored Israeli schoolchildren to steal cars and go for joyrides – and kibbutz children weren't immune to boredom. But this recent spate just didn't seem to fit the pattern. Not least because on the farms themselves, kibbutz children as young as 13 and 14 got to drive tractors and even light pickups to their hearts' content as part of their regular after-school and summer vacation work schedule. Most kibbutzim even owned several all-wheel-drive off-roaders for farm work; small, nimble four-wheeled motorcycles, really, that could do some pretty heavy agricultural work. So kibbutz kids usually had ready access to all the four-wheeled fun they wanted. Joyriding stolen kibbutz vehicles simply didn't make sense, even though Benny Hart was the first to acknowledge that over the years there had been several recorded cases of kibbutz children taking vehicles off the farm for longer-distance trips – strictly against both kibbutz rules and the law of the land.

But there was another sector that was partial to the theft of motor vehicles, over and above the casual 'take-and-leave' of irresponsible kibbutz youngsters.

Some Bedouin Arabs of the Negev seemed to observe a rather loose interpretation of the law of possession. Taking someone else's possessions – particularly those of the Jews – was OK. So long as you weren't caught. It was only theft if you were caught. If you weren't caught, then it was merely a strategic rearrangement of custodianship.

The *kibbutzim* and *moshavim* of southern Israel, in particular, had grown accustomed to and generally turned a blind eye towards a low, steady trickle of theft. Harvests, implements, fencing (sold for their scrap metal value), cattle and horses even, had a habit of disappearing. But always at a more or less manageable rate.

Not vehicles.

Further north, in the villages, towns and cities along the Green Line that separated the disputed Jewish provinces of Judea and Samaria from the rest of Israel, car thefts were a common problem and sometimes took on epidemic proportions. Arabs from the Palestinian Authority area would enter Israel, either legally or illegally, steal vehicles and then drive them into PA-controlled territory where they would be speedily taken apart, dismantled down to their smallest component parts for resale as 'second-hand spares'. Car insurance premiums were higher in these areas just for this reason. And the police both in Israel and the area run by the Palestinian Authority undertook routine operations to stamp out this scourge, including with the use of electronically tagged bait cars so they could be followed all the way to the chop-shops where stolen vehicles were dismantled for recycling as spare parts.

Sometimes the police operations succeeded, more often they didn't. Of course car theft was nothing unusual, most of the western world suffered from the problem of cars being stolen, often to order.

The police learned quickly to look for patterns. Particular makes, particular models, sometimes even particular colours. There had even been one epidemic a number of years ago in which every second car that was stolen seemed to be a white Subaru, because back then the most popular import in Israel was Subaru, and the most common colour was white. The second-hand market was awash with used body panels in that one colour.

Although car theft was certainly not part of Benny Hart's remit, anything that had a possible link to illegal and/or terrorist activity along the Gaza seam line was. Because in this volatile area, what may seem like just regular criminal activity could also have a security aspect.

So he did what his uniformed colleagues did when faced with a spate of car thefts: he looked for a pattern.

And didn't find one.

Or rather, he did, but it was only a pattern because it wasn't.

Which was a kind of pattern in its own right.

All the vehicles that had been stolen in recent weeks from the local towns, villages and farms were relatively old. Nothing newer than ten years old.

Was that because newer cars with their electronic wizardry were more difficult to steal? Or because of some other reason?

Benny Hart leaned forward and reached for the phone. He needed to find out if there had been any other types of unusual activity in recent weeks along the Gaza Strip seam line.

Al Fukhkhari, Gaza Strip

Adan Hamati put down his binoculars, tore his eyes away from the scene in front of him and surveyed his immediate surroundings.

He already knew the lie of the land beyond the security barrier ahead of him. "Thank you Google Maps!" he muttered fervently to himself.

The Americans and their allies were truly idiots. Anything just to make a fast buck. Back in the bad old days before the Internet, none of what he was planning would have been even remotely possible. But the Americans had come up with a fantastic military tool, something called the Internet that allowed them instant access to any kind of information the world over. And instead of keeping it to themselves for military purposes, some bright spark realised he could become a millionaire and – hey presto! – everyone and their pet donkey now had access to the same advanced tool that the imperialists had.

True, the Zionists had it. But then so too did ISIS, al Qaeda, Hamas, Hezbollah, al Shabbab, Boko Haram, Islamic Jihad.

And Adan Hamati.

Today, it was extremely difficult to keep things secret.

The point was to exploit the openness, the availability, of the Internet, to use the easy penetration it invited, while at the same time concealing your own footprint.

It was difficult, but it was possible.

And the sharpest tool in that toolbox, in keeping things secret, was size.

Because it turned out that in the digital age, size really did matter.

But not the way most people believed.

Because smaller was better. The fewer people involved, the better. The less time you spent online, the better your chances of working undetected.

The Internet was a marvellous tool for law enforcement, uniformed police and various clandestine security services alike.

But the downside was that the more a society relied on digital tools for keeping things running, the more vulnerable it was.

Not least because anyone who didn't figure on the Internet, usually didn't leave behind a trace.

And therefore didn't exist.

It was a situation that suited Adan Hamati perfectly.

"Sderot!" he grumbled to himself, referring to the small Israeli town just off the northern edge of the Gaza Strip that had taken a battering from Gaza rockets and mortars in recent years. "That's all the media talk about. Like the Jews are the only people suffering! What about the hundreds of Palestinian martyrs from the Zionist occupiers' attacks against our children? Nobody talks about that!"

There was nobody to hear Adan Hamati rage silently to himself. And what he was raging about wasn't strictly true, because even blatantly biased BBC and CNN reporters knew they were an eager and willing part of the slick pro-Palestinian propaganda machine. They seldom, if ever, reported on Hamas and Islamic Jihad attacks against the Israeli town of Sderot, so tantalisingly close to the Gaza enclave yet so far away owing to the security fence. And the foreign news media always, almost without exception, did an excellent job of giving massive coverage to injuries and fatalities among Palestinian Arabs that could be blamed on Israel. This naturally included Israeli air and artillery strikes against *jihadi* terrorist operations, but also what were euphemistically labelled 'work-accidents' in which Arab terrorists accidentally blew themselves up while making or transporting bombs for use against Jews.

So Hamati's rage was not entirely justified, although even a quick glance at the discrepancy between the standard of living in the hemmed-in Gaza Strip and the flourishing open areas of Israel beyond the security fence highlighted the frustration most Gazans felt at their situation.

"They can keep focusing on Sderot, they can keep piling in all their resources there. I have a different surprise for them, the bastards!" exclaimed Adan Hamati as he took up his binoculars once again to survey the enemy territory beyond the fence.

He panned slowly from left to right – north to south – taking in any changes there might have been since last he had been here, just two days previously.

Nothing new.

Apart from the tall blond man in civvies standing on the roof of a dusty, rather battered Israeli army Land Rover Defender. He was glued to a pair of binoculars and was looking through the fence into the Gaza Strip.

That was odd. Because like virtually everywhere else along the border, this section was rife with Hamas snipers. Why would an Israeli take the risk of showing himself so openly, so relatively close to the border?

It was out of the question for Adan Hamati to take a shot at him, because that would reveal his own position and he would be killed in the resulting exchange of fire. In the good old days he would have given a signal to his compatriots to fire on the Jew from a totally different angle as he made good his own escape. But the very nature of this operation meant that Adan Hamati had no compatriots on whom to call for assistance.

Not yet.

As he slithered back down the sandy rampart behind which he had been crouching, Hamati was conscious that something niggled him about what he had just seen. Either the man or the vehicle on which he was standing had triggered a memory. Vague, indefinable. But there was something there that was reaching out long tentacles to sift through the archives of his mind. He paused on his way back down, pondering, recalling. Nope, nothing. He shrugged and continued crawling back down the sandy hill until he was well below the line of vision of the tall blond man standing on top of the army Land Rover.

And that's when he remembered.

Gothenburg, Sweden

The engine cut out and all was silent, save for the quiet ticking of the hot exhaust system as it cooled down in the rainy weather.

The three youngsters sitting in cab of the van looked at each other. They said nothing.

Then they heard the impatient banging on the wall of the cargo section behind them.

Aisha Naddi did not appreciate being put in the back of the van while the three guys rode up front in the comfort of proper seats. And heating. She on the other hand was freezing in the back of the van, and almost asphyxiated by the overpowering smell of petrol, used cooking oil and other chemicals in the sacks that Zahir Tafesh had carefully prepared.

"Let me out of here you idiots!" her muffled voice came from the van's cargo area as she thumped on the steel dividing wall.

Zahir Tafesh, Ghalib Ajrour and Amir Assaf looked at each other, smiled at their success in putting the girl in her place, and got out of the cab. Aisha was going to have to learn to cope. The Sweden of her birth was going to disappear. She was going to have to get used to the new Sweden, where women would learn to keep their mouths shut and do what they were supposed to do. And that usually involved providing services of a more horizontal nature.

But there was no point in making an issue of it now, that time would come. Soon.

They walked to the back of the van and Ghalib Ajrour opened the door. Aisha could of course have opened it from the inside, only she wasn't strong enough to work the stiff latch. More evidence, if any were needed, that women needed to realise their limitations – do what they were told and leave the rest to the men.

They'd been through the plans so many times there was no need to speak. Each quickly and smoothly slipped into their allotted role and started moving.

Ghalib Ajrour and Amir Assaf each carefully shouldered two sacks of chemicals, thoroughly wrapped up in large, stout black plastic bin-liners, and made their way to the main door of the apartment building. Zahir Tafesh carried the black sacks containing the old clothing doused in petrol and oil, the lighters and associated paraphernalia. Aisha Naddi brought up the rear with a backpack containing several rolls of ultra-strong gaffer tape, rope, assorted tools, hooks and a small battery-powered drill in case it was needed.

With the cargo area empty and the van's rear door shut but not locked, Aisha went back to the cab, opened the driver's door and placed the ignition key on the floor under the rubber mat as agreed.

The four teenagers walked to the main entrance of the apartment building.

Gothenburg, Sweden

As always, SÄPO conducted an advance security analysis of the addresses that the Israeli ambassador would be visiting while on her visit to Gothenburg. The hotel venue was fine, it had been used before and all the serving staff and kitchen personnel had undergone background checks and both uniformed and plain-clothes officers would be placed around and inside the building.

The synagogue was also fine. The security service had plenty of previous experience in securing the synagogue and that operation swung into action with well-oiled precision.

The private address in downtown Haga, however, was a different matter. There were no established security protocols for this particular venue.

Five days before the ambassador's visit, Mats Knudsson of SÄPO's Gothenburg office phoned and made an appointment with Anna Berkowitz and her husband Isaac. Just routine, he assured them. They wanted to get a feel of the place ahead of the ambassador's visit so they would know what to expect.

Anna Berkowitz felt inordinately proud. Not only would she play host to the Israeli ambassador and her husband, now she was being visited by SÄPO! So exciting! It was almost like being in a James Bond movie! She simply had to tell her friends, they would doubtless be really envious of all the attention she was receiving.

Mats Knudsson and his extremely taciturn colleague Alexander Sandström turned up exactly on time. Introduced themselves. In Alexander Sandström's case with a curt nod of the head as he looked around the little hallway of the Berkowitz apartment.

Mats Knudsson put his hosts at ease. Yes, he would love a cup of coffee while he went through the details. His colleague would look around the apartment if that was all right with Anna and Isaac.

It was.

Mats Knudsson explained.

"Thank you for making time to see us. We've been notified that the Israeli ambassador Mrs Ronit Gottlieb and her husband will be visiting you on Thursday evening for dinner. This is just a routine visit so we can see for ourselves what your apartment looks like and work out whether there are any details we need to take into consideration."

This was a SÄPO euphemism for checking out what exactly the potential weak points were, possible points of penetration by terrorists, the location of a temporary safe room if one was viable, an emergency evacuation route should this be necessary, and all additional conventional points of entry into the premises, that is to say windows, doors and balconies.

Anna Berkowitz smiled. This was delicious! This was the stuff of thrillers and spy movies! Her husband Isaac looked at the light shining in her eyes and his mouth curled in distaste. What had he ever seen in her? She had about as much intelligence as a bag of damp cotton-wool, and about as much personality too, for that matter. He had no intention of disrupting her reign as President of the Jewish Community of Gothenburg, but once her current term was up next year, whether or not she intended to campaign for re-election, he was going to file for divorce. He'd earned a life of his own after so many years of putting up with her nonsense. Enough already!

Isaac Berkowitz tuned back in, was startled to note that the conversation had gone on without him even being aware of it.

"Thank you very much Mr and Mrs Berkowitz. My colleague has taken all the photographs he needs. We'll do our analysis and if we have any reason to get back to you we will, but I don't expect we'll need to bother you again. Once again, many thanks, and you really needn't have gone to such lengths with seven different sorts of home-baked cookies! Now we'll need to get back to the gym to work it all off!"

'What a charming young man!' thought Anna Berkowitz to herself. 'And here I am stuck for the rest of my life with this old goat instead. Still, at least Isaac brought money and a good name. But we'll have to see after my re-election, once that's in the bag I'll have to get rid of him. Hope he doesn't demand a messy divorce, what would my friends say?'

All that to herself. Out loud she said with a broad, almost sincere smile: "But a fit young man like you can certainly put away all that and more, I'm sure. Looking forward to seeing you on Thursday night, I'll cook you up something extra-special!"

There was an embarrassed silence as Mats Knudsson and Alexander Sandström exchanged glances and tried desperately to suppress their smiles. Isaac noticed the look that passed between them and cringed in embarrassment. Not only was this old hag coming on to the two young men – in front of her husband! – she was also not even bright enough to understand that these two were the advance team who analysed the premises; the bodyguards accompanying the ambassador would be different people entirely. What an idiot she was. Divorce would be a real pleasure, something truly enjoyable to look forward to...

Mats Knudsson neatly side-stepped the indelicate situation by asking: "Just before we leave, Mrs Berkowitz, can you show me once again the room where the bodyguards will be sitting while you host the ambassador and her husband? The bodyguards will need to know that they have a direct line of sight on their car outside."

What Isaac Berkowitz heard was a diplomatic way of avoiding an embarrassing explanation. What Anna Berkowitz heard was a request by the handsome young man to show him into the deserted spare bedroom.

She walked into the room, swaying her hips just that little bit extra. Forcing himself to keep a straight face Mats stayed rooted to the spot by the open doorway and exclaimed "Ah yes! That was the room. Sorry, I'd forgotten. Great, no need to look at it again, we have the photos."

And with that he quickly brushed past the other two men and made it through the front door before the Berkowitz woman realised she'd lost her prey.

Thanking the Berkowitzes once again, the two agents walked down the stairs, not bothering to wait for the elevator. It would give them the chance to check the names on the front doors of the apartments as part of their security sweep.

Safely out on the street and approaching their unmarked blue Skoda Superb department car, it was, uncharacteristically, Alexander who burst out laughing. Giggling uncontrollably, in fact.

"So!" he gasped between bouts of body-shaking mirth. "You escaped – but only just! That one's something special. I feel really, really sorry for the Stockholm guys who are on the ambassador's security detail! What a man-eater, she'll chew them up and spit out their bones!" And he gave way to more snorts of laughter.

Mats Knudsson smiled wryly. "Never been on a more dangerous mission in my life! When I get back to the office I'm putting in for a transfer to front-line patrols in Syria – give me ISIS any day compared to this one! At least with them you have a sporting chance of escape!"

And with that they got into the car, Alexander Sandström almost crashing the car as his spasms of laughter caused him to pull the wheel over to the right and then overcompensate by wrenching it over to the left, narrowly missing an elderly couple in a white Ford Fiesta returning home with their weekly shopping.

"Get a grip, Alex!" exclaimed Mats in mock annoyance, nevertheless smiling broadly. "Our insurance doesn't cover 'death by giggling."

The two SÄPO agents had survived the most unexpected attack of their careers – they'd almost died laughing. All in the line of duty.

Central Israel, Mossad Headquarters

Amira Hart examined the spreadsheets, scrutinising them for traces of a pattern.

It was nothing new or surprising. It had been widely known for at least a year now that young radicalised European Islamists were making their way from all over Europe to various conflict hotspots to participate in what they saw as an organised, integrated, global *jihad* against everything non-Muslim, but which the Western world desperately tried to convince itself was nothing of the sort. It was, the West's political leaders whined on and on, just a ragtag bunch of disaffected youngsters doing what disaffected youngsters always had done since the dawn of time: rebelling against what they perceived as the structure and hierarchy of society.

The police, however, had a very different view of the situation. In common with just about anyone in uniform who had to deal with the 'disaffected youngsters' on their European home ground – police officers, fire crews, ambulance personnel, nurses, social workers and others – they saw the problem for what it really was: youngsters of Muslim background, mostly but worryingly not only men, were getting increasingly aggressive in the face of everything that represented mainstream society. And this aggression often took the form of gang wars, aggravated rapes and gang rapes, anti-Semitic outrages against synagogues, schools and cemeteries, wanton destruction of both private and public property, usually but not only in the form of arson attacks that saw anything up to forty cars set alight per night.

And the clandestine security services had yet another take on the situation: in addition to the overt acts of destruction and the terrorising of large swathes of civil society – not terrorism for political purposes but terrorising of civilians in order to impose dominance – they noted that there was a lot of fluidity in the movement of radicalised youngsters in and out of Europe.

Nowhere was this more clearly visible than in Sweden, which over the past few years had admitted an annual average of about 100,000 asylum-seekers into the country and almost immediately granted the overwhelming majority of them Swedish citizenship. These numbers swelled the already growing ranks of second- and third-generation Muslim immigrants who felt they had been overlooked by a largely failed, mostly non-existent Swedish integration policy.

The two groups – recent arrivals and established radicals – intermingled and did not always get on well together. There were turf wars. But by and large, their unofficial leaders had noted the massive potential synergies available from this restless, heaving mass of disaffected humanity now firmly entrenched in the heartland of the European Union. They were, quite simply, ripe for indoctrination, weapons training and preparation for war. War in the form of global *jihad*.

Indoctrination took place at home – whether that home was in England, France, Germany, Sweden or elsewhere. But weapons training and the subsequent preparation for all-out war required facilities far from the prying eyes of Western security services and politicians usually desperate not to see what was staring them in the eye.

On this specific day, however, one particular security service agent was staring intently at the data on her screen and comparing it with the printouts she had been continuously receiving from sister services throughout the Western world.

What Amira Hart was looking at was a veritable travel agency specialising in *jihad* tours. Based in a town called Jönköping in Sweden.

"Jönköping Jihad Journeys, that's pretty much what we have on our hands," muttered Amira Hart to herself as she leaned back in her chair.

She picked up her mobile phone and selected a number from memory.

It rang just once at the other end before her call was answered.

"Calev. What's up Amira?"

Calev Mizrachi was a man of few words. What he lacked in verbosity he made up for in clinical, single-minded efficiency.

Calev Mizrachi was the Mossad's head of European 'dry' operations – activities that involved research, monitoring, surveillance and the supply of vital information to the service's 'wet' division which carried out the surprisingly few targeted assassinations actually executed by the Mossad. At just 36 years of age, he was also the youngest person ever to head the desk in the organisation's history.

It was highly unusual for someone as low down on the food chain as Amira Hart to have direct access to a man of Mizrachi's prestige. It wasn't a question of rank – the Mossad was famously informal almost to the point of insubordination. It's just that the paths of two such different people were very unlikely ever to cross in the course of their work.

However, after Amira Hart's return to Israel from her impromptu and somewhat unofficial mission in Sweden the previous year, Calev Mizrachi had insisted on personally attending her debriefing.

Because, as he pithily put it, unfortunately within Amira's earshot, "We can't have some jumped-up schoolgirl straight out of training college jeopardising our security relations with the most volatile country in Europe."

Amira Hart gave her superior a tongue-lashing that went down in the annals of the service as one of the most inventive, descriptive, biological and colourful ever heard, involving as it did what she thought of Calev Mizrachi's mother, his supposed father and their pet dog, with a lot of unnecessary detail thrown in about the mutual physical relationship between the three. She rounded off with a few well-worded comments about jumped-up schoolboys leaping to conclusions without bothering to wait for information – which any 14-year-old schoolchild knew was the proper way to do things. Of course, she went on, many men were susceptible to premature release without waiting to get to the point...

By the time Amira had finished lambasting her superior for his disparaging comment, she didn't know if she would be given enough time to clear out her personal belongings from her desk or whether she would be physically ejected from the building without her feet touching the ground.

As it turned out, neither happened. Mizrachi broke out into one of his rare smiles, then spoke briefly.

"I gather I may have upset you. Feel better with that off your chest? Now let's get on with the debriefing. And from now on you report personally and directly to me. Every time. Got it?"

Amira Hart got it.

Which was why she was reporting directly to Calev Mizrachi on what she saw as a possibility and a pattern.

"I can send you a bunch of files and printouts, but really it would be better if you came down here to look at it all in my office," she said. "I reckon we're seeing signs of an influx of European Islamists into both Syria and, believe it or not, maybe even directly into Israel. Something might be afoot."

Calev Mizrachi spoke at length:

"Give me five minutes." Amira's phone clicked off.

"Four words!" she said to herself. "If he continues making such long speeches I'm going to have to lay on bottles of mineral water to soothe his dry throat."

Four and a half minutes later Calev Mizrachi knocked on her door and walked in without waiting for a reply.

"You have ten minutes," he said, pulling up a chair and sitting beside her. Not opposite her – he was not in the business of receiving information but of checking it out as it was being delivered. Especially when the information came from Amira Hart, he reflected as he ruefully recalled the first time he had come up against her – and lost.

Calev Mizrachi wanted to see for himself, not just hear what she had to say.

Amira Hart explained. Quietly, unhurriedly, methodically.

"Here's the situation: in Sweden, *jihadis* with Swedish citizenship are exploiting their citizenship and freedom of travel to go to Turkey, Syria and Iraq for training. From there they are making their way to the borders of Israel and lying in wait.

"That's bad enough," Amira continued, "but it's nothing we didn't already know. What *is* new, however, is that many of these European *jihadis*, in particular those with Swedish passports, are making their way into Israel as 'tourists'. Not all of them are Arabs or Muslims from other Islamic countries, some are native-born Swedish converts. All this makes our job that much more difficult."

Calev Mizrachi leaned back in his chair and looked Amira Hart over slowly, top to bottom.

"So? What's your point?" he asked.

'My word,' thought Amira to herself, 'another four-word speech! At this rate, there'll be no shutting him up!'

Out loud she was somewhat more circumspect. "My point is twofold: One: a couple of years back we already had trouble with Swedish politicians who came here to Israel, joined forces with various anti-Semitic European-funded NGOs in Israel and the Palestinian territories. We had to deport a couple of them. Including one who tried to invade Israeli territorial waters on a ship owned by a Turkish Islamist organisation. But relatively speaking all that was pretty harmless – we knew who they were even when they left home after breakfast in Stockholm, and we had our eyes on them the whole way.

"What we have now, however," Amira continued, "is a far greater threat. Because we don't know who these people are. All we know is that suddenly, in the midst of our current downturn in tourism, we are seeing a surprising upswing in tourists from Sweden. Yet Swedes have for the past ten years and more avoided coming to Israel. Most of their travel agencies don't even include our top tourist sites in their destinations – not the Dead Sea, not Jerusalem, not the sun and sand and sea of Netanya or Eilat."

Amira paused.

Calev filled in the gap. "Nuuu? So what's your point?"

'Five words now!' thought Amira. 'There was no stopping the man, he's positively gushing.'

"The point," said Amira slowly, "is that we are currently – already – being invaded by people who we have reason to suspect don't mean us well. Unfortunately, we realised it too late. They're already here. It's too late to lock the gate because they're already inside. But it's not too late to monitor who's here, and keep a far better watch on who enters from now on. We're not seeing a sudden influx of young Swedish tourists into Israel because they've suddenly discovered a love of our famed Bauhaus architecture, our historical heritage or our pristine beaches. They're here for something else. To paraphrase one of Sweden's most notoriously fickle and unprincipled politicians, I'll eat my right shoe if I'm wrong."

Calev Mizrachi rocked his chair on its back legs. Not a good idea because it creaked ominously. Amira eyed the chair somewhat nervously.

"OK," he said.

"These are the Border Control dockets from Tel Aviv-Ben Gurion Airport for the past month," said Amira, pointing to her computer screen. "Scan the barcodes and you'll see just how many Swedish visitors we've had. Look at the border exit section. Apparently, our Swedish tourists love our country so much, not one of them has left Israel. We can't do anything about that because tourists are allowed to stay up to three months without requiring a visa, so for up to ninety days after their arrival who knows where they are or what they're up to. As you are well aware, the typical overseas tourist comes for either a week or a fortnight. People simply don't have longer vacations or more money to spend on one single vacation at one single destination."

"OK," repeated Calev.

'Aha,' thought Amira to herself, 'now at least he is back to his talkative self. A full one-word sentence.'

"You know the drill," continued Calev Mizrachi. "Notify uniform and also Shin Bet. If it takes place on our soil, it's officially out of our hands. Liaise with them both, offer them any help they want, but no territorial squabbles – this is their pigeon and you take orders from them."

There was a pause as Calev Mizrachi recovered from this, probably the longest speech in his professional career. "Cancel that. You take orders only from me. But you hand over operational responsibility to uniform and Shin Bet. Let them work out who's in charge. Questions?"

Amira Hart didn't have any questions.

Except maybe that she wanted to ask her boss if in fact she had just witnessed two records being broken, one after the other. The legendarily taciturn Calev Mizrachi had just spoken joined-up sentences. Not once, but twice. Nobody would believe her.

Gothenburg, Sweden

Aisha Naddi tucked her hair firmly under her bobble hat and donned the large tinted glasses she had purchased cheaply at a charity shop. She pulled up the collar of her jacket to hide as much of her lower face as possible, put on her mildest smile, looked once again to her left to make sure that Zahir Tafesh, Ghalib Ajrour and Amir Assaf, black ski-masks pulled down to cover their faces, were well out of the line of sight from the apartment door spyhole, and then rang the doorbell.

From inside the apartment she could hear the sound of a chair scraping on a wooden parquet floor, then shuffling footsteps approaching the door.

The spyhole didn't darken – whoever was in the apartment was already fumbling with the door lock. It was amazing that in this day and age people – especially the elderly – were still so trusting as to open their doors without first verifying who was there.

The door opened slowly and Aisha smiled disarmingly.

"I'm sorry to disturb you, but I see I've made a mistake. I was looking for my aunt Anna, I reckon I got out one floor too early."

As soon as she finished speaking she stepped aside and the three boys rushed in.

Ghalib Ajrour clamped a large hand across the old gent's mouth and propelled him, none too gently but not unnecessarily roughly, back into his apartment.

Zahir Tafesh and Amir Assaf dumped their bags just inside the door and while Zahir went back out to the landing to bring in Ghalib's bags, Amir walked swiftly through the apartment, moving from room to room in search of the old man's wife.

Empty.

"Where's your lady?" demanded Ghalib, propelling the old man backwards into an upright kitchen chair. Aisha handed him a roll of silver gaffer tape.

"You ... you can have what you want, I won't call the police. My wallet is on my nightstand. Take it!" The old man's eyes were big and white with terror.

Ghalib quickly bound the man to his chair, wrapping swathes of the sturdy tape around his arms, chest and the chair back. He then repeated the procedure with the legs, putting down the roll of gaffer tape only after the man's calves and ankles were securely strapped to the chair's legs.

"We don't want your money. Where's your wife?" Ghalib asked again.

He didn't feel particularly happy or proud of himself at this moment. In the entire plan, this was the bit he'd dreaded the most. He was up for any amount of violence, killing even. But there was something deeply uncomfortable about targeting innocent and defenceless old people.

But the cause was what mattered. He shook his head to rid himself of all thoughts apart from his mission.

Eggs.

You can't make an omelette without cracking eggs.

He looked again at the old man, doing his best to look menacing and threatening.

"Speak up old man! Where's your wife?" he demanded.

"She's … she's not here!" he moaned, spittle flying from the corners of his mouth. A wet patch was spreading across the front of his trousers. A mild odour of ammonia revealed that the old man had wet himself, and soon enough a trickle of urine puddled on the floor at his feet, leaving a tell-tale vertical stain down the inside right leg of his baggy trousers.

"I can see that!" snapped Ghalib steeling himself to ignore the pitiful sight. "Where is she? When is she returning?"

"She went to stay with her sister in Karlstad. She left yesterday. She won't come back for another week. Please," he sobbed, "take my money. Here! This watch," he nodded towards his bound left wrist. "It's gold! I got it after working for 50 years at Volvo. It's solid gold, I promise. Take it. I won't say a word. I'll tell her it must have slipped off my wrist when I went out shopping."

Ghalib and Amir exchanged looks of incredulity. The old man's life was hanging by a thread but he was more concerned about upsetting his wife over a missing watch.

But this did solve a major problem. Actually two problems.

For one thing, they now had only the old man to contend with, not his wife too.

And for another, only one innocent martyr would be sacrificed for the greater good.

Although nobody said a word, all four were relieved.

Almost tenderly now, Ghalib placed a strip of gaffer tape somewhat loosely across the old man's mouth. But not before asking him if he would like a drink of water first. The old man stared, uncomprehending.

The tape was put across his mouth and the four youngsters got to work.

Zahir packed two of the sacks along the outside of the inner bearing wall. While he was doing this Amir and Ghalib each grasped the built-in fridge and freezer from the bottom front, raising the units onto the small castor wheels at the back and sliding them out of their snug enclave.

The wall behind the two units was the rear of the same retaining wall on the other side of which Zahir had packed his two sacks. He now placed the other two sacks on the inside, sandwiching the retaining wall.

He primed the fuses. And waited.

The old man must have understood what was happening. Not why, but what.

He started struggling in vain against his restraints.

Ghalib and Amir grabbed one side each of his chair, with him strapped firmly to it, and carried him into the bathroom.

There was one window in the bathroom. Good. Amir opened the window wide. At least this would even out the pressure wave somewhat, which meant the old man had a slight chance of surviving the blast.

They then lifted the man, still strapped to his chair, and laid him with his back down inside the bathtub. It wasn't a comfortable fit and his knees and lower legs protruded above the rim of the tub, strapped as they were to the front legs of the kitchen chair, but it was better than nothing.

They left the bathroom, leaving the door wide open to allow for unrestricted movement of the pressure wave from the blast.

Once the old man was safely out of the way in the bathroom, they pulled off their ski-masks and stuffed them in their jacket pockets. Now they would wait until the time was right. Whatever terror was screaming through the old man's head, at least he was no longer able to watch their preparations and ponder over the manner of his possible death.

At 5.30 pm on the dot a small convoy of two cars pulled up to the kerb outside the building where Anna and Isaac Berkowitz lived.

The lead car was a marked police patrol car, lights and sirens switched off. It was followed by an unmarked black Volvo S80. Impossible to tell apart from any other civilian Volvo in the city where Volvos were built and where such cars were a very common sight on the city's roads. Except that like all police and security service cars, marked or otherwise, there were a few tell-tale signs. The small extra rear-view mirror attached to the top of each door mirror, for instance. The discreet extra antenna integrated into curved roof panel. And, in the case of armoured cars used for carrying high-value political and diplomatic personnel, there was the fact that however much the engineers at Volvo beefed up the suspension to cope with the added weight of the surprisingly lightweight body panel and glass armour, the car still squatted somewhat lower than its civilian counterparts.

And of course, there was no visible tailpipe. The exhaust system on armoured cars ended up well short of the rear bumper to avoid the risk of someone putting something unsavoury into the tailpipe. It wouldn't even take a bomb or a grenade to render such a car undriveable – merely blocking the exhaust outlet would prevent the engine from being started owing to the increased backpressure. A simple, cheap, and highly effective way of immobilising a car.

The front doors of the police car opened and two uniformed officers got out. Nishtiman Halabjaee stayed by the driver's door while Per-Olle Pettersson walked to the main door of the apartment building and pressed a button. Anna Berkowitz answered.

"Good evening," said Per-Olle Pettersson. "This is the police. You're expecting visitors this evening and we want to advise you that they are on their way up to you. Please do not open your apartment door until you receive a phone call on your landline asking you to do so. They will be with you in a minute."

Anna Berkowitz buzzed open the door and Per-Olle Pettersson held it open while Nishtiman Halabjaee beckoned to the occupants of the black Volvo and then joined her partner by the building's front door.

The Volvo's front passenger door opened and Isabella Kronlind got out. She walked to the rear nearside door and opened it.

Just then a silver Toyota Avensis drove slowly up behind them and stopped. The driver and front seat passenger got out and walked briskly to the offside rear door of the Volvo, opening it.

Israel's ambassador to Sweden Mrs Ronit Gottlieb got out of the rear of the armoured Volvo at the same time as the plainclothes SÄPO officers from the Toyota helped her husband Dan out from the other side. Isabella Kronlind walked them both briskly to the front door as Henrik Winqvist slipped out from behind the wheel of the black Volvo and joined them, speaking discreetly into his cuff mike.

Ronit and Dan Gottlieb smiled their thanks to the uniformed officer holding open the front door of the building, while their SÄPO bodyguards nodded crisply in their direction and hustled their charges straight to the elevator.

The door to the apartment building closed shut with a heavy click and Per-Olle Pettersson and Nishtiman Halabjaee started walking back to their car. Reaching their marked police car they got in without exchanging so much as a look with the two SÄPO spooks who still stood between their silver unmarked car and the black armoured Volvo.

"Wave goodbye to Batman and Robin," said Per-Olle to Nishtiman Halabjaee as they pulled away. Nishtiman laughed.

There was no real love lost between the uniformed branch of the nation's law and order officers, and the behind-the-scenes men and women who seemed to revel in playing action scenes from *The Bourne Ultimatum* or some third-rate James Bond knockoff filmed in China.

Job done until it was time to pick up the ambassador after her dinner, Nishtiman Halabjaee and Per-Olle Pettersson headed back out on patrol up and down the main thoroughfares of Avenyn past Brunnsparken, the downtown areas of Gothenburg where things always tended to get a bit heated when the clubs opened in a couple of hours, and then again around 3 am when they closed. Meantime it was just a matter of showing a police presence on the streets of central Gothenburg. Thankfully today they were not patrolling in Biskopsgården or Bergsjön, or any of other the 55 districts in Sweden that were no-go areas for the police.

Stockholm, Sweden

Marita Ohlsson realised she was facing an uphill struggle. Not because what she was saying was inaccurate or unacceptable.

It was going to be an uphill struggle because what she had to say was politically incorrect and diplomatically hypersensitive in what was still – albeit increasingly marginally – the democratic state of Sweden.

"Look," she tried again. "I'm not proposing a coup, or a revolution, or anything like that. We're not the military, we're police officers without the benefit of a uniform. And, crucially, we're not politicians. It isn't our job to take account of the political niceties of a given situation. Our job is simply to identify the situation and, if that situation is problematic, propose a remedy. We're duty-bound to suggest the most effective way of dealing with the problem. Refusing to identify or name the problem for reasons of political correctness is not part of our job description. So let's focus!"

Nobody seated at the conference table disagreed with her. But crucially, nobody agreed with her either. Not because they didn't agree with her, but because they didn't want to be seen to be doing so.

This was Sweden, after all. Sweden, where Political Correctness had been elevated to the status of a national religion, an unassailable tenet that determined how the nation would avoid dealing with embarrassing or troubling problems.

Marita Ohlsson valiantly tried again. "Our job isn't to create policy, but it is our duty to point out to those who do make policy, what the dangers facing our society actually are.

"And right now," she continued, "the dangers are twofold: firstly, the rapid increase in Islamic radicalisation in this country. And secondly, the equally rapid increase in mostly right-wing opposition to Islamic radicalisation. Remember the turf wars between those two neo-Nazi motorcycle gangs about a decade ago, which spilled over from Denmark into southern Sweden and then the rest of the country? Well, let me tell you, if we don't address this current issue robustly – and immediately," Marita Ohlsson tapped the table, "you're all going to look back fondly on those halcyon days of biker bloodletting as a wonderful era of peace and universal brotherhood. Because," she carried on, pressing home the point while everyone stayed silent, "what's in store for Sweden is carnage on an unprecedented scale unless we can convince our politicians that burying their heads in the sand is no longer a solution. On the contrary, that is precisely what is fuelling the rabid troublemakers on both sides. They've got the measure of us, they know we won't respond because our hands are tied by the politicians."

Jens Marklund, formally her immediate superior and the person responsible for liaison with Rosenbad, the seat of Swedish government, cleared his throat.

"Maybe," said Jens, looking slowly around at the assembled faces, "just maybe the best thing would be to let them at each other, give them a free hand, let them cull each other, while we mobilise to ensure that the violence doesn't spill over too much into the civilian population."

He took in the startled expressions from all around the table.

"Look, I'm just playing the devil's advocate here. I'm not actually proposing that we tacitly agree to oversee a battleground on Swedish soil. We can and in fact we have penetrated the right-wing groups, the bikers and neo-Nazis and what-not. They aren't the problem because we're keeping tabs on them from the inside. Virtually anyone around this table," he looked at the people sitting in the room, the vast majority of whom were fair-haired, light-skinned and blue-eyed, "as I say, virtually anyone here could be inserted into these right-wing groups and would blend in perfectly. Our problem is the other side, the Islamists. We have few of our own people on the inside. We have neither the language skills, nor the cultural mind-set, nor indeed the physical appearance, to penetrate these groups. For instance, we have one – just one – SÄPO agent of Iranian descent, some of you may know him. He's worth his weight in gold when it comes to analysing information about the Iranian community, but he can't be used for clandestine work within that community. For one thing he's now thirty-seven years old and therefore not suitable for insertion among the young radicals in the Iranian-Shia extremist community, and for another he's spent the past couple of years travelling around the country speaking to young Iranian Muslims about the dangers of radicalisation. Everybody knows and recognises him, so he can't be used for any kind of undercover work. And that's just the Iranian connection, which in turn is only one portion of the Shia-Alawite connection, which in turn is only one part of the wider Muslim community, which includes but is not limited to the Sunni and Ahmadiya divide too, all of which is in addition to the ongoing conflict between Sunni and Shia Muslims. Here. On our streets. The whole thing is far more complex than we're accustomed to dealing with.

"But," Jens Marklund continued, "I want to make one thing clear to everyone around this table: we work on the clear assumption that Swedish Muslims who are law-abiding, and that's most of them," he looked up sharply as someone snorted in derision, "and that's most of them," he repeated slowly and with added emphasis, "are either too scared, or too uninvolved, or too busy trying to earn a living, to deal with the radicals in their midst. And yes, we know that there are many seemingly moderate Swedish Muslims who very likely secretly agree with the more hard-line, Sharia-embracing approach of the radicals but who don't want to acknowledge it in public. They are admittedly a problem. By definition they are a problem that is difficult, if not impossible, to quantify.

"But," continued Jens Marklund, "that does not absolve us from dealing with the issue as best we can. Marita," he said, turning to her. "Put that slide back up, the one with the panorama view of Islamist-linked attacks in Sweden this past twelve-month period. People, hold judgement, let's just break it down into manageable chunks of information."

Marita Ohlsson scrolled through a series of thumbnail icons on her laptop until she found the slide she was looking for.

She hit a key and the slide slid onto the large white wall at the end of the room.

It didn't take a lot of imagination to see a clear picture, one that emerged quickly and seared its image on the consciousness of the people assembled in the conference room.

Whatever the reason – and one might speculate as to whether the motivation was frustration, or a sense of segregation, or absolute refusal to integrate, or quite simply a racist, arrogant perception of native Swedish women as deserving of rape and Swedish men as weak-willed Westerners ripe for domination by radical Islam – whatever the reason, there was no doubt that what the country was witnessing was a sharp spike in violence perpetrated by young people with a Muslim background, and that the overwhelming majority of their victims were white ethnic Swedes.

The crime statistics provided by police districts all over the country made for chilling reading. There was the usual undercurrent of violent crime: biker gangs and their turf wars, usually about where each gang had its unwritten franchise to sell drugs; young Swedes whose parents had long abdicated their roles of responsibility and who indulged in binge-drinking every single weekend, with predictable results on the roads and wherever teenagers got together; violence by roving gangs of teenagers stealing mobile phones and money from the elderly and from vulnerable youngsters walking home alone.

None of that was remarkable, and none of that was peculiar to Sweden – the same patterns of behaviour could be noted in most, if not all, European cities.

What was remarkable, however, was the additional layer of crime that went with no name.

It had no name because nobody was willing to be the first to break the taboo on mentioning the unmentionable.

Islamist-influenced violence. On the streets of Swedish towns and cities throughout the length and breadth of the country. From Östersund in the north where a group of refugees, recent arrivals from Syria and Iraq, had gone on the rampage, tearing up their asylum facility because they didn't like the cold weather in northern Sweden and demanded to be moved further south where the weather was more to their liking; to Malmö in the south where the local slang for

Swedish girls among large swathes of the city's younger Muslim population was 'white mattress'. A none-too-delicate allusion to the way native-born girls were regarded and, increasingly, treated.

Marita identified some of the salient points.

"It may be politically inexpedient to say so, but thankfully I'm not vying for public office so I'm not one bit concerned about political sensitivities. We here all have a job to do, and that job has nothing to do with politics. We identify security-related problems, and pass on our recommendations for dealing with these security issues. That's it. Other people make the decisions based on our recommendations, and that's their responsibility, not ours. So let's get going, and let's be honest about what we think we see. And also about what we don't see – we don't want to be alarmist after all. Here goes.

"We're not in the business of generalising," she went on before anyone else could interrupt, "but we do have to use the tools available to us. Name-recognition software used on lists of perpetrators of violent crimes reveals an alarmingly high proportion of foreign names. Not just foreign, Muslim. Wait!"

Marita held up her hand to ward off the impending storm of protest. "This is not a qualitative or racist judgement. It is merely a statement of fact. The computer software does not make judgement, it simply calls up data. Impartially.

"Data analysis," she went on, "reveals a preponderance of young people involved in violence. Eighty-seven percent of violent crime, including attack rape – that is to say rape carried out by a perpetrator not known to the victim – is carried out by people below the age of twenty-five.

"Vehicular attacks – with cars being deliberately used as battering rams to kill and maim people – has become something of an epidemic. Not only in the big cities, even in the smaller towns. People are being mown down while waiting for buses, crossing the road, coming out of stores.

"And there's more: almost ninety-three percent of all bodily assaults including vehicular attacks, violent robberies and sexual crimes are carried out by males.

"And there's still more. We've all read the papers, seen the TV news about the increase in anti-Semitic attacks, both verbal and physical. As you know, many of our uniformed colleagues were pulled off their regular patrol beats and pressed into guard duty outside synagogues, Jewish schools, Jewish old-age homes. Many even had to pass refresher courses with the MP5 assault rifle before they were put out there to safeguard Sweden's Jewish population – and the last real gun some of these officers had ever handled was probably a British Lee-Enfield of First World War vintage…"

Marita Ohlsson paused while the assembled group chuckled at the memory of rusty officers being press-ganged into front-line SWAT-type guard duty following the recent spate of terrorist attacks in Brussels, Copenhagen, Paris and Oslo.

"But seriously, folks," continued Marita. "Our statistics once again point to an overwhelming majority of these attacks being carried out by young people, almost without exception male, whose origins are the Middle East or North Africa. This all makes for uncomfortable reading, I know, but I repeat: we are not making qualitative judgements, just calling up the recorded data. The data does not lie. So what does this data reveal?"

Marita Ohlsson paused, taking in each and every one of the faces seated around the table. She took a sip of water, put down her glass carefully, and then continued speaking, slowly and with the trepidation visible in the way she held herself, audible in the strained tone of her voice.

"The picture that emerges," she said, "is of young Muslim males on a violent rampage. Their targets are sometimes the elderly, but more often young Swedes, both male and female, and rape is prominent. None of this is news to any of you, I'm sure. What will be news is the following,"

Marita punched a key and a new slide appeared.

"Overlaid on this wave of Islamist violence against Swedes is the inter-Muslim violence that we are also witnessing but which our political masters are doing their best to disregard. Because if they take notice of it they fear they may be required to do something about it. Better then to ignore the problem and hope it goes away. But as our colleagues in blue note every single day on the beat, the problem isn't going away. Rather, it's growing.

"That problem is Muslim-on-Muslim violence here in Sweden. The Shia-Sunni divide within our Muslim community. The wars they started fighting and subsequently fled from in Lebanon, Syria, Iraq, Israel, Gaza, wherever – they've imported those battles here. Onto our turf.

"We're seeing it," continued Marita, "not least, in the recent spate of attacks on mosques. I don't need to remind anyone here that the recent death of a Shia imam in a basement mosque in Kristianstad has brought matters to a head – the first fatality in this spate of hate-crime attacks. And I'm very afraid it's not going to be the last, unless we adopt a robust policy to deal with the issue. For goodness sake, we're seeing Muslim attacks against each other's mosques involving arson, tampering with electrics, homemade bombs. There was even that scare with the white powder sent to the Sunni mosque in Malmö. Glad it turned out to be just flour, but the note that accompanied it made it clear that the next batch would be rather more potent."

Marita paused, and looked around the room.

Jens Marklund spoke. "We all know what the term 'hate-crime' usually means. It's those goddamned white supremacist neo-Nazis who believe skin colour somehow determines IQ. You know what? In their case they're probably right – you'd have to have the IQ of a cucumber to be a Nazi sympathiser. And most Nazi sympathisers are white."

He was rewarded with grins and nods of assent all round.

"But in the new reality facing us, today's wave of hate crime doesn't refer to the racist acts being carried out by gangs of white-supremacist thugs with a collective IQ somewhat lower than that of a pile of cow-dung. No, the hate crimes we're encountering are the attacks being carried out by Shia thugs on Sunni thugs. And vice versa. Here – in Sweden. It's their battle for domination of the Muslim community here that is probably the most worrying right now, because if this is the way they treat each other, one fears for the way the ultimate winners of that battle will treat the people that both sides openly regard as *dhimmis* or 'non-Muslim subjects living in Muslim society' – that's us native-born Swedes, whether we are Roman Catholic, Church of Sweden, Jew, Buddhist, Hindu, Zoroastrian, Sikh, atheist, whatever. That, my friends, is the other layer of the problem with which we have to deal. Provided, of course, our politicians even allow us to mention that this is in fact a problem..." His voice faded away.

Marita Ohlsson filled in with the words nobody wanted to hear.

"It's all going to come to a head before the elections. Because that's what this is all about. Each side in the Sunni-

Shia divide wants to get ahead of and crush the other so that on September 20th when the country goes to the polls, Swedish Muslims will know for whom to vote. And whom to avoid. On pain of – well, we've all seen the pictures and the statistics."

Pursing her mouth in a grim smile, Marita added: "It's not going to end well – and that's just the religious aspect, the fight for domination between these two groups. We've still got to deal with the wave of violence both sides have unleashed via the country's disaffected Muslim youth, the other layer of the problem we are facing. Because on election day, *that* problem, ladies and gentlemen, is going to propel this country not into the arms of the Islamists, as they believe. It's going to propel the nation into the arms of an increasingly strong, increasingly strident, right wing."

Jens Marklund put it most succinctly. "Which means we have three wars to fight, simultaneously. Firstly, young radicalised Islamist thugs bent on dominating Swedish youngsters. For racist reasons, pure and simple. Secondly, Sunni and Shia radicals pursuing their vendettas against each other here on Swedish soil. And thirdly, whichever of these two wins, the imposition of their will on the rest of Sweden."

"Which brings us neatly to the fourth dimension of the war facing our society and our country," filled in Marita Ohlsson. "The right-wing parties – some of which used to be centrist parties not so long ago – won't take any of this sitting down.

They will respond – far more violently than we have seen so far."

The group of people around the table looked at each other, and everyone turned to Jens Marklund. He was the person with the unenviable task of bridging the reality gap with the nation's politicians in Rosenbad. No easy task bearing in mind the strong Islamist component in the current Swedish government.

Jens Marklund stood up. "Anyone here feel the situation analysis is unduly alarmist, inaccurate, not based on proper data sets, anything?"

There was no answer apart from a unanimous shake of heads.

"OK, I'll schedule an appointment with the powers that be and get back to this task group as soon as I have anything to report. Thanks for coming, back to work now."

The meeting broke up and the participants disappeared.

Sweden's problems didn't.

Gothenburg, Sweden

Anna Berkowitz was sitting at the head of the table with her husband Isaac opposite her and Ambassador Ronit Gottlieb on her left, and the ambassador's husband Dan facing her.

As Ambassador Gottlieb excused herself to visit the bathroom, Anna left the open-plan dining room-cum-living room to pay a quick visit to the spare room. She wanted to ensure that the SÄPO bodyguard sitting there had enough to eat and drink. It was the tall, attractive girl. Isabella something, if she remembered rightly. Anna Berkowitz asked if Isabella's colleague would like to come up and have something to eat too but was assured that he would stay at his post in the car. Yes, he had plenty to eat and drink with him in the car. Yes, she was quite sure, this was the way they always worked. One stayed close, the other stayed with the car. If Henrik Winqvist who was in the car needed to come up to use the bathroom he would call up a local patrol car to swing by and stay with the armoured vehicle while he made use of the facilities. No, really, there was nothing to worry about. Yes, she would be happy to take a piece of cheesecake for her colleague at the end of the evening.

Isabella Kronlind looked out the window. All was quiet. The black Volvo was still parked in place, the driver's window open halfway and there was an eerie, subdued blue glow from the driver's seat. Henrik Winqvist was probably texting his girlfriend Marie or engaging in some kind of online skulduggery to purchase a rare five-dimensional postage stamp or something as implausible as it was boring. Isabella watched as a young girl came into view. Must have come from the same building she herself was in. Wearing a light-coloured coat with a hood pulled over her head, hands in pockets as she made her way quickly, almost running, towards a white van with garishly coloured pictures of fruits and vegetables painted on the side. Isabella couldn't make out the text on the side panel.

Isabella smiled to herself. Probably some girl off to have an evening out with her boyfriend. Or, as she recalled from her distant youth and the fun she'd had with one particular boyfriend whose father owned a carpentry business and, most importantly, a van, more likely an evening in with her boyfriend. In the van.

Isabella smiled briefly at the memory and started to turn away. Didn't want to intrude on the young generation, even in her thoughts. She turned her attention to her plate. This really was excellent cheesecake, she was definitely going to have to spend some extra time in the hotel gym tomorrow morning...

She noticed a young man following the girl towards the same van. That was the boyfriend, obviously. Uh-oh. Hold on. He wasn't alone, there was another man with him. Both were big. One even bigger than the other. OK, there went her brilliant theory – no secret tryst between two young lovers in the back of a van. Unless it was a threesome...

"Get a grip on yourself!" she muttered to herself, "not everything's about sex!" She turned away from the window and contemplated her empty plate and the remaining piece of cheesecake. Surely Henrik wouldn't know how thick or thin the slice had originally been? And what he didn't know, he couldn't possibly miss. She reached for the knife.

Anna Berkowitz returned to her seat, smiled at the ambassador's husband, Dan Gottlieb, and was reaching over to pass him the carafe of water when the blast tore through the floor directly behind and beneath her.

The explosion sent the free-standing fridge and freezer units surging first upwards into the air, hitting the overhead kitchen cabinets and then crashing down onto Anna's head. The impact smashed her skull like a pumpkin and killed her instantly.

The sudden impact of the heavy fridge and freezer also caused the end of the table to buckle down, crushing the table legs and see-sawing the other end of the table up a number of centimetres into the air. The leaf of the table caught Isaac Berkowitz under the chin and rattled loose three of his teeth. The pain was indescribable and he fainted almost immediately, blood pouring from the gash in his lower gum and lacerated lips. These were relatively minor injuries, however. What killed him was the massive coronary failure brought on by the sudden attack.

Dan Gottlieb was rocked backwards off his chair by the force of the blast, cracking his head on the edge of the ebony-and-inlaid-ivory coffee table behind him. As the light dimmed from his consciousness he recalled wondering if this was it – he wouldn't get to hold his one-year-old granddaughter ever again, he wouldn't get to attend the *bar mitzva* of his oldest grandson in just six weeks' time.

In the bathroom, Ronit Gottlieb heard and felt the explosion and immediately dropped to the floor, squatting on her heels behind the washstand. She looked quickly around – was there a bathtub here in which she could take protection? Or was this one of those modern bathrooms with just a glassed-in shower cubicle?

No bathtub. Glass shower cubicle. The last thing she needed in a situation where there were explosions was glass above and behind her. She got up, moved swiftly to the back of the bathroom and crouched beside the washing machine and tumble-dryer, which formed a tower placed one on top of the other.

She could hear someone trying the bathroom door. She looked around for a weapon and saw the heavy glass-topped bathroom scale. Hefty. That would do very well. She reached out and grabbed it, pulling it toward her with her left hand and then grasping it firmly in her right, ready to throw into the doorway.

"Mrs Ambassador!" she heard through the door. "Answer me! Are you OK?" It was Isabella Kronlind.

Without waiting for an answer Isabella threw herself at the door shoulder-first. It splintered and gave way a bit but did not yield. She took a step back, measured the distance and lashed out with her right foot in a low swinging arc rising up at ever-increasing speed until it connected with the hollow wood panel just beside the lock and handle mechanism.

The door gave way and fell in with a crash.

Isabella barged in, right hand reaching simultaneously into her jacket and emerging with a dull dark-grey hand-gun.

She reached out her left hand. "Come!" she commanded. Ronit Gottlieb dropped the bathroom scale on the floor and rose to follow her bodyguard.

"What happened? How's Da..."

"There's no time. Stay with me, put your right hand on my right shoulder and never, ever, break physical contact with me. You go wherever I go, always one step behind me, and always with your right hand on my shoulder. Can you walk? Any injuries?"

Ronit shook her head. "But what's..."

"No time now!" snapped Isabella Kronlind and started speaking into her cuff mike. She finished speaking and, her right hand raised and her left clasping the right for added support, she swept her handgun in the direction of the apartment's front door.

Nothing, no movement there. So no attempt to penetrate the apartment as yet.

As the dust started settling, she surveyed the scene. There was a jagged crater where the fridge and freezer had stood. She had no intention of approaching the hole to see who or what had caused the explosion. That would be asking for trouble.

She spoke into her cuff mike once again, waited for the response and nodded.

Henrik Winqvist had been about to pour himself some hot coffee from the steel thermos in the cupholder beside him when the explosion flashed bright yellow and deep orange, blowing out a couple of windows and the entire glassed-in balconies on the second and third floors.

Henrik dropped the thermos on the floor of the car, opened the car door with his left hand and whipped out his hand-gun with the right. He raised his left hand to his mouth and spoke into his cuff mike.

No answer.

He tried again. Relief. Isabella Kronlind answered. She was fine, the ambassador was not injured. No situation assessment regarding the others, or the cause. She was going to initiate an extraction via the front door of the apartment. No, only the ambassador. Her husband was not their security concern.

Henrik got back in the car and fired up the engine. Spoke again into his cuff mike. He was asking for uniform backup. Immediately. Whatever was in the area – traffic police, canine unit, anti-terror squad. Hell, even parking wardens, whatever. Anything in a uniform. Now, immediately.

Ronit Gottlieb spoke urgently to Isabella. "I have to get my husband, where is he? I can't see through the smoke!"

Isabella Kronlind answered tersely, speaking quietly but urgently. "No way Mrs Ambassador. We are exiting. Right now. I'll send people back for everyone else, including your husband. Now focus! Hand on my shoulder, follow me and look neither right nor left. Just keep with me."

And she moved forward, left foot leading and right foot following in its track, sidling forward swiftly yet unhurriedly, her hands clasped firmly on her sidearm and heading for the front door.

As she put her hand on the door handle, she cast a look behind her. From the smoke and dust she could see a figure moving slowly, difficult to see who it was. No time to find out, her responsibility was the ambassador and nobody else. She pressed down firmly on the door handle with her left hand, twisting open the security lock with her right, which still held her gun in a firm grasp.

She stepped outside onto the landing and was hit by a thick, oily blast of acrid-smelling smoke billowing up the stairwell from downstairs. The apartment below must have suffered a catastrophic explosion and fire, she thought, not sure whether accidental or deliberate. Except that in her line of work, there were no coincidences or accidents, only threats that had to be dealt with.

Blocked. Which meant the stairwell was out. And of course the elevator.

She half-turned to the ambassador, who was in a semi-crouched position behind her with her right hand on Isabella's right shoulder.

"Right!" shouted Isabella. "Back into the apartment! Go!"

And with that both Ronit Gottlieb and Isabella Kronlind made their way back into the trashed apartment and locked the front door behind them.

In the road outside, Ghalib Ajrour slipped behind the wheel of the van, noted that Aisha had already taken the middle seat of the three-seat cab, and smiled grimly to himself. The other two boys would have to sort out who was sitting where, but if there was any bickering between them about who was going in the back, he'd just drive off without them. This was no time for schoolyard nonsense.

He needn't have worried. Zahir opened the rear door and climbed in quickly, shutting the door on himself in one fluid movement. Amir got in the cab beside Aisha. Shut the door and spoke just one word.

"Go!"

Ghalib went.

Gothenburg, Sweden

Leaving the Volvo's engine idling, Henrik Winqvist ended his barked conversation with police despatch and ran to the front door. A marked police car was on its way, probably accompanied by other uniformed units and the fire service. He could already hear sirens in the distance.

He pulled up short.

The door handles of the apartment building were locked together with a stout steel chain and massive padlock. He gave the chain a rattle. It wouldn't budge.

The SÄPO bodyguard didn't bat an eyelid. He stepped back ten paces and sprayed five rounds into various parts of the glass door panel. It splintered and showered the ground with large chunks of broken glass. Kicking in a huge sagging sheet of fractured glass hanging crazily from a corner of the shattered door frame, Henrik stepped into the building's entrance lobby and started running up the stairs, speaking all the while into his cuff mike.

Once past the first floor he was met with an impenetrable wall of black, oily smoke. Pungent, acrid, roiling up into the ceiling of the landing and on up the stairwell.

He wasn't going to make it through this, this was a job for the fire department, requiring proper breathing apparatus.

Henrik turned swiftly as first one and then a second explosion rocked the stairwell. These were definitely smaller than the first devastating blast that had demolished the floor of the Berkowitz apartment and the glassed-in balconies.

He ran back down the stairs, gun in his right hand held halfway out in front of him, ready to face what came.

But there was nobody there.

He ran outside, back to the car. The engine had cut out because when he entered the building the car's keyless-go ignition system had put the remote he carried in his pocket out of range. He yanked open the driver's door, reached in his right foot, stepped on the brake pedal and, dropping his gun onto the driver's seat, fumbled for and pressed the red "START" button in the dashboard. The powerful turbocharged diesel engine fired up immediately, settling to a quiet idle.

Grabbing his gun again, Henrik Winqvist spoke once more into his cuff mike. Reported the situation in the stairwell, heard that Isabella Kronlind had seen and heard exactly the same thing from three storeys higher up in the building.

What to do?

Henrik looked about, quickly and calmly assessing the situation. The balcony windows had been blown out and there was glass everywhere, but crucially the stout aluminium beams supporting the balcony windows were intact. Slightly buckled, but intact.

"Get the curtains!" Henrik barked the instructions into his cuff mike. "It'll be fine. Knot them two and two together to double their strength, and tie them to the horizontal rail on your balcony. I'll bring the car directly beneath the balcony – it won't be much of a drop onto the car's roof. Move."

Isabella surveyed the situation. Their two hosts were either dead or seriously injured. At any rate they weren't moving. The figure that was moving in the apartment turned out not to be a terrorist emerging from below via the smashed floor, but Dan Gottlieb. He seemed dazed and was bleeding from somewhere around his head or face, not sure which, but he was responding coherently and was able to walk under his own steam. Which was good, because Isabella was not going to wait a single second for him. If he could make it out on his own together with her and Ronit Gottlieb, that was fine. But her sole mission was Ronit's security. Nobody else's.

Isabella Kronlind tucked her gun back into its skeleton holster, ripped the beautiful full-length curtains off their rods, bringing the entire fitting crashing to the floor. Fingers working with lightning speed, she knotted the fabric together and tested the strength of the knots. Perfect.

She ran to the spare room and repeated the procedure. Full-length ceiling to floor curtains here too as this room also faced onto the balcony. Perfect. Yanking the curtains off the rods she repeated the procedure, then strode back to the living room.

Isabella quickly tied the two lengths of curtain to each other, tugging hard on either side of the new join to see if the knots held.

They did.

She unlatched the smashed frame of the balcony door and threw it open, stepping out onto the balcony as a marked police car came screaming into view, lights flashing and siren blaring. Before the car had come to a complete stop the passenger door flew open and Per-Olle Pettersson hurled himself out of the car. As the engine died his female colleague Nishtiman Halabjaee snapped open the driver's door and stepped out. Both had their right hands on the grips of their side-arms, which remained securely inside their holsters.

Per-Olle shouted to Henrik. "What's the situation? You need help to get the ambassador out?"

"No!" shouted Henrik Winqvist. "I'll deal with the ambassador, you and your partner keep everyone else at bay until more help arrives. The stairwell's on fire but I'm sure there are people inside the building who need to get out quickly." And with that he got behind the wheel of his armoured Volvo.

Nishtiman Halabjaee and Per-Olle Pettersson charged into the building intending to get the occupants out to safety. No answer from either of the ground-floor apartments. They made their way up the stairs to where the smoke seemed to be thinning out, ringing on doorbells and ordering tenants on the first floor to leave immediately, down the stairs and out into the roadway. As they made their way up to the next floor a third explosion ripped their legs out from under them. The last of the three gas canisters had blasted apart at the seams owing to the intense heat, releasing the high-pressure gas contained within.

Neither police officer had a chance. Their blood loss through the shredded tatters of what remained of their lower legs was so massive that they bled out before their brains even fully realised what had happened.

Following the killing of their first civilian victims, Anna and Isaac Berkowitz, the four terrorists had now added the murder of two young police officers.

Meantime, her fingers working efficiently and firmly, Isabella tied one end of her emergency curtain ladder to the stout aluminium rail that until minutes before had secured the bottom of the balcony's large glass panels.

She looked over the edge of the balcony. Henrik had driven the car up onto the verge and positioned it directly below.

Isabella turned to the ambassador, speaking urgently but quietly. "You're going down first, Henrik is below waiting for you. I can't see how far down the curtain reaches, go as far as you can and jump the rest of the way onto the car roof. Henrik will catch you. Go!"

"But what about Dan?" asked Ronit Gottlieb. She knew her question was pointless, because she knew the drill, but she asked anyway. SÄPO had one priority, and only one. The ambassador. Not her husband. The Israeli ambassador was not going to plead, not least because if their roles were reversed she would have made the same decision.

"If Dan can manage it himself, he'll go after you. If he can't, I'll follow you and uniform will come back for him. Now go!" And she physically pushed the Israeli ambassador towards the edge of the balcony.

Ronit Gottlieb climbed over the low beam holding the curtain rope-ladder. Slipping off her high-heeled shoes and kicking them over the edge, she started climbing down. It wasn't as bad as she had feared. Houses and apartments in Sweden weren't as tall as they were in Israel, where ceilings tended to be somewhat higher to allow for the freer circulation of cool air in the hot summer months. Here apartments had lower ceilings, designed to keep the heat in.

Great when you were shimmying down a makeshift escape ladder to a waiting car.

Ronit Gottlieb felt her stockinged feet hit the cold metal roof of the car well before she was ready for it. Her knees buckled from the unexpected jolt but Henrik Winqvist was there to steady her and help her step down from the roof onto the car's sloping boot-lid and from there he unceremoniously placed one hand on each of her hips and swiftly lifted her down, hustling her straight into the back of the armoured Volvo and shutting the door securely on her.

He looked back up, straining his eyes through the thick clouds of oily smoke belching up through the apartments on the second and third floors. If Isabella wasn't already on her way down, he'd leave her to fend for herself and get the ambassador to safety. That was his sole priority.

Isabella wasn't on her way down. Dan Gottlieb was. Henrik barked into his cuff mike. "Bella! What the hell is going on? Leave him behind! Where are you?"

Isabella Kronlind's voice came through, calm, authoritative and clear. "He's moving on his own. I'm fine. There's nothing going on here, no further penetration into the apartment. The Berkowitzes aren't moving. I'll come down as soon as Dan hits the ground."

As she finished speaking Dan Gottlieb dropped onto the roof of the Volvo and stumbled down to the ground, wrenching his ankle as he did so. Henrik Winqvist ran around to the other side of the car, opened the rear door and swiftly bundled the ambassador's husband into the car, slamming the door shut as soon as he was in.

By the time Henrik was finished there Isabella had already dropped onto the car roof, rolled with remarkable acrobatic ability down across the windscreen and onto the bonnet, gaining her feet with an unexpected agility for someone so tall. Her feet struck something. Looking down, she saw a pair of black high-heeled shoes. The faintest trace of a smile crossed her face as she bent down, picked them up in her left hand, swept the area with her right, gun in hand, and shouted to the growing crowd of onlookers to stand back and call the police, fire service and ambulance service.

With that, she wrenched open the front passenger door, climbed in and threw the shoes into the back, simultaneously shouting to Henrik "Go! Go! Go!"

Henrik went.

He took off so fast the car's forward motion swung the front passenger door shut.

With a scream of four tortured tyres scrabbling for purchase on the wet asphalt, the four-wheel drive Volvo S80 armoured sedan shot forward, narrowly missing an elderly woman who had misjudged the car's distance and speed.

Disaster averted – for the time being – Henrik Winqvist concentrated on driving as fast as the turbocharged diesel engine would spool up, while Isabella Kronlind issued a stream of instructions via her cuff mike and received precise information regarding the route to their designated safe house.

The main police headquarters in Gothenburg at Ernst Fontells Plats in the heart of the city.

Al Fukhkhari, Gaza Strip

Adan Hamati was a man on a mission.

Or, more accurately, two missions.

The first was personal: the tall blond giant, the Zionist officer who had plagued his life in Sweden last year, and who had turned up once again right across the fence from him in Occupied Palestine. Because that's who it was who had been standing on top of the dusty Land Rover.

The second was sacred. Occupied Palestine was going to be freed.

It was going to cost lives. Lots of lives. Both in Gaza and in Zionist-Occupied Palestine. Muslims were going to be martyred, and Jews were going to be slaughtered. Both for a higher cause. Allah would welcome the Muslim martyrs, who would go to their deaths unaware of the immense honour being bestowed upon them.

And as for the Jews … Adan Hamati spat on the dusty ground, the spittle forming a bubble of human waste on top of the dry soil before sinking slowly into the sands of Gaza. The Jews consistently refused to recognise either God or His prophet and messenger Mohammed, peace be upon him, so there would be nobody to welcome them where they were going.

Adan Hamati laid out his plans. Not on paper, not in a colourful PowerPoint slide. Everything Adan Hamati planned, every last detail that he put into place, was inside his head. Communicated to nobody, neither by word nor in print.

Not until the time was ripe.

And that time was fast approaching.

Because despite the Zionists' much-vaunted destruction of Hamas' attack tunnels leading from various parts of the Gaza Strip into Israel, and the Egyptian Army's wholesale destruction of Hamas tunnels between Gaza and the Egyptian Sinai Desert, there were tunnels leading into both Egypt and Israel that were still intact.

Intact, but dormant.

Dormant because both the Jews and their cursed dogs the Egyptians were fast developing advanced new subterranean listening devices to monitor the slightest trace of sound underground.

Adan Hamati was like an obscenely wealthy man with more gold goblets than he knew what to do with, but without a drop of water with which to fill them. Rich, but desperately thirsty.

Because Adan Hamati had plenty of attack tunnels, but as yet no possibility of using them.

That would change soon enough but in the meantime, he would have to be patient.

Gothenburg, Sweden

The van slid to a gentle stop and all four got out. They didn't shake hands, hug or embrace. Each just looked at the other, smiling grimly and nodding somewhat nervously. It was Aisha who broke the silence.

"Right, we'll split up. Go home like nothing happened. We'll watch the news in surprise. Let's see how many of the pigs died, I'm hoping above all the two Zionists got it. Later." And with that she turned on her heel and left.

Zahir Tafesh, Ghalib Ajrour and Amir Assaf watched her go. She was just a girl, and she had more of a mouth on her than they cared for, but you had to hand it to her: she had nerves – and balls – of steel. The three boys embraced briefly and parted.

If they thought the subject was dead until they watched the TV news in feigned surprise, they were wrong.

Just about everything had gone their way.

Just about.

They had set the bomb, armed and triggered it, set the fire and activated the delay charges for the gas canisters that would prevent or at least slow down rescuers arriving at the scene, they had locked the main door of the building to further slow any rescue efforts, and all four of them had made good their escape. Unhindered.

But not unnoticed.

Isabella Kronlind had noticed them leave the apartment building. She'd even seen the van they used, with its distinctive fruit and veg. markings.

And in the armoured SÄPO Volvo S80, the outward-facing dash-cam and passenger-compartment digital recording device had both been up and running as per established security protocol.

There wasn't much for the interior audio recorder to catch apart from Henrik Winqvist turning the pages of his newspaper, and the occasional beeps and whistles as he answered texts and messages on his smartphone, as well as his regular security checks with both Isabella Kronlind in the apartment and police despatch in downtown Gothenburg.

It was the dash-cam that provided the break. First a girl, then in quick succession three young men – boys really – following hard on her heels. The dash-cam was fixed, pointing ahead although taking in a wide angle. It did not see where the four were headed.

But Isabella Kronlind did.

It didn't take long for face recognition software to identify the four young people. In Sweden, everyone is required to carry an ID card or, if they have one, a driver's licence. Both are digitally produced in a high-security tamperproof system, and both prominently feature a photograph of the card holder. The interlinked computer systems of the police, licensing authority and security services make short work of putting names, addresses, current work details – even outstanding parking tickets – to anyone with a Swedish ID number.

Cross-referencing the greengrocer's van with the four faces yielded one match – the same surname was shared by the van owner and one of the three male suspects: Ajrour.

Things were ready to move into high gear.

The first inkling the four had that things hadn't worked out quite to plan came in the breaking news on national TV. The incident was labelled an anti-Semitic act against the well-known head of the Gothenburg Jewish community, Anna Berkowitz, and her husband Isaac. Both had died in a combined bomb and arson attack at their home. There were no signs of any racist slogans or graffiti but there was no doubt they were the target – and they were the only fatalities apart from the two police officers who had arrived later. An elderly man had been bound and gagged by four attackers who had broken into his apartment one floor below, but oddly they had not killed him, nor stolen anything, and had even taken the trouble to give him some kind of rudimentary protection by placing him strapped to a chair inside his bathtub, flat on his back. Flying debris had caused considerable laceration to his lower legs as well as his face and chest, and he was not yet able to speak. He was in critical condition.

The news report made no mention of any political targets, and only four bodies were carried out – those of Anna Berkowitz and her husband Isaac, and the two police officers, Per-Olle Pettersson and Nishtiman Halabjaee. There was little doubt among media talking heads this was an anti-Semitic attack and the police were not contradicting that assumption.

Uniformed police identified the two civilian victims and the two police officers, and said that SÄPO was involved in hunting down the vicious perpetrators. There were however no leads. At all. The public was asked to be extra vigilant in case of any repeat and/or copycat attacks, and to come forward with any information they had regarding this incident.

Swedish Prime Minister Mahmud Sadeghi made a brief noncommittal statement in which he reiterated his government's declared position that all monotheistic religions were recognised by the state and that everyone had the right to observe their religious practices, within recognised limits and provided they did not mock other religions. He declined to make any further comment and quickly returned to his interrupted meeting with His Royal Highness Prince Farooq, the visiting head of state of Qatar.

Sitting in the back of a marked police Volkswagen van with blacked-out windows – the sort of van regularly seen patrolling the streets of most Swedish cities – Israel's ambassador to Sweden Mrs Ronit Gottlieb was in rapid conversation with her embassy security staff in Stockholm. Her husband Dan sat beside her. Isabella Kronlind and Henrik Winqvist sat in the front beside the driver, and in front and behind the ambassador were four heavily armed members of a SWAT team, two to a bench. The van drove slowly up the exit ramp out of the police garage, waited while the heavy security gates opened, and exited into the traffic. It was a regular police van like any other, nothing to attract any undue attention. Up ahead, first one, then another unmarked police car, both rented Opel Insignias from Avis, led the way. There was going to be no question of any further surprise attacks on the ambassador. Not if the Swedish Security Service, SÄPO, had anything to do with it.

Quietly, discreetly, another three unmarked police cars with blacked-out windows trailed the police van. A BMW X5, a Range Rover and an Audi Q7, powerful off-roaders each manned by one driver and three fully equipped – and extremely heavily armed, black-clad and balaclava-wearing – Close Protection Specialists.

The police and security services in Gothenburg were determined to deliver the Israeli ambassador back to Stockholm safe and sound.

And if anything, they were even more determined to apprehend the terrorists behind the killing of their uniformed colleagues and the attempt on the ambassador's life.

Because whatever the nation's indecisive politicians did or, worse still, whatever secret agenda the politicians might have behind their public façade, the security establishment had absolutely no intention of absorbing any more attacks or disruption to law and order, neither by right-wing extremists nor Islamist thugs.

Irrespective of whether it was for political, financial, territorial, religious or other gain.

The police and SÄPO in Gothenburg, at least, were going to impose order in the fast-expanding chaos – the lame Donald Duck government in Stockholm be damned.

Ambassador Ronit Gottlieb and her husband Dan were driven swiftly but without fanfare in an impenetrable and invisible security convoy all the way to Säve Airport outside Gothenburg, on the island of Hisingen. The string of six vehicles stopped outside the terminal building, where the entire Airport Bus platform and the normally bustling taxi rank had already been cleared of waiting passengers, buses and taxicabs. The doors of five cars opened, the heavily armed drivers stayed behind the wheels of their vehicles while the entire security detail fanned out between the marked police van and the staff-only security entrance in the fence at the side of the building.

Once the security gate was opened, the rear doors of the police van opened and the ambassador and her husband, along with their two civil-clad SÄPO agents, were hustled out amidst a sea of black-clad security agents dressed in full body armour and Kevlar helmets. The couple were whisked through the gate, which clanged shut behind them, and they almost thrown into the back of a waiting red Mercedes minibus. The security agents piled in around and on top of them.

The minibus sped across the apron to a waiting business jet.

Not just any business jet. This was a Gulfstream G550. And it sported the three crowns of the Swedish coat of arms. This was no less an aircraft than State Flight II – one of two aircraft, one based in Stockholm and the other in Gothenburg – used exclusively by the Swedish King, the Swedish Prime Minister and selected Swedish government ministers of suitably high rank.

And used now also to extricate the Israeli ambassador from a dangerous situation in Sweden's second-largest city, Gothenburg, and deliver her to Stockholm, Sweden's capital.

Somebody at SÄPO Gothenburg must certainly have some serious pull. This unprecedented use of the State Flight probably involved not so much a word in the right ear, as threats and probably no little measure of blackmail in the wrong one. The Swedish security establishment, it seemed, had no intention of witnessing the debacle of overseas diplomats being assassinated on its territory. Ronit and Dan Gottlieb were walked briskly up the stairs and into the aircraft, led by their SÄPO bodyguard Isabella Kronlind and followed by Henrik Winqvist. The ambassador's black-clad escort bundled quickly down the stairs again, boarded the red minibus and sped back to the security gate. Before they even climbed out of the van the aircraft doors had closed and the jet was taxiing out for take-off. A Ryanair flight to Stansted was put on hold as the Gulfstream jet was given top priority to take to the air.

As the three crowns on the tailplane flashed by the terminal building and the aircraft lifted into the air, the collective sigh of relief from the Gothenburg security establishment could almost be heard over in Stockholm, 550 kilometres to the east.

Right. One liability off their hands in Gothenburg. Now they would deal with the terrorists responsible for the death and destruction and racist violence that had taken place on their patch.

The net was closing.

Aisha Naddi, Zahir Tafesh, Ghalib Ajrour and Amir Assaf all realised the net was closing. Because nobody was saying anything about the ambassador. That could mean she hadn't died or even been injured, but the fact was that two other Jews had perished. So had two police officers who had come to rescue the building's tenants – that was all over the news. It was obvious the government would do everything imaginable to toe the politically correct line and hunt down Jew-killers. It was the wrong Jews who had died – not the

Israeli Jews but the Swedish ones. And with the added complication of two dead police officers – and still no Zionist victims – the tacit sympathy and support they could have expected from Sweden's current and, above all, next government would not be forthcoming. It probably also meant that nobody in the Muslim community would dare offer them help or shelter – right now it was simply too risky.

Which meant that Aisha, Zahir, Ghalib and Amir would be targeted and have nowhere to hide.

This wasn't part of their plan, but when needs must…

It was Aisha who phoned.

"Hi, it's me. I'm going away for a while. Just thought you should know."

There was a silence as Zahir Tafesh pondered over this piece of news.

"Where are you going?" he asked.

"Tell you what," replied Aisha, avoiding the question. "Get the others together and meet me at the usual place and we'll discuss it. I'd recommend everyone brings their passports."

There really wasn't much to discuss, they knew they'd most likely been compromised. There was nothing unusual about people with Middle Eastern names having Swedish passports – Sweden had been allowing in so many immigrants and asylum-seekers from the Middle East over the past few years that the past half-decade alone had seen Sweden's population swell by an unprecedented 450,000 new citizens. And their passports were genuine. All that remained was to decide where to go.

"Gaza," said Ghalib Ajrour when they finally met up. "We'll be safe there, the Palestinian government won't give us up or extradite us, in fact they'll probably reward us. We just have to get there. Best bet is a flight to Turkey, and from there perhaps to Egypt. Turkish Airlines flies from Landvetter Airport every day – and they're the cheapest airline out of here."

They didn't require much persuasion. An airport bus from Korsvägen in central Gothenburg would take them to the airport, where they would buy tickets to Ankara and leave all the fuss behind. Only problem was, Korsvägen was perilously close to the main police station of Gothenburg, and not all that far from Haga, where the attack had taken place.

But nobody was looking for them. At least not in the heart of Gothenburg, a mere stone's throw from the scene of the explosion. The bus carried them swiftly to Landvetter Airport and it was easy as pie to purchase four tickets to Ankara. Asked about their luggage – or lack of it – they plastered smiles on their faces and said they were all cousins attending another cousin's wedding in Istanbul, they were just going there early for some fun time and that their parents would be bringing the entire family's luggage with them later that week.

It was perfectly plausible.

But in the age of Islamist terrorism with its penchant for blowing up aircraft and moving terrorists around an increasingly shrinking globe, it also meant that at least two crucial alarms were triggered with their exit from Sweden.

They were youngsters travelling alone, to Turkey. A well-known transit point, a hub for departure to the Islamic State strongholds of Syria and Iraq.

And they were travelling without luggage.

Two parameters that automatically triggered a digital recording of all their personal details, including their travel arrangements.

Only problem was, being automatically flagged was not the same thing as being physically stopped. The system merely locked the stable door after the horse had bolted.

Which is what Aisha Naddi, Zahir Tafesh, Ghalib Ajrour and Amir Assaf did. They bolted. Not from a stable, but from Sweden.

First stop Turkey. Next stop Egypt. Then hopefully Gaza.

Meantime, they were all flagged as being on the Jihad Express from Sweden via Turkey to the spreading, and increasingly bloody, atrocities being carried out by Islamic State aka Daesh in Syria and Iraq.

If the Swedish security establishment had its way, they wouldn't return to these shores.

Al Fukhkhari, Gaza Strip

There was nothing wrong with the plan.

Adan Hamati went through every detail in his head. Simplicity was best. This plan was immensely simple. The fewer people in the know, the fewer working parts that could go wrong, the better.

The plan itself was fine. It was the people involved who would make the difference. Adan Hamati hadn't yet found the right people. He would, of course. This was Gaza, after all. A cesspit of human misery, with a vast depository of people who had lost all hope – first with the accursed Jews who had denied them a national home but now, even more so with the wretched Hamas leaders who lived in palatial beachfront mansions while the people lived among sewage ditches. There was no money to build proper sewage treatment facilities, claimed the Hamas bigwigs, because the Zionists wouldn't allow the entry of sufficient amounts of concrete, cement and iron reinforcement rods for construction purposes. There weren't even enough building materials to construct bomb shelters to protect the people of Gaza in the routine exchanges of fire between the Islamist regime and the Jews on the other side of the security fence, claimed the Hamas leaders from deep inside the secure underground bunkers they had built for themselves beneath Shifa Hospital.

So how come there was enough cement and concrete and other materials to build the hundreds of Hamas attack tunnels leading under the fence and into Israel, wondered Adan Hamati.

He shook his head in disgust. Not that he was against this policy – in his hands, those tunnels were finally going to be of some real use. But there was no arguing with the Hamas rulers who had colonised the best properties in the Gaza Strip, occupying the choicest beachfront territories and evicting poor fellaheen into the narrow, already overcrowded hinterland of the narrow Strip. Hamas claimed to want the best for the people of Palestine, but so far the only people in Palestine who were doing well were the rich and increasingly obese Hamas leaders living behind high security walls and shopping in exclusive, well-stocked malls. When they weren't stuffing themselves at the many fancy, high-priced seaside restaurants where a plate of humus and pitta, if they even served such simple fare, cost more than the monthly wage of the average Palestinian Arab labourer. For the forty percent of the workforce even lucky enough to have a job at which to labour, that is...

Adan Hamati shook his head once again to clear his thoughts.

All that would change. But only once he had succeeded. His plan would be successful. But that first of all required finding the right candidates to help him.

People without hope, without a future, with no home to go back to. Crushed between the equally oppressive yokes of the Zionists on one side and Hamas within, with the might of an increasingly aggressive Egypt on the emerging front to the south, there was plenty of choice for Adan.

Adan Hamati wanted the best. So he waited and continuing scouting for the talent he needed.

Stockholm, Sweden

Following the attempted assassination of Israel's ambassador to Sweden in Gothenburg and the murder of two police officers, the security establishment pulled out all the stops to locate the culprits.

They already knew their identities. But visits to their homes to bring them in for questioning had resulted in massive rioting, as word of the attempted arrests spread like wildfire and family members and friends descended on the suspects' homes to prevent the police from executing the arrest warrants. Sweden's political Left and the increasingly strident Islamist parties, which many analysts predicted would be in government after the elections on September 20th, cried 'foul' and wheeled out the charge of 'Islamophobia'. Their battle-cry was deliciously simple and appealing: as soon as a Jew got hurt, the police always picked on the nation's Muslims. It was time for long-suffering Muslims to stand up for their rights, to fight back. Today with sticks and stones, but in the political tomorrow they would be fighting back from within the system, as members of the government. But only with the help of the nation's Muslims, and only provided all right-thinking Muslims rallied together and fought as one – physically and politically.

The result was a failed attempt to arrest any of the four suspects, but with scenes resembling a veritable battleground. Molotov cocktails were hurled at police vehicles, firecrackers were aimed straight into the faces of the riot police horses, dozens of cars were torched, shops and pizzerias – mostly owned by hard-working fellow Muslim immigrants who themselves had recently fled war-torn countries – were smashed and looted. Three apartments housing Roma families were ransacked and the occupants driven away with home-made clubs and rocks. The fire service could not deal with the conflagration because firefighters were being attacked with rocks and petrol bombs.

It was only when the commissioner of police announced that martial law would be declared at midnight, with a blanket curfew throughout the embattled area, and that the military would be given orders to shoot to kill on sight if anyone dared contravene the curfew, that the violence fizzled out. Frustrated at being made the target of agitators and violent youths triumphantly howling '*Allahu Akhbar*' in their faces, first one and then more and more fire crews started turning their high-pressure hoses on the retreating bands of thugs, the massive horizontal shafts of water knocking the rioters off their feet and sending them skimming along the road into the gutters.

At midnight calm descended – without the military being called out of their barracks.

Sweden still maintained a semblance of civil society, she still remained an electoral democracy.

But all that was taking place in Gothenburg.

In Stockholm, Marita Ohlsson had been recalled to work despite the late hour and was at her desk collating the incoming information. Anything related to her specialist area – the steady stream of Terror Tourism from Sweden to the Middle East.

And the day's events in Gothenburg had flagged up four new names to add to the 572 already on her list.

Aisha Naddi, Zahir Tafesh, Ghalib Ajrour and Amir Assaf.

They didn't fit the profile.

They didn't fit any profile.

They didn't figure on any terror watch-list.

They were simply regular kids. Kids who had grown up in Sweden. Who had just completed high school and were on their way into adult life, either to continue studying at college or university or to get jobs of one sort or another.

It's not as though they had escaped the radar – they'd never even been on the radar.

Exactly the same as all the other 572 young Muslim men and women on Marita Ohlsson's watch-list.

Her Terror Tourism hall of fame.

Marita Ohlsson stamped her foot impatiently as she sat at her desk. They'd missed the four by just a couple of hours. Not a couple of hours after the four had taken off from Gothenburg's Landvetter Airport, because then they could have asked the Turkish authorities to put them on the next plane back to Sweden. Turkey, led by a staunchly pro-Islamist and anti-West regime, would probably have refused the request but it would still have been worth a try.

No, Marita had only received confirmation two hours after their flight had landed in Ankara.

Which meant the trail had gone cold. There was no point in even asking for assistance. Once Sweden's – and the rest of Europe's – aspiring young *jihadis* had left their home shores there were no means of tracing their whereabouts unless they posted something on social media, which they were surprisingly often prone to do from their operational centres in Syria and Iraq, apparently unfazed about being tracked by Western security agencies.

Like everyone else in the security establishment, Marita Ohlsson knew why this was. It was because most of them had no intention whatsoever of returning. They intended to live and die fighting for Islamic State. Those few individuals who over the years had attempted to leave Islamic State had been summarily executed by the Islamist masters they had once sworn to serve.

They'd been executed the same way infidels were executed by Islamic State: beheaded with deliberated dulled knives so that the process of dying was immeasurably more painful, indescribably more excruciating. The method had its effect, on infidel and would-be turncoat alike. Nobody wanted to cross the Islamic State barbarians.

Which is why Islamic State, which also went by the name of ISIS, ISIL and Daesh, among others, was winning the day in large swathes of Iraq and Syria and even making inroads into Jordan. In fact, their black banners had been seen right up on the north-eastern border of Israel.

Marita Ohlsson shuddered. It was bad enough that Swedish youngsters were using their Swedish passports to travel to Turkey and on to territories conquered by Islamic State. But if Islamic State succeeded in creating serious problems for Israel, the Swedish security establishment's only dependable ally in the region and its only conduit of vital information about Swedish *jihadis* in the Middle East, then Sweden was going to face a far worse problem than it already had.

Because exporting Swedish warriors to the Middle East at least had the benefit of getting them out from under SÄPO's feet.

The flip-side was that the terrorists' return – as full-fledged Swedish citizens, but now battle-hardened and fully experienced in the art of war – was an even bigger problem. Not all wanted to return – most wanted to live and die by the sword and gun in Syria and Iraq. But there were enough making it back to Europe to pose a serious threat. And it was their black flags that were increasingly often seen flying on the streets of Swedish cities.

There was no country anywhere in the Middle East that was either interested in or capable of keeping tabs on these Swedish exports.

Except the embattled state of Israel.

Sweden's politicians loved to hate the Jewish state. Doing so was a cheap vote-catcher in a country with an ever-climbing number of Muslim immigrants, many of whom were bullied and threatened, very much against their will, into toeing the pro-Sharia Islamist line – even on Swedish soil, as the Swedish government continued to turn a blind eye.

But Sweden's security establishment enjoyed excellent, cordial and particularly fruitful relations with the Jewish state. Relations of benefit to both, but of particular benefit to Sweden, some of whose radical elements Israel monitored closely when they entered the Middle East arena.

Marita Ohlsson hit the 'Send' button and despatched the message to her opposite number in Israel.

She rubbed her tired eyes, then stretched her arms wearily above her head as she stifled a yawn.

Another four names on her Terror Tourism watch-list, another four Swedish youngsters travelling on the Jihad Highway.

You could think up any number of amusing, sardonic names for the phenomenon but it didn't do anything to hide or downplay the reality: Sweden had a very serious problem with the steady stream of youngsters eager to learn the skills of war. Short of kicking democracy out the window and placing all at-risk youngsters in internment camps as a means of deterrence – a measure barely contemplated even in times of outright war – there was no way of adequately dealing with the problem.

Aisha Naddi, Zahir Tafesh, Ghalib Ajrour and Amir Assaf. Marita Ohlsson did not know where they were, but she hoped her opposite number in Israel, Amira Hart, sister of the delectable Benny Hart, would do some magic via Israel's covert information sources in Turkey.

Egyptian Rafah, Sinai Desert, Egypt

Every once in a while, the Egyptian authorities would relent and open up the border crossing between Egypt and Gaza. Traffic usually went in one direction only – Gazans desperate to get out from under the increasingly onerous yoke of the Hamas regime.

Egypt was rabidly mistrustful of Palestinian Arabs after it emerged that Gaza's Hamas and Egypt's Muslim Brotherhood had jointly engaged in several acts of terrorism to overthrow civic rule in Cairo and the Sinai Peninsula. Even so, many Gaza Arabs felt they had a better future in Egypt than under their own Hamas leadership.

If for no other reason than that Egypt at least offered a springboard to the world beyond – the Muslim world and the West.

Occasionally, not very often, there were people seeking to enter Gaza from Egypt. University students returning home to their parents. Middle-aged patients returning home following medical treatment in Cairo. Radicalised youngsters with Swedish citizenship making their way to the relative safety of a Hamas-controlled Gaza that would never extradite them following their brave attempt to blow up a Zionist ambassador.

Aisha Naddi, Zahir Tafesh, Ghalib Ajrour and Amir Assaf found, to their surprise, that entry into Gaza, where they all had extended family, was not particularly difficult. All they needed to do was to present their Swedish passports to the Egyptian border guards, state that they were visiting family in Gaza, and then repeat the procedure with the Hamas border guards. Swedes were universally loved in Gaza on account of Sweden's rabid dislike of the Jewish state. No questions would be asked. On the contrary, they would be – and were – feted wherever they went.

Once again it was Aisha who took the initiative, about a week after they had entered the embattled enclave and were beginning to relax in the knowledge that here they were beyond the reach of Swedish or any other authorities.

They met at the house where Aisha was staying with her aunt and uncle. It was still possible for a single girl to go out alone and without a chaperone, but under the fiercely Islamist regulations of the Gaza Strip it was becoming increasingly difficult to do so.

"So, we didn't entirely succeed," said Aisha as they sat sipping hot mint tea. "We got two Zionists, but the wrong two. The question is, where do we go from here? Any ideas?"

They looked at each other. It was a very valid question. They'd made it to the comparative safety of Gaza, but there wasn't a whole lot for them to do here. No mixing freely with friends of the opposite gender, no going out clubbing, no bars for the boys to frequent, no girls for them to pick up. It was very different to life in Gothenburg.

And to be perfectly honest, life was beginning to get a bit boring. Because there was nothing on the horizon – there was no change in sight. Ever.

It was Zahir, ever the objective, analytical member of the group, who put it into words.

"Fact is, we've kind of backed ourselves into a corner. Coming to Gaza was a safe move in an emergency because here we're beyond the reach of the Swedish police, but on the other hand the road to Gaza is a bridge going nowhere – it leads here and nowhere else, and we can't turn back."

Amir Assaf looked thoughtful. "So, like, what next? Here we're OK, but then what? We can all get by with our Arabic, we all grew up speaking it at home, but I for one can't read it very well, certainly not enough to understand a newspaper. So that's studies out of the question. And even if I could read fluently, where would I study – and why? To get a degree from Al-Azhar University here in Gaza City? Great – where's the job after that? There are no jobs here. Unless you want to enlist with Hamas as a fighter."

Ghalib joined in. "That's not such a bad choice. It's not as though we backed away from violence to achieve our goals. We blew up a building and a few people, for heaven's sake! Jews and police! We did it in Sweden, so we can do it across the other side of the fence in Israel."

Brought up in Sweden, he had no trouble using the Zionists' own name for their self-declared country – 'Israel'; only the local Palestinian Arabs refused to call the country by its real name, referring to it in a variety of pompously propagandistic terms such as the 'Imperialist Entity', the 'Zionist Entity', the 'Racist Colonial Entity' and all sorts of combinations thereof.

Aisha shot back immediately: "I have no intentions of becoming a *shahida*! You can if you want, I want to live."

Zahir spoke quietly, persuasively. "It's not a question of becoming a martyr and dying for some cause. But we do have to look at our situation realistically, analytically. What's our future here? The Egyptians didn't let us in out of the kindness of their hearts – they probably knew exactly who we were but didn't want any political fallout from the Arab world by handing us over to Interpol. So they let us in. They let us in to what is arguably the world's biggest jail. And we walked in voluntarily. No, wait," he said, holding up his hand, palm facing outwards to forestall discussion as the other three started arguing vociferously.

"Let me continue, then you can all have your say. We don't decide for each other – everyone makes up his own mind about what he wants to do." He smiled self-deprecatingly as Aisha snorted in disgust. "I stand corrected – everyone makes up his *or her* own mind. OK?" He smiled again at Aisha, who just looked away, although her body stance relaxed visibly.

'Arab men and their macho self-concern,' she thought to herself. 'We sure need a revolution, but it's not a political one between Gaza and Israel – first we need a social revolution in the mind-set of Arab guys whose very vocabulary needs to be kicked right up their arses.'

But she said nothing out loud.

Zahir continued, laying out their situation and their prospects with chillingly concise objectivity.

"So we walked into Gaza. You can bet your last piece of Marabou chocolate," a brief smile crossed his face as he referred to one of the Swedish delicacies that the band of four found themselves strangely nostalgic over, now that they couldn't get it here in Gaza, "that the Egyptian authorities have informed the Swedish security police about our presence here. For them it's a win-win situation: they don't get into trouble with the Arab world by giving us up – in public – while at the same time getting into the West's good books by aiding the West's security services with information about our whereabouts."

The other three looked gloomily at each other.

"Here we're safe. Hamas won't give us up, ever, not even to their biggest supporter and financial backer, Sweden. But what's our future? We either rot away here, forgotten for the rest of our lives. Or," he eyed them all carefully, "or we go on the offensive, turn our disadvantage into an advantage."

"How?" demanded Aisha, strangely intrigued by the persuasive words of Zahir Tafesh, their engineer, their bomb-maker, and their quietly persuasive spokesman.

"Well, one way would be to go out into the open and let the world know – from our own mouths – that we're here, in Gaza. Go on Facebook, let our parents know where we are and that we're fine. That this is where our future is, and that all true, patriotic Muslims and Palestinians should join us in the struggle to free Palestine. Tell the Swedish police they don't have to pretend that they're still looking for us – they know where to find us and they can't do a thing about it."

Ghalib spoke up. "That doesn't make much sense. Why give up our anonymity? Why potentially embarrass our Hamas hosts? Where's the gain? True, the Swedish authorities probably have a good idea by now as to just where we are, but they don't know for sure. Why give away that element of uncertainty? It just doesn't make sense to me."

Amir nodded in agreement.

"I'm not saying we should do that, just that this is one way of going about it – showing open defiance," explained Zahir patiently. "The other way is equally valid," he continued. "Continue letting everyone, including our families, stay in the dark. We can't be in touch with our families because whatever message we send, however we send it, there's always the risk that it can be traced back to us, revealing our whereabouts.

"So we do the very opposite: stay out of the picture. Cover our electronic footsteps. That means no use of credit cards, bank accounts, social media, mobile phones or even landlines. And we look for a way of exploiting the fact that we have Swedish passports, and our credentials of having already carried out an attack on a leading Israeli political figure, and see if we can't build on that. Not suicide missions, but attack missions. There are people my family know in Hamas who will listen to us."

He looked round expectantly.

It was Amir who broke the silence.

Looking strangely sheepish.

"We, er, that is to say, I mean, we may, kind of, be a little late there."

They all looked at him questioningly.

He looked down at the floor and seemed acutely embarrassed, the tips of his ears flushing bright red. "I've been using my bank card to empty my Swedish account."

If looks could have killed, Amir Assaf would have volunteered to climb into his coffin within ten seconds of having spoken.

The other three all started in on him, berating him for his stupidity and for endangering them all without first coordinating such a move with them, since what any one of them did also by definition affected the other three.

"But it's not my fault!" he retorted angrily. "Not everyone has rich relatives high up in Islamic Jihad or Hamas, not everyone has beachfront properties or owns a string of luxury shopping malls like some others I could mention," he shouted, his eyes blazing in the direction of his cousin Ghalib Ajrour. "Some of us have to live by paying our way!" he shouted.

Ghalib balled his right fist over the stinging jibe at his wealthy family's connections and the influence it had amassed through years of highly profitable corruption in Gaza. As he started forward, Zahir stepped calmly in to defuse the situation, putting a very gentle hand on Ghalib's bulging right biceps. Not enough pressure for it to be perceived as an attempt to physically restrain him – that would only exacerbate the situation and redirect Ghalib's wrath – yet just enough pressure for Ghalib to register that someone else was stopping him from escalating the situation so he wouldn't lose face when he backed down.

"I can understand that," said Zahir smoothly and quietly. "Nobody's accusing anyone of deliberately endangering the others. What's done is done, we need to look ahead now. I have an idea. My father has a cousin whose son is here, looking for a few good people. He's obviously in Hamas, but he's not *with* Hamas, if you know what I mean – he pretty much keeps himself to himself but I've heard a rumour that he knows a thing or two about military matters and was wanted by the Israelis in the West Bank before he escaped to

Gaza. He made it in here himself, without outside help apparently, so perhaps he can get us out the same way. Let me have a word with him, see if he has anything to suggest."

It wasn't so much that this was a good idea; it was more a matter of not having any other ideas to suggest.

The other three sullenly agreed that Zahir should make the contact and get back to them when he had something to report. They weren't hopeful.

But then they hadn't yet met Adan Hamati.

Central Israel, Mossad Headquarters

Amira Hart leaned back in her chair, her excitement mounting.

First there was that interesting message from Benny's Swedish flame, the female SÄPO agent in Stockholm. Marita Ohlsson. A decent person. They'd worked together before – more by chance than by design – on that Palestinian terror attack against Gothenburg's bridges some time back. Capable. Quick-witted. Very intelligent. Not someone who was prone to see connections where there were none, and definitely not the kind of operative who leaped to conclusions. Measured – that was Amira's assessment of Marita Ohlsson. Measured.

And here was Marita, in contact not even forty-eight hours later, saying she had confirmation that at least one of the four people wanted for questioning in connection with the attack on Israel's ambassador to Sweden was next door in Gaza. Marita Ohlsson had it on good authority, via the Swedish banks' joint ATM monitoring system, that Amir Assaf had been withdrawing sums of money in Gaza. Just a stone's throw away from Amira Hart's brother Benny's monitoring station in the Israeli town of Ofakim, on the other side of the security fence separating Israelis from Gaza Palestinians.

Marita Ohlsson's report stated that two of the young men, Amir Assaf and Ghalib Ajrour, were cousins and were usually inseparable, had been all the way through school.

If Amir Assaf was in Gaza, the chances were his cousin Ghalib Ajrour was with him. And if, as seemed likely, the two cousins were in Gaza then the chances were also pretty good that the remaining two, Aisha Naddi and Zahir Tafesh, were also nearby. They were all Palestinians, and they all had families in Gaza. Tafesh also had family in the West Bank town of Kafr Jibrin.

The town's name rang a bell for some reason.

After pondering futilely for a moment or two, Amira Hart put the elusive connection out of her mind.

Four young Swedes of Palestinian Arab heritage, wanted by the Swedish police for questioning in connection with a fatal assault on the Israeli ambassador in Sweden. Fatal because two innocent Swedes, Jews, had died. Along with two Swedish police officers. Now even the old man found gagged and tied up in his bathroom one floor below had succumbed to his wounds.

Having so many fatalities was tragic. Because it had been planned and executed as an attack on the head of an Israeli diplomatic mission overseas, it was a Mossad responsibility.

Yet because all the tracks led into neighbouring Gaza, it was more likely a Shin Bet reconnaissance responsibility.

With the Israeli Defense Force, the IDF, doing the field work of extracting the four suspects in order to bring them to justice.

After which the Israeli Foreign Ministry would have the delicate task of deciding whether the four suspects, if safely brought into Israel, would be questioned by Israeli security services for a suspected crime against an Israeli asset, or turned over to the Swedish authorities for a crime committed on Swedish soil.

It was the sort of diplomatic nightmare that made Amira Hart glad she worked behind a desk and in the field for Mossad rather than for the Foreign Office.

However Israel proceeded, the situation had all the ingredients of a massive diplomatic storm in the making.

What everyone agreed on, however, was that this was unavoidable.

Israel had to first verify that some or all of the four suspects were in Gaza, as the Swedish Security Service claimed.

Secondly, Israel had to find out how they had entered Gaza. Because if they had gotten in, they could probably get out and escape the same way.

And finally, Israel had to work out the quickest, smoothest, least violent and most effective way of extracting the four suspects from Gaza and delivering them to waiting hands – and cells – in Israel. Or possibly Sweden. The legal and diplomatic bigwigs could wrangle over that.

Amira glanced at the time on her smartphone. Not yet a quarter to nine in the morning, and already she had a splitting headache.

She wondered if her Mossad boss Calev Mizrachi would be inclined to give her the task of liaising between SÄPO's Marita Ohlsson and Shin Bet's man on the spot in Ofakim, her own brother Benny Hart.

There was a lot at stake. If she played her cards right, Marita and Benny might get to work together on this case.

And she might get to work closely with Calev Mizrachi.

Amira Hart reddened under her smooth dark skin as she reached for her phone.

Gaza City, Gaza

Adan Hamati was not used to people accosting him at home.

Well, the place he currently called home.

Home at the moment was a small room, bare but for a single bed, a wooden table and two plastic chairs, and a small gas cooker on the stone top of the kitchen counter that he used to make his early-morning cup of thick, sweet, aromatic coffee which he drank piping-hot out of a small glass. That was his daily ritual, and the one luxury he allowed himself.

There was a bathroom and toilet next door, used also by the family that owned the house.

Adan Hamati was meticulous about using the bathroom facilities only after the family went to bed and before they woke up in the morning. During the rest of the day, Adan Hamati used bathroom facilities wherever he found them – at a small restaurant if he stopped by to eat a simple meal, at one of the fancy new air-conditioned shopping malls that were popping up all over Gaza City and elsewhere in the Gaza Strip, or behind a dune or a clump of dusty date trees if he was out in the field on one of his innumerable reconnaissance missions.

Adan reflected on his situation. How on earth had this man – this boy really – with the strangely accented Arabic found out his whereabouts? It meant his security had been compromised and it was obviously time for him to move on.

He'd make sure he found a new place before the day was over. And he wouldn't be leaving a forwarding address.

Meantime, he had this boy to contend with.

Zahir Tafesh spoke again.

"My father always spoke highly of you back in Sweden. He knows what you did last year in Gothenburg. And my uncle, with whom I am living here, said I should never contact you or in any other way bother you, that you are a highly regarded hero in the Resistance and that you would not like being approached out of the blue. But even though he warned me off ever trying to locate you, even when I came here last year on holiday, he also always spoke of you with the utmost respect and admiration."

Zahir paused, respectfully. When Adan Hamati didn't oblige by easing the silence, he filled in:

"I'd like to speak with you."

Silence.

"Only with your permission, of course," he continued.

The man looked down at the boy. He opened his mouth for the first time.

"I know your father. And your uncle. We are distantly related. And they are right. I do not appreciate this one little bit. Go home and do not dare ever again to try and make contact with me."

Adan Hamati's glare was enough to freeze the blood in his visitor's veins. But Zahir knew that this was his – well, their, really – only chance to claw back some good out of the increasingly desperate situation in which he and his three friends found themselves.

"Two minutes. Just listen to me for two minutes. After that I will leave and if you don't want to see me ever again, I will of course respect that. I haven't told anyone I was coming to see you." This was not even remotely true and Zahir hoped from the bottom of his heart that the feared Adan Hamati wouldn't take the trouble to verify his claim. "I promise that once I leave, you will never see me again. Just two minutes, that's all I ask."

There was something about the young man's earnestness that triggered Adan's curiosity. Allowing himself the luxury of satisfying that curiosity, he indicated one of the plastic chairs with a gesture of his left hand.

Seating himself nervously on the edge of the chair, Zahir started speaking.

"I have come from…" he managed to say before he was interrupted by Adan.

"You have one minute to make your point. If you anger me before that minute is up, I'll return you home myself – in pieces. Family ties or not."

Zahir gulped, sweat starting to bead on his forehead.

He started speaking. Quickly.

"I have come from Sweden. I was the person who made the bomb and set the fire that killed two Jews and two police officers in Gothenburg but seems to have missed the main target – the Israeli ambassador to Sweden. That's all I have to say. I did it with three friends. We are all here now, we ran away from Sweden after the operation. We can never go back there because the police want us. We want to help the Resistance in Palestine. For that, we need to enter Occupied Palestine, not remain trapped here in Gaza. I was hoping you could help us."

He stopped speaking, sat quietly, nervously waiting for the other man to speak.

Then he added, in what was the biggest gamble of his young life: "That was less than a minute, and you haven't yet killed me. I hope you will think about how we can help – and how you can help get us into Occupied Palestine."

Surprised at his own reaction, Adan Hamati's face creased into something resembling a smile. Gothenburg! Sweden! There was a God after all – even in this confounded place. This could be the break he was waiting for!

"You've got balls, I'll say that for you," he said. "That was you? That thing in Gothenburg? I've got news for you: there was nothing about any ambassador, just two old Jews who died in a fire. And two cops trying to rescue them. And some old man. You march up to me claiming some sort of grand conspiracy that you put together, and you don't have a shred of evidence, not even a result or any kind? You want me to believe you … why, exactly?"

Zahir Tafesh opened his mouth, nothing came out.

He gulped.

"Speak, boy!" thundered Adan Hamati. He had heard rumours on the Palestinian grapevine, eyewitness statements of an emergency evacuation from the bombed and burned-out apartment, of a mysterious black car whose occupant or occupants had helped pull two survivors out of the wrecked apartment and whisked them away at high speed. The news blackout didn't quell the rumours, only strengthened them in the Palestinian and Islamist communities. This had the smell of a true story, but Adan Hamati wasn't about to let some little kid think he held sway. It was vital to put the fear of Allah into him and his compatriots so it would be abundantly clear to them that he owned them, not the other way round.

"Speak!" he commanded once again.

And Zahir Tafesh told his story, from the beginning, leaving out no details. He only started relaxing once he fell into his stride, recalling the components of the chemical bomb he had detonated in the apartment – this, after all, was what he knew best. This was his home ground.

Adan Hamati knew he had found an able replacement for his long-dead master bomb-maker Haydar Murad, who had perished at the hands of that accursed Zionist, the tall blond one he had seen just the other day atop the army Land Rover. This boy here was not only a skilled young man, he was a young man with two major assets: a Swedish passport, and three Swedish friends. Albeit Arabs, but that just made it all that much easier. They were, first and foremost, Swedish citizens. That meant ease of movement.

Just what he needed.

This was shaping up to be a very good day. A very good day indeed.

Stockholm, Sweden

Marita Ohlsson had her orders. The hard-line political establishment in Sweden were perfectly content with Israeli ambassadors being blown up. In fact they wouldn't have minded one bit if the Israelis withdrew their ambassador indefinitely 'for consultations' – diplomatic-speak for expressing outrage over a breach of protocol, a lack of trust or plain and simple rudeness. Unfortunately for the politicians, however, the security establishment played to different rules.

If you started allowing politically inspired mayhem on the streets of Sweden, there was no telling where it would end.

That wasn't strictly true – SÄPO and uniformed police both knew pretty well where it would end.

And they had no intention of letting it end that way, with Islamist thugs, right-wing gangsters or left-wing anarchists ruling the streets.

In addition to which, neither SÄPO nor uniform had any problem with the State of Israel. On the contrary, like most people in Sweden who worked in any branch of law enforcement or who wore any kind of a uniform or had any position of public responsibility to uphold society's amenities, they had a sympathetic understanding of Israel's embattled position and in fact had a good working relationship with the Jewish state.

So SÄPO wanted the matter cleared up. Publicly, openly, done by the book to the very last letter of the law. No stone left unturned, no expense spared. The four suspects would have to be brought in for questioning so they could either be publicly cleared of any involvement, or alternatively charged with the killing of the two elderly Swedish Jews and the pensioner, the manslaughter of the two police officers, and the attempted murder of the Israeli ambassador and her husband.

End of story.

Marita Ohlsson put down her phone and smiled. She was heading back to Israel. For the second time in less than a year. Upon arrival she would first report to the Swedish embassy at Asia House on Weizman Street in Tel Aviv, and then check in to her hotel, the beachfront Renaissance Hotel on Ha-Yarkon Street in the same city.

She put her desk in order, looked around her small office once more to make sure everything was neat and tidy, added some water to her potted plant, left a note on her desk for the cleaner asking him to water the plant just once a week on Fridays, then switched off the light and walked out, closing the door behind her.

'Tel Aviv, here I come,' she thought to herself. 'And I sure hope it's sunnier and warmer there than it is here in Stockholm.'

She needn't have worried.

Lufthansa flight LH686 winged its way steadily eastwards. It crossed the Israeli coastline, where the sparkling turquoise of the Mediterranean Sea met the glistening yellow sands and glittering white houses of Tel Aviv, the skyline breached by a number of remarkable commercial skyscrapers and residential high-rises, architectural wonders spearing their way high into the crisp azure skies.

The Airbus A321-200 started slowing down and began to describe a large arc in the sky as it descended, looping over the beautiful new city of Modi'in perched picturesquely in the Judean foothills halfway between Tel Aviv on the coast and the Israeli capital, Jerusalem further to the east.

The lumbering aircraft completed its loop, heading west once more and came in to land at Ben Gurion Airport, touching down gently and racing ahead until the pilot reversed the engines and began slowing down the aircraft.

And just like the last time she had landed in Israel, many of the passengers burst out into a round of wild applause. Marita Ohlsson looked around, amused. What was that about? Were the Israelis on board just happy to be back home with their families and loved ones, or did they know something about the pilot that she didn't? She hadn't seen any obvious "Learner Pilot" signs inside or outside the aircraft...

As the aircraft came to a halt and the seat belt sign was switched off a member of the cabin crew came up to her and told her she was to disembark before any of the other passengers, using the stairs at the front where she would be met on the apron and escorted through passport control.

Marita Ohlsson looked up, surprised. This was not something she was expecting. The cabin steward looked even more bemused – there had been nothing about this passenger that suggested she was a VIP or bigwig of any sort.

After picking up her small overnight case, which contained her laptop and other essentials, Marita made her way down the stairs of the aircraft, where she was met by Amira Hart.

"Welcome back to Israel. Hope your stay here is long enough to get your job done, but short enough to leave you with some extra time to visit anyone you may miss." Amira smiled disarmingly.

Marita shook hands with Amira and they both broke into peals of laughter. Benny's sister had a wicked sense of humour, Marita reflected.

"How is, you know, how are things?" Marita asked.

"Oh, *things* (Amira emphasised the word) are fine. *Things* is waiting impatiently for the weekend so *things* can get to meet you. *Things* can't stop talking about you. And *things* reckons he might have some information for you."

The two looked at each other and smiled companionably, chatting as they got into a small white Skoda Fabia with amber flashing lights on the roof. The driver sped off and deposited them at a dull grey metal door leading into the terminal building. He got out and swiped his electronic card unlocking and opening the door for Amira Hart and Marita Ohlsson.

"Straight through along the long corridor and go to the lobby and the counter marked 'Cabin Crew'. They're waiting for you," he said over his shoulder as he made his way back to the car.

The two women made their way down the corridor to the passport counter. Amira Hart presented her Mossad ID, was told to report to the security desk to recover the weapon she had had to check in earlier, while Marita Ohlsson's passport was examined and she was issued with an electronic entry visa just like all other visitors to Israel received.

In and out in less than four minutes. The advantages of working in the security service of a friendly ally.

Well, an ally anyway.

"Are you fixed for transport?" Amira asked as they waited for the baggage carousel to bring Marita's suitcase.

"I have to pick up a rental car from Avis," replied Marita.

"OK, I guess you have official business to attend to first. Give me a call when you're done. But remember, this is Israel. Here every car is equipped with the three essentials: horn, accelerator and, in the case of an absolute emergency, a brake pedal. In that order of priority. So watch the traffic. Including when the traffic light is red – some people here seem to regard red as an advisory only."

Marita smiled and replied: "I've visited Tehran and Calcutta – if you can survive traffic in those cities, you're brave enough to face anything with four wheels," she said confidently.

Amira looked at her. "You're really that naïve, are you? Call me from the hospital…" and with that they both burst out laughing as they headed for the Avis car rental counter.

"Give me your mobile phone," said Amira as Marita Ohlsson dealt with the car rental paperwork. "I want to download an app that you'll find very useful when driving in Israel. It's pretty much the unspoken religion here – forget Judaism, Christianity, Bahai'ism or Islam. In Israel, once you get behind the wheel of a car, you pray to Waze."

"Ways?" asked Marita. "Ways to do what?"

"Not Ways, Waze". Amira smiled. "Yes, they sound the same but spelt differently. It's W A Z E. An interactive app in your smartphone or tablet that finds the best ways to get to your destination. Forget the satnav that Avis gives you – that's static and just shows you the route to take to get to your destination. Waze is interactive, everyone who uses the system inputs information as they drive, pinpointing road hazards, roadworks, traffic jams, animals on the road, police speed traps, cyclists on the motorway – yes, you'll believe it when you see it! – and so on. The software takes all this information into account and instantly computes your current position, speed and destination and works out the best route to your destination, the quickest way to get there in hours and minutes – which is not always the shortest route in kilometres. It prioritises time to destination, not distance to destination. Learn to trust it – it goes against the grain when you think you know a shorter route or your Avis satnav suggests an alternative route, yet Waze recommends you to take a different direction entirely. But the system knows if there are traffic snarls up ahead, which you don't. Learn to trust it and you'll always get to your destination in the quickest way possible.

"Here," continued Amira and handed back Marita's phone. "I've programmed it so the menu and the audible voice commands are in Swedish. Although the place names are in English and sometimes in Hebrew. Plug it into your car's cigarette lighter socket because the system uses a lot of battery power, and off you go. Give me a bell when you're done."

And with that Amira Hart raised her arm over her shoulder in farewell as she walked off toward her own car in the Orchard car park at Ben Gurion Airport's Terminal 3.

Marita Ohlsson looked down at the screen of her smartphone. Amira had already programmed in three destinations: Benny Hart's place of work in Ofakim, his home in Ashdod (well, his and Amira's parents' home), and the Swedish embassy on Weizman Street in Tel Aviv.

Amira hadn't asked for or programmed in the name of Marita's hotel in Tel Aviv.

For some inexplicable reason Marita found herself blushing over the deliberate omission.

Ofakim, Israel

"This is just too boring for words," said an exasperated Benny Hart to nobody in particular. Because there was nobody else in the room.

Benny Hart was trying to make sense of something that made no sense at all. Or at least didn't seem to.

Car thefts. Mostly in the rural south, but also in the centre of the country, where most of the population lived.

And that was when he began to see the pattern that was emerging. Yes, they were all older vehicles. Yes, there were fewer thefts in the centre of the country, despite the fact that the population density – and therefore the number of cars – was far higher there.

What did that mean?

It probably meant that in the relatively more affluent urban sprawl of the centre of the country, a higher proportion of cars, and a larger number of cars in absolute terms, were newer. People here were more upwardly mobile, their cars were factory-equipped with all the latest electronic immobilisers, and the more expensive luxury models were fitted with tracking devices.

And unusually, at least compared with the rest of Europe, it wasn't these more attractive models that were being stolen. It was the simpler ones, older, more run-down, beat-up second cars in large families, in fact even large seven- and eight-seat minivans and pick-up trucks. Hard-working vehicles.

And nobody knew where they were going.

Benny Hart grabbed his phone and made a call to a good friend of his at Traffic. Just eight months ago, Mariyam Gavriel of the National Traffic Police Directorate had lost her husband Yussuf, a serving Shin Bet officer, in a terrorist attack on a deserted stretch of Highway 90 that ran along the shore of the Dead Sea to the east and the hills of the disputed West Bank to the west. The couple were Israeli Christian Arabs. Which made them, in particular Yussuf, a target for both Israeli Islamists and West Bank Palestinian Islamists who insisted that it was the duty of all Arabs, Muslims and Christians alike, to hate the Zionists and to drive them from the land. Going over to the dark side by joining not just the police but, worse still the security police, the Shin Bet, was the most evil kind of treachery imaginable as far as the extremists were concerned.

Yussuf Gavriel was hit in a classic ambush – the terrorists knew who they were waiting for, having let several cars pass by before picking the one he was driving. Somebody in the Palestinian Authority on the West Bank with close ties to Israeli security was obviously passing on information about the movements of Israeli police and Shin Bet officers – and Israel had not yet located the source. That night Mariyam Gavriel became a young widow.

After the phone rang twice Benny heard it being picked up. "Mariyam," he spoke into his handset. "How's it going? Your twins behaving themselves or do you want me to come round and pinch their cheeks for them? Just let me know and I'll be round.

"Meantime, I have a question. Anything unusual popped up regarding this spate of stolen vehicles, any pattern you reckon you can see, any trace of where they are being taken? I'm assuming there's no particular increase in the movement of stolen cars between Israel and the Palestinian territories, or we'd have heard something from your lot?"

"Benny, what do you take me for? Of course you'd be the first to hear if we found anything worth reporting. The only thing I can say for sure is that we can see no particular pattern of increased trafficking of stolen cars going east to the West Bank. That means they're either being chopped inside Israel, I'd guess maybe in Ramle or Lod, or that they're making their way south to the various Bedouin towns and villages in the Negev Desert. In either case, they're finished, we'll never see them again.

"The problem," she continued, "is that without some form of conclusive proof as to the cars' whereabouts, the insurance companies aren't paying out, and that in turn means there are lots of people who are without their cars and no financial means of replacing them. So this really, really, needs to be sorted out double-quick. And yes, the twins could definitely benefit from someone pulling their noses, so bring Amira and come around some time. There'll be cheesecake in it for you."

After salivating for a few moments and chatting about nothing much in particular Benny hung up.

Why did he get the distinctly uneasy feeling that everything was starting to point toward the south of the country?

And which part of the south? All the way to Eilat on the Red Sea coast? Or just the northern part of the Negev Desert, abutting the Gaza Strip, where he himself was based in the small town of Ofakim?

It wasn't as though there was a whole lot else in between the two, just desert. And the city of Beer Sheva. That was a large city nowadays, plenty of space to hide a bunch of stolen vehicles, when you thought about it. And there was the Mitzpe Ramon crater, but that was a nature reserve, you couldn't get several dozen stolen cars down into the depths of the crater. For what reason, anyway?

There was the small town of Arad, but the operative word was 'small'. 16,000 souls – and that was only if everyone was at home on a Friday night eating dinner at the same time. People in a small town this size knew everyone else's business, from the size of their shoes to who was going on the latest diet fad. So if stolen vehicles started turning up someone was bound to start asking questions.

Finally of course there was the small, dusty town of Dimona. Nothing much happened there.

Except for the fact that it housed what Israel consistently denied it had: a nuclear reactor capable of producing – or perhaps already having produced – a stockpile of nuclear weapons. Israel's policy of plausible denial, fashioned over the decades by the country's one-time Defence Minister and later Prime Minister and even later President, Shimon Peres, had served Israel well. It had kept Israel's Islamist foes off-balance. It had made Israel's self-professed allies wary of giving the Jewish state's enemies enough diplomatic, military and financial leeway to implement the genocidal mayhem that was always on the Islamist menu.

But in this day of the Internet and instant access to digital information, that open secret was scarcely any longer a secret. Plausible denial was no longer the deterrent it once was.

Benny leaned back in his chair, biting his lip in concentration. In a worst-case scenario, why would anyone be interested in a bunch of beaten-up old jalopies in or around Dimona? Stealing low-tech cars and stockpiling them in or near what was probably Israel's most high-tech – and best-secured – defence hub?

It didn't make even remote sense.

Which was why it was well worth investigating.

If the name of the game was low-tech, Benny Hart was going to approach it the same way.

He rummaged in his drawer and found what he was looking for, a large road map of Israel, courtesy of Eldan Car Rentals the last time he had rented a car to drive down to Eilat. That was a year ago, when Marita Ohlsson had flown in after their impromptu mission in Sweden, for what turned out to be a remarkably memorable five-day stay in the beautiful Red Sea resort.

Well, memorable was stretching it a bit. Marita had said afterwards that she couldn't remember all that much of Eilat because they hadn't actually left the hotel all that much. They'd spent most of the time in their room, with the "Do Not Disturb" sign hanging firmly on the outside door handle, surfacing only to cast themselves ravenously over the lavish evening buffet in the large poolside hotel dining room on the ground floor.

Benny shook his head. She was supposed to be arriving here any day now, Marita. Was it going to be just business, or would they have some more quality time together? And how would he keep his nosey-parker sister Amira out of his life for the duration?

Benny chased all other thoughts out of his mind and focused on the task at hand.

The Eldan map took up most of his desk after he moved his keyboard and mouse pad out of the way.

He turned it to the southern section of the country, on the flip side.

Mentally he put on a *keffiyeh*, the chequered headdress favoured by the Palestinian Arabs as a kind of national symbol even though it differed little from the headdress worn by Arab men all over the Middle East, from Syria to Iraq, from Lebanon to Saudi Arabia. Adorned in his imaginary *keffiyeh* he viewed the map as a local Bedouin Arab might do. What was he looking for?

Benny tried to picture what he would want to do if he were aiming for mayhem and he had a bunch of rundown old cars at his disposal.

And that's when the pattern became crystal-clear to him.

It was idiotic that he hadn't seen it before. And that nobody else had seen it either.

Because a free, giveaway paper map showing the roads of Israel also showed how the attack would take place, and what it was that would be attacked.

Gaza City, Gaza Strip

Adan Hamati surveyed the four youngsters as they sat facing him.

They were in the ground-floor apartment of a prominent Hamas militant, Salem Rajoub.

Salem Rajoub was one of these immensely rare people with vision. Vision beyond the strictures and harsh interpretations of the Sharia. He realised the importance of coming out of nowhere to do a job and then disappearing equally unnoticed.

To do that, you had to be prepared to turn your back on certain givens. For instance, the Islamic beard for men. The modest hijab for women. If you wanted to blend into the society of your unwitting hosts, you had to look like them, dress like them, talk like them, even do the things that appealed to them.

And that meant practice.

Because it was difficult to live like an observant Muslim your whole life, and then switch overnight into a different persona to carry out a mission. The human psyche didn't work like that, it didn't adapt that fast.

What you needed, if you wanted to successfully insert yourself into your unsuspecting host society, was to live the life of your host society.

And there was no better way of doing that than by using people who had lived that way all their lives.

Like the four young people currently sitting opposite Adan Hamati.

Adan hadn't introduced the four to Salem Rajoub – the five had never met. It hadn't been necessary. Adan had outlined his plan to Salem, described the four youngsters, their background and their bungled operation in Sweden.

And Salem Rajoub had given Adan the go-ahead. Salem didn't need to meet, and for security reasons didn't want to meet, the four youngsters. He was just the facilitator. And financier.

Permission for the mission had already been secured from higher up the Hamas hierarchy. As Hamas was officially in the Palestinian coalition government, this would not be a Hamas operation but one run by Islamic Jihad. Different name, same goal: dead Jews. Salem Rajoub would be coordinating it all. And he would finance the operation via the revenue generated from one of Hamas's very few remaining, undiscovered, smuggling tunnels still operating under Rafah into Egypt.

The fact is that preparations had been under way for weeks now. Months, if you included the aftermath of that last war of aggression the Jews had undertaken against the martyrs of Gaza.

'Protective Shield' is what the Zionists called it. Well, it hadn't protected them much. The Palestinian mortars and rockets had pulverised half of Israel and brought that country to an economic and industrial standstill, while the tunnels had kept the Jews guessing as to where the brave Hamas fighters would appear next, popping up out of the ground to kill and maim Zionist Occupation Force soldiers or anyone they came across – young or old, man, woman or child.

The Jews had destroyed the tunnels in an operation that had cost them many lives, and calm had been restored to the border communities on either side of the security fence.

Or so the Jews thought.

Hamas had not contradicted Israel's belief that the destruction of thirty-odd tunnels leading from Gaza into Israel had ended the problem.

The Zionists were going to get a lesson in belief that they would never forget.

In fact, to put it more accurately, if Adan Hamati had his way, there would be no Zionists left to have any belief. Not in the Holy Land, anyway. The unassailable power of *jihad* would teach them a lifelong lesson.

And his tools were sitting right across the table from him.

Adan Hamati started speaking to Aisha Naddi, Zahir Tafesh, Ghalib Ajrour and Amir Assaf.

Mossad Headquarters, Central Israel

"You can be sure they didn't enter Gaza from any Israeli land crossing, or from the sea," said an exasperated Calev Mizrachi, defiance edging his voice.

"But we know that at least one of them – or someone with access to both his bank card and his PIN code – is in Gaza. We have the withdrawals to prove it," said Marita Ohlsson as mildly as she could. She didn't want this to develop into an inter-agency pissing contest. SÄPO wanted this wrapped up as quickly and neatly and quietly as possible, but they had to establish how one or possibly more Swedish citizens had gotten into the Gaza Strip without apparently crossing any border control points apart from entry into Turkey, a thousand kilometres to the north-west.

"Look, we have two indices," intervened Amira Hart. "Use of the bank card at a Gaza ATM, and the 'anonymous' tipoff from an untraceable phone number with a '+20' international prefix calling code. Plus 20 is Egypt. It's a safe bet that they entered via Egypt. Either via a smuggling tunnel that the Egyptians don't know about under Rafah or somewhere nearby, or more likely via the official border crossing at Rafah but without being officially processed. A few dollars exchanging hands and the Egyptian border guards will let anyone into Gaza – they're a lot more difficult to persuade when it comes to letting people out of Gaza into Egypt."

Calev Mizrachi looked at Amira Hart, and Amira looked around the assembled group. Nobody disagreed with her.

"So now what we have to do," she continued, "is to try and find out if the other three are there too, and then how best to apprehend them so that the relevant Swedish authorities can question them regarding any possible role they might have played in the attack on Swedish soil. And of course we will want to question them ourselves regarding any possible role they might have played in the attack on Israel's top diplomat in Sweden. So let's work together."

"We don't have any intelligence assets on the ground in Gaza," said Calev Mizrachi, looking steadfastly at his shoes.

Marita Ohlsson smiled discreetly and ignored this blatant lie. The Israelis obviously weren't prepared to compromise their information sources inside Gaza just to apprehend four young hoodlums, albeit hoodlums with blood on their hands. Their Gaza sources would only be deployed for issues relating to real and present security threats to the Jewish state and its citizens.

Marita sort of understood this, although it was galling not to get the assistance she had hoped for. They'd have to find a different way of locating the four Swedish murderers and would-be assassins.

Neither SÄPO's Marita Ohlsson nor Mossad's Calev Mizrachi counted on getting help in their task from an unlikely source: Hamas in Gaza. Unwittingly, but help nevertheless.

Gaza City, Gaza Strip

Adan Hamati knew he had just one single opportunity to set the tone, the tone that would make or break his plan.

These four spoiled brats needed to know who was boss, who called the shots – but they also needed to feel as though it was all their voluntary decision, that it was actually a good idea and in fact the only workable idea.

"You know you're burned. You can't ever go back to Sweden to meet your families, even if you wanted to. You'll be done for manslaughter, murder and also attempted murder. You can't go anywhere else to meet your parents secretly in another country because you can't get out of here. The Jews have this border sealed tight to the north and east, and if anything the Egyptians in the south are even worse. Not only that, the Egyptian security agents will either arrest you when you show your passports, or more likely they'll just tip off Interpol so they don't have to dirty their own hands."

Adan Hamati surveyed the four glum faces opposite him.

"So what are you saying, we're stuck here for the rest of our lives? Why do we need you to tell us this? We've worked that out already," Aisha Naddi blazed defiantly.

Adan looked at her mildly. Let her have her say. She thought she could live in Gaza and behave like a headstrong western girl living in Sweden? She'd learn soon enough. But not right now. Right now he needed to get her on side.

Because, much to his surprise, Adan Hamati was fast learning that it was this tiny little slip of a girl who actually set the tone for the group of four refugees.

Swedish refugees in Palestine! A quick, almost imperceptible, smile flitted across the dark features of Adan Hamati's face as he savoured the delicious irony of the situation.

But back to business.

"That's not what I am saying. What I'm saying is that the conventional ways out are closed. All you have left is to swim out to sea and make your way to Europe, hoping you won't be detected by the Zionist gunboats patrolling this entire coastline. Frankly, I wouldn't give you particularly good odds on that."

"OK, I've got that. Why are we here then?" persisted Aisha. The three young men, still in awe of being in the presence of Palestinian resistance legend Adan Hamati, had not yet uttered a word since entering the room apart from mumbled greetings.

Adan liked the girl's guts, she definitely had leadership qualities. What Aisha lacked in physical strength she made up for in a directness, a willingness to tackle confrontation head-on instead of beating about the bush. He liked that, it was a mind-set that would stand her in good stead.

But meantime she would have to learn her place if her outspokenness wasn't going to antagonise her compatriots, wasting their energy and diverting their focus. Adan Hamati could already see the signs. He'd take her under his wing and give her the necessary psychological training when the time was ripe.

Out loud he said: "You're here because I want to show you the way out. Yes," he held up his hand to forestall the barrage of questions that even the boys had plucked up the courage to ask. "Yes," he repeated, "there is a way out. On your part it will require intelligence, strength, an ability to plan and stick together, courage. And one other thing." Adan looked at them, one at a time.

"What is that?" ventured Ghalib Ajrour.

"Commitment," replied Adan Hamati. "Dedication. And you've already shown that the four of you have all of this, and more besides. You carried out an operation that you planned all by yourselves. And it worked perfectly. It only missed its target by some freak of chance. But it worked! And that's because you had a plan, rehearsed it, implemented it exactly as rehearsed, and then left the scene. I couldn't have done that part better. What I offer you now is a chance to do all that, and more. But on a much grander scale."

He looked at the four expectant faces, wondering not for the first time if he had made the right choice. He was convinced he had – that wasn't the problem.

The problem was ensuring that they carried out his plan exactly as he intended, without succumbing to the western penchant for deviating from the orders of one's elders and betters. Arabs and Palestinians though they undoubtedly were, they were also Swedes. And Swedes were accustomed to thinking for themselves.

Adan Hamati had no place in his plan for people who thought for themselves.

He proceeded to lay out his plan for the four youngsters.

After first assuring them that as of now, they would not be able or allowed to venture out of the house on their own.

As of now, they were in training.

And so their training began.

Ashdod, Israel

"So you're saying there are two separate missions that are ongoing right now?" Marita Ohlsson asked.

She was sitting at an outdoor café on the paved *tayelet*, the promenade which snaked along the beachfront of the southern Israeli port city of Ashdod. Seated at the same table were Amira Hart and Benny Hart.

The brother and sister looked at each other.

It was Amira who broke the silence.

"Look," she said. "This is entirely off the record because officially we will deny everything if any of it comes out, and there's every likelihood that any leak will also end all liaison with SÄPO on the recovery of your four Swedish murderers in Gaza – if indeed they are there." She looked down very pointedly, closely examining the red and grey paving for no reason whatsoever and saying not one word more.

Marita felt her interest mount. "You mean you have eyeball confirmation that all four are there? In Gaza?"

Amira said nothing. Benny spoke. "Mossad neither can nor will speak on this issue, and Shin Bet will not officially confirm any sighting. All I can say, entirely unofficially of course, is that if SÄPO wants to be sure of getting their hands on the four suspects with Swedish citizenship wanted for the deaths of those people in Gothenburg, it will probably be worth your while to stick around so you will be on the spot should they appear in the very near future. SÄPO should count on trying to get an interview with them on Israeli soil before," he paused, and looked straight into Marita's eye, repeating slowly, "before, the Swedish embassy in Tel Aviv or, worse still, the Swedish consulate in East Jerusalem, is notified. If the embassy is involved, there will be all sorts of red tape to cut through. If your Arab-loving consulate staff in Jerusalem get wind of the story, if and when such a story emerges, then you won't be dealing with red tape but with rivers of red blood because they'll whip up the Palestinian Arab population into a frenzy of violence. It's what your East Jerusalem consulate people do best. They're hate-mongers, pure and simple. The problems we have with our home-grown extremist Islamists is child's play compared with the problems that your East Jerusalem consulate deliberately cause us, their rabid incitement every single day from behind the diplomatic security of their consulate walls." He leaned back in his chair, looking out to sea.

The sea used to be his father's domain. His father, Dov, had been a naval engineer and had worked on sea tests, verifying the seaworthiness of many of Israel's cutting-edge attack surface craft. Even so Dov could never get enough of the sea. On the Sabbath he would take his children out in their small boat, teaching them to sail and fish while his wife Sarah enjoyed a well-earned day to herself at home.

As a child Benny had known that his father worked in something to do with the military, but back in those days, to a child at least, that didn't mean very much. Everybody's dad was in the military – all men served for three years and then did up to one month of reserve duty every year. His dad went to work, and when he was home they had fun together. Who would have thought that almost three decades later both he and his sister would be more or less following in their father's footsteps, working and living in a far-flung security apparatus necessitated by the many and varied threats facing the Jewish state.

Benny sighed imperceptibly. His mind was wandering. He needed to focus. Focus on the job – the official bit – and on the unofficial, behind-the-scenes smoothing of relations that actually made the official job possible: sitting in a café setting out the parameters of the upcoming mission.

And he needed to focus on trying to get some quality time with Marita Ohlsson on the day all this was over.

Whatever that day brought.

"So you're saying I should stick around in case there are developments that may interest SÄPO, but you don't know if there is something in the offing, when, what or involving whom. Have I understood you correctly?" Marita asked.

"You understood perfectly! That's what happens when you receive a crystal-clear presentation that is strong on detail, leaves no questions unanswered and lays out all the facts with immense clarity," replied Benny with a wicked smile.

Marita Ohlsson smiled wryly. "Yeah, right. I've gotten all the information I'm going to get, now all I have to do is to sit around and wait."

"You don't exactly have to *sit*," said Amira, emphasising the last word as she got up from her seat. "I'm off up north for a late evening in the office so you two have the house to yourselves for a few hours. I'll call before I head back home," she said as she grabbed the small backpack she always used in lieu of a handbag. Some Swedish habits were hard to kick.

"You're paying!" she flung over her shoulder to Benny as she made her way to the car park and left the two to themselves.

Benny considered his options. Work in the office, or an afternoon of liaising with the delectable Marita Ohlsson at home.

Marita made up his mind for him by putting her hand on his and asking if his parents were home or still overseas on holiday.

Gaza City, Gaza Strip

"Run through the plan once again," commanded Adan Hamati.

Surprisingly, there were no sighs of impatience or frustration. He'd gotten them all on board.

Strike one.

Aisha Naddi, Zahir Tafesh, Ghalib Ajrour and Amir Assaf looked at each other and started ticking off on their fingers as they repeated the procedure they had spent the past few days learning by heart.

It wasn't particularly complicated, and there wasn't a whole lot to learn. It simply had to be done in the right order, and at the right locations. That was all.

It was Zahir who started speaking.

"When we get the signal, we move out, two to a tunnel. Amir and I in the 'Al Quds' tunnel and Ghalib and Aisha in the 'Deir Yassin' tunnel."

Amir took over. "When we get to the end of our respective tunnels, where the screwdrivers and hand-shovels have been left in position for us, we sit and wait until we get the second signal. We don't move until then. We can drink water, but we can't do anything else. Literally no moving in case we are detected."

Ghalib filled in. "When we get the second signal, I grab my screwdriver and start drilling out the bolts retaining the hinged metal panel above our heads, in the vertical part of the shaft. In the other tunnel, Amir does the same. Once the bolts are out and the panels are loose, we swing the horizontal bracing strut 90 degrees to align with the hinged section in the middle and let the metal panel collapse in on itself, folding it in half along the hinge and dropping it on the floor."

Aisha continued. "Make sure you don't drop the panels on our heads, they're made of steel and they're heavy. In each tunnel, we then use the hand-shovels to dig the remaining distance up through the soft soil until we penetrate through to open sky. The last fifty centimetres of the vertical shafts are not shored up with cement, so there may be some caving in, but at that depth the soil is fairly moist since the farmers irrigate at night. Damp soil will tend to stick, preventing collapse. Ghalib gives me a leg-up and I climb out, then he climbs out after me. I give him a hand if he needs it."

That brought a snort of derision from the muscle-bound Ghalib Ajrour. He wasn't going to need help from a girl, what did Aisha think she was, a female James Bond? After all this was over he was going to have to put her right.

"In our tunnel I climb out first," said Zahir, "and I don't need to help Amir out of the tunnel because he is a big strong man who can look after himself." Everyone burst out into spontaneous laughter, even Ghalib smiled wryly at his own expense. He'd had it coming, he supposed. But he was still going to teach that *bint* Aisha a lesson when all this was over. Embarrassing him like that in front of everyone.

"OK, that's enough. Focus!" said Adan sharply, but his mouth was still twitching slightly at the corners. He really liked this girl, she could stand up for herself. But if he read the meat-head Ghalib's body language right – and Adan was seldom wrong when it came to assessing people – there was trouble in store between these two. Bad blood that might actually lead to bloodshed. He'd have to have a word with Ghalib – and he'd have to give Aisha a few additional lessons in self-defence.

"What comes next?" he demanded.

"Like the others, we strip off our dusty overalls, drop them back down the tunnel opening, gather together any shrubbery we find nearby and cover the tunnel opening," said Amir. "We're already inside the kibbutz perimeter fence in the area where they are building new houses, across from the road running parallel with the back of the school building. Zahir and I make our way directly to the kibbutz factory," said Amir. "We plant the two small backpacks as agreed, Zahir's at the six-inch pipe where it dips down below the ground just beside the building's outer wall, mine I keep with me until we get to the row of cooking-gas canisters at the back of the kibbutz kitchen, which in turn is at the back of the big communal dining room. The timers have already been set, the phone batteries have already been fully charged. We just place the bags and leave, making our way to the meeting-point with Ghalib and Aisha. We still have our other four small backpacks with us, two each, as well as the grenades and the pistols."

"Really?" asked Adan Hamati. "And what vital step have you forgotten in all this?"

Zahir and Amir looked at each other in consternation, going through their mental checklist.

Nothing was missing from their recollection of the plan, which they had recited step by logical step from the very beginning to this point.

Aisha filled in the missing what was missing.

"Between the first and second person climbing out the tunnels, the person remaining below has to hand the backpacks up through the hole to the person up top. We both forgot that. But we do know that's all part of it," she added lamely.

"There's no 'knowing' anything," snapped Adan Hamati. "You repeat every single step of the plan until you have it pat, nothing omitted, nothing added. We'll go through this three more times today. But in the meantime, continue. What comes next?"

"Aisha and I make our way to the white Mazda 4x4 pickup parked at the end of the field under the row of eucalyptus trees," recounted Ghalib. "The ignition key will be on the hollow inside of the steel front bumper, on the right side. Aisha sits in the passenger seat, I drive to the T-junction where the road from Kibbutz Sadot Darom leads to Road 250 as it makes its way between Ashkelon and Beer Sheva. At the junction two point four kilometres further east where a small road leads right to Kibbutz Margalit, we place one of my small backpacks behind the concrete bus shelter, covering it with sand and a few dead eucalyptus branches."

"Then what," Adan asked.

"By now we are ready to move into the next phase of the operation," said Aisha. "Ghalib and I drive down to Road 2591, turn left and make our way to the parking lot outside the Rami Levi supermarket in Ofakim. There we will find a white Peugeot panel van, ignition key on the floor under the rubber mat on the driver's side. I take the van and Ghalib and I drive on to rendezvous with Zahir and Amir."

Adan nodded, satisfied thus far.

"We cut the wire fence surrounding the kibbutz about 100 metres to the south of the main gate," Zahir said, recalling the details with ease. "After we crawl out, we bend the jagged edges of the cut fence inward so it looks like we broke *into* the kibbutz, not out. This simple ruse may not stand up to a detailed forensic analysis of the site but in the short term it will keep the kibbutz in lockdown and the police and military will be busy looking inside the kibbutz for non-existent intruders. They won't be looking outside where we are."

Amir filled in. "We walk all the way down to the main road, taking care to keep in the shadow of the eucalyptus trees lining the road on either side. We split up for the walk there, one on each side of the road to present a smaller target should we be seen. At the main road, there should be an old white Ford Transit van parked by the side of the road with its emergency flashers going and the rear end jacked up, with the right rear tyre off the road as though it has a puncture. I take the wheel, Zahir stands outside to make sure I do it right."

"It shouldn't be a problem," Zahir added. "Just get in, start the engine and drive off the jack – it's a front-wheel drive van so it should easily pull you ahead by the front wheels. I make sure the jack hasn't caused any problems with the underside of the van, throw the jack into the ditch at the side of the road and climb into the front with you. You drive straight for just under nine kilometres until we hit Road 264 and then make our way north to Rahat. As we enter Rahat there is a Sonol petrol station on our right. In the parking lot out back there will be an old blue Hyundai minivan with glass side windows. The ignition key will be on the driver's seat under an old newspaper. That's our new ride."

The session went on and on throughout the day and evening until Adan Hamati was certain all four knew every single detail of their mission by heart. There was no room for mistakes, in fact no room for thinking. He needed them to do exactly as planned without hesitation.

His plan depended on it.

Ofakim, Israel

For once both the Israeli military and the top politicians were in touching agreement.

Never again would Israel suffer the indignity, the demoralising debacle, of seeing millions of citizens having their lives torn apart, disrupted for 50 days by a Hamas terrorist organisation operating largely on a shoestring budget and using workshop-made mortars and Qassam rockets, with some Iranian-built range extenders in the form of the more advanced Grad, Fajr-5 and M-302 Khaibar missiles.

The next time conflict broke out, and all the indications were that there would be a next time, quite soon in fact, the targets had already been selected by Israel's military top brass with the full backing of the country's political echelon.

If Palestinian terrorists ever again chose to attack Israeli civilians *en masse*, military and civilian infrastructure belonging to Hamas, Islamic Jihad and Fatah had already been pre-marked for total annihilation. From wherever the terrorist attack originated: from Gaza City or Ramallah, from an open field or a hospital. From now on, there was total consensus in the Israeli leadership: there would be absolute repayment in kind for every act of violence against Israeli civilians, if necessary repayment in the form of random targeting of infrastructure in the terrorists' heartland until the terrorists got the message and ceased their wanton attacks. The new Israeli policy would lead to wholesale destruction on a scale never before witnessed in the region.

The Israeli leadership's reasoning was as appealing in its simplicity as it was lacking in nuance. Nuance was for those who could afford it, and Israel couldn't afford nuance in a neighbourhood where the country was under constant and increasing attack by terrorists, who in turn received diplomatic and financial backing from a Western world whose political leaders – but not their military strategists – turned a blind eye to constant, escalating, Islamist aggression against the Jewish state and its citizens.

An increasingly embattled Israel felt that she went to war in the most humane manner ever conceived by mankind, including warning in advance of forthcoming pinpoint attacks to take out enemy positions. These enemy positions were almost always illegally concealed and deployed from within civilian infrastructure. Even so, the world community consistently responded by roundly condemning Israel. And then proceeded to reward the terrorists with billions of dollars in aid to rebuild, replenish, restructure, ready for the next round of genocidal violence against the Jewish state. That was the perception in Israel, and it was backed by most of the Israeli population.

So the new doctrine in Jerusalem dictated that if Israel were to be ostracised, penalised, sanctioned and threatened even if it went to war with one hand tied behind its back out of humanitarian concerns, it might just as well go all the way and get the job done, once and for all – the Jewish state would attract exactly the same amount and type of criticism anyway, no matter how it conducted its self-defence.

This new policy was known to Israel's Security Cabinet and a few field officers on the nation's front line as "The Apocalypse Scenario". Either Israel got to live in peace with its neighbours – not an absence of war but actual peace – or there would be no neighbouring infrastructure still standing from which terrorists could attack under cover. Wholesale destruction. Egypt was applying just such a policy towards Gaza, with wholesale destruction of its Rafah border community, and the tactic was paying off for Egypt. Israel intended to take a leaf out of the Egyptian book.

In Israel's northern Negev sector that bordered the Gaza Strip, it was Benny Hart's unenviable – some said impossible – task to ensure that the Apocalypse Scenario never played out.

Because it was Benny Hart's task to prevent the sort of major Hamas and Islamic Jihad attacks that would trigger this kind of massive Israeli response. There were of course the almost predictably sporadic sniper attacks and infiltration attempts from Gaza but if Benny Hart had his way they would stay just that – low-key and sporadic.

What Benny Hart didn't know was that the Middle East was on the brink of a permanent game-changer – if Adan Hamati had his way and Benny didn't.

Tel Aviv, Israel

Marita Ohlsson left the Swedish embassy with her ears still ringing.

She'd always seen herself as a calm sort of person, analytical and clear-thinking and not overly given to impetuousness or thoughts of violence.

But on this particular day, she was glad that she was not in Sweden where she would have been armed as per SÄPO protocol.

Because she was not entirely sure she would have been able to resist the temptation to put a bullet between the eyes of the Swedish ambassador to Israel.

Yes, Marita knew that the politicians in Stockholm weren't entirely enamoured of the Jewish state. But she, Marita, was an officer of the law serving the Swedish public in the vital area of national security – she was neither a politician nor a tool for politicians to play with.

And she didn't appreciate being told not to do her job.

Least of all by a jumped-up little tart of a woman. A Swedish ambassador to Israel whose sole qualifications for the job seemed to be that she disliked the Jewish state only slightly less than she disliked the prospect of having root canal work done by a dentist wielding a Black & Decker drill.

The idiot! The vindictive, bigoted, blinkered fool of a woman! Christ, if this ever got out!

But of course it never could get out. Because as a professional, Marita Ohlsson knew she would never reveal the depravity, the naked, undiluted racist hatred, of the Swedish state's top diplomat in one of the world's most sensitive countries.

She didn't feel there would be any point in reminding the ambassador that two serving police officers had also died in the attack. Swedish police officers' lives apparently didn't merit a thought for the Swedish ambassador.

"Look, let's examine this objectively," Ambassador Gunhild Hofström had said. "It was just a couple of old Jews who died in Gothenburg. These people are used to it by now. Let's face it, it's what they do best – die and then put the squeeze on the world community to obtain massive reparations for their fellow-Jews by way of compensation."

Marita Ohlsson had said nothing. Hands behind her back, she had actually pinched her bottom with the thumb and forefinger of her right hand to check if she was awake and really was hearing this, or whether she was in the midst of a particularly horrible nightmare.

Unfortunately, she felt the pinch and winced. Ambassador Hofström saw the look of pain that flitted quickly across her face and misinterpreted it.

"You think I'm exaggerating? D'you even know how much we have had to shell out via our taxes over the decades just to 'protect' Jewish institutions in Sweden? It's in the millions – every single month and year, from 1945 and down to this very day. As for Germany..." Gunhild Hofström almost looked as though she would spit on the carpet in disgust, stopping herself only because the carpet was emblazed with the Three Crowns of the Royal Swedish Coat of Arms.

"The Germans have had to pay through their noses ever since World War Two, even having to give the Jews" – she apparently couldn't bring herself to use the term 'Israelis' – "attack submarines at cut price so they can terrorise the neighbouring states. But of course that's the Jews' other great skill – bargaining." And this time the spittle actually flew from the corner of Ambassador Gunhild Hofström's exquisitely made-up mouth.

Marita Ohlsson reflected idly that the ambassador must give herself a particularly generous cosmetics allowance, bearing in mind the amount of lipstick she probably went through every day in the Jewish state as she lambasted Jews for having a state.

The good ambassador went on to inform Marita that the SÄPO officer was on the ambassador's territory, she was not at home running around playing at cowboys and Indians. She would not tolerate any diplomatic embarrassment at the hand of a SÄPO loose cannon who thought she was on a mission. Ohlsson's job was ceremonial – she was here to demonstrate goodwill by, well, simply by being here. She was not here to assist in any way, to provide intelligence from Sweden, or drag the embassy into any compromising situations.

Marita Ohlsson listened aghast. Not provide intelligence from Sweden! This was a SÄPO issue, a police matter in other words, not part of an underhand political agenda!

More of a natural diplomat than the highly-paid ambassador sitting opposite her, Marita Ohlsson smiled warmly, said she understood perfectly and added she would keep the embassy informed if and when there was anything to report.

"I don't expect there will be anything for me to do or say," she lied cheerfully, "so you may not hear from me all that frequently or in any great detail. After all, if I have nothing to contribute to their investigation," she smiled wickedly, "then I have nothing to report to you."

Ambassador Gunhild Hofström wasn't quite sure whether the SÄPO operative had wholeheartedly agreed with her, or had in fact done the precise opposite. With a vague sense of unease she got up from behind her glass desk, stretched herself to her full height of one metre sixty-one and offered her right hand in what was intended to be a firm, intimidating power handshake to the salaried officer sitting opposite her.

She was a bit taken aback when Marita Ohlsson drew herself up to her full height of one metre seventy-nine – her black

Gucci heels (on fifty percent sale at the NK department store in Stockholm) helped – and pumped the ambassador's hand vigorously, almost wrenching her shoulder from its socket.

"I'll be sure to be in touch if there's anything you need to hear," she smiled sweetly at the ambassador who was slowly massaging her right shoulder with her left hand. "This is such a lovely office you have here," she added as she made her way to the door. "You can see almost the whole way to the beach from here. I think I'll go there for a walk and a coffee. No point in overdoing things, eh?" And she winked as she left, shutting the door quietly and deferentially behind her.

Swedish ambassador Gunhild Hofström had absolutely no idea whether she had just won a battle, or lost a war.

Hilton Beach, Tel Aviv

Marita sat in the warm sunshine at Aroma Café. She sat picking at her Greek salad. What was it with Israelis and their huge portions? Benny had warned her that she should never, ever, order more than a child's portion for herself, or just one regular portion between two adults. He'd been right. And his sister Amira had been right about this fantastic Waze app in her smartphone. Just tap in the destination and it guided you to your destination – not necessarily by the shortest route but definitely by the quickest one. Brilliant! The Israeli high-tech industry was definitely alive and kicking.

Marita pushed back her half-empty plate and asked the waiter for a second cup of Turkish coffee. This was good stuff, strong, thick, with a gentle hint of cardamom and with a kick to it that sent your eyeballs spinning in their sockets. But it kept you awake for hours.

And right now Marita Ohlsson wanted to keep very awake, very alert.

She was obviously going to have a problem with the ambassador. What she needed was a way of ensuring she could stay out of the embassy's reach, but legitimately. She would simply have to manufacture a problem with her office-issue smartphone and try and get herself another phone for the duration of her stay in Israel, with a local number that only a few select people would have.

The first of those people would be Benny Hart. She picked up her Samsung S6 and called Benny. She needed a burner – a cheap prepaid phone with a local number that couldn't be traced. If a leading Shin Bet operative working on his own home turf didn't know where to lay his hands on such a device, he wasn't worth knowing.

Benny Hart was definitely worth knowing. He gave her the address of a phone operator near her current location that supplied such phones to tourists and other short-term visitors.

Marita Ohlsson paid her bill, leaving a tip which must have been way too big judging by the delighted smile creasing the young waiter's face. "Welcome back!" he said happily.

"I'll have to ask Amira or Benny what sort of tip the locals leave, I have no intention of paying for that waiter's dental work for the rest of his life," muttered Marita as she made her way to her parked car.

She tapped in 'Azrieli Center Tel Aviv' and made her way to the triple towers of the shopping and office complex. After undergoing the regular security check of her car's luggage compartment at the entrance to the underground car park, she found a suitable parking slot on level two and made her way to the massive multi-storeyed shopping mall. At the Cellcom store she bought two burners, simple smartphones with few frills but with the major benefit of unregistered numbers. She also bought a car cigarette lighter phone adapter with twin USB sockets.

Back in her car, she plugged in her new USB adapter and then connected both phones to charge them. By the end of today, once both phones were fully charged, her SÄPO-issue Samsung would develop a mysterious fault that would take, oh, at least a week to repair.

If Marita wanted to do her job properly, she needed to be on the grid with SÄPO and her Israeli liaison counterparts, but totally off the grid with a Swedish ambassador hell-bent on placing Swedish-Israeli connections firmly in the bottom drawer of the diplomatic freezer.

Still using her office Samsung, Marita Ohlsson scrolled through her Waze menu until she found 'Hart Ashdod' and checked it.

The intelligent, interactive navigation system guided her down Arlozorof Street and Jabotinsky Street until she hit Route 2, which swept her through the heart of Tel Aviv until it merged with the fast multi-lane Ayalon Highway and finally Highway 4 heading for Ashdod and Ashkelon, where the speed limit rose to a satisfying hundred and twenty kilometres an hour as the smooth blacktop of the wide-open motorway carried her south.

On her left, the fast-expanding towns of Rishon LeZion and then Yavne flashed by as she headed ever south, past the sands of Palmahim between the highway and the sea. On her right, the sun danced and sparkled off the shimmering blue waters of the Mediterranean Sea as she sped south towards Ashdod, a mere 45 kilometres away.

She'd give her hotel maid at the Renaissance Hotel Tel Aviv an easy time – one less bed to make in the morning.

Gaza City, Gaza Strip

This was the beauty of the electronic world's marvellous opportunities, thought Adan Hamati to himself. People got accustomed to the easy life offered by the thousand and one amenities made possible by advanced electronics, and that suited him just fine.

Advantage and disadvantage, upside and downside, good days and bad days. Or in the pithy Arabic vernacular *yom assal, yom bassal* – 'one day honey, the next day onions'.

Adan Hamati was all set to deliver a massive load of stinging, eye-watering onions to the Zionists. By the time he was finished with them, the Jews were going to have a really, *really* bad day.

And it was all going to cost about as much as ... well ... pretty much no more than a few kilos of onions, to be honest.

Adan Hamati smiled in satisfaction. The most delicious part of it all was that it was the Zionists' own vehicles, their own advanced electronic systems, their own over-reliance on advanced gadgetry, that was going to do Hamati's work for him.

Well, that and four Swedish youngsters, aided by a number of strategically positioned Israeli Arab patriots dotted around Occupied Palestine.

Everything was in place, or soon would be.

Adan Hamati went through his mental checklist once again, ticking off each item in his head as he reviewed the list.

Nope, there was nothing missing, everything was set, waiting for the starter's signal.

His signal.

He made his way on foot to a small coffee shop in the heart of the city. Sitting down at one of the five empty tables, he waited until the owner came over and ordered a cup of coffee for himself, with a side-order of chaos in Occupied Palestine.

The man nodded twice, one for each order, and hurried away to prepare the coffee and pass on the second message verbally to an assistant who in turn would run to an address a few streets away to relay the word, after which a third person would make up the chain and deliver the order. All so as to ensure the least possible chance of traceability. No phones – landlines or mobiles – were involved.

Not until the final two links in the chain of communication. The first a phone call placed to Gothenburg, Sweden, and the second from 'Sherif' instructing his cousin 'Ahmed' to 'sell his car' in Ramle, Israel.

The message from Gaza City in the Gaza Strip to Ramle in Israel, a distance of 60 kilometres as the crow flies, took almost twenty-four hours to get there, covering several thousand tortuous kilometres to bridge the short gap between the two cities.

But for Adan Hamati, it was worth the wait.

And in the meantime, he had his cup of steaming fresh coffee to enjoy before he went home.

Ramle Police Station, Israel

Chaim Azulay put down his mug of mint tea – his fourth of the day – and scratched his spreading tummy.

Fifty-four years old and looking forward to the day when he could hang up his police sergeant's uniform and start enjoying a life in retirement, he smiled ruefully and shook his head in wonder.

He thought – not for the first time as pangs of hunger gnawed at his insides on this, his third day of wife-induced diet – whether it wouldn't really be much more humane to just walk under a bus rather than put his body through such torture.

But of course two things held him back from such drastic action. First, the sheer effort involved in walking all the way out the police HQ, down the steps and out onto the road, then making a left turn and walking a massive seventy or perhaps even eighty metres till he got to the main road where the number thirty-seven and eight-two buses ran.

And who could manage so much effort without sufficient sustenance in his body?

Secondly, and much more importantly, his wife Bracha had an eagle eye and was the moving force behind Chaim's diet. She was in uniform and on duty, working the front desk. He'd never make it past her.

And in any case, if he were to overlook the hopefully temporary discomfort involved in losing a few extra kilos, he had one major goal to live for. His daughter Malcha and her husband Itai had been blessed with a gorgeous little daughter, Re'ut. A smiler and a giggler if ever there was one. Luckily, the little doll didn't seem to have inherited her looks from her maternal grandfather, so the girl had at least some chance in life…

Chaim Azulay looked hopefully at the plate beside his empty mug and verified, for the third time, that the plate was as empty as his mug was. So much for the power of tele-transportation from the fridge to his plate, he thought.

Ah well, back to the order of the day, he thought to himself. Time to pay that car repair workshop a visit. The police station had received information that it was serving as a front for a chop-shop, cutting up stolen cars to provide used parts for the second-hand market. Someone down south in Ofakim had requested that officers from Ramle police station pay the garage a visit to have a poke around. Nothing official, no search warrant since there was no probable cause. Just make the police presence felt, keep the light-fingered element of the motor trade on their toes.

Chaim Azulay sighed and reached for his sunglasses, calling the front desk to ask for a partner to come along for the trip.

Bracha Azulay despatched a young rookie just out of police academy, Ofer Dahan, to keep her husband out of trouble. Chaim walked past his wife just as she finished her call.

"Don't forget you're meeting Malcha straight after work to take her and the baby to the clinic – I'm on late shift all this week and Itai is still on reserve duty," Bracha reminded her husband.

Chaim rolled his eyes in mock desperation and replied testily but with a smile playing across his round face. "Yes ma'am. I know ma'am. I won't forget ma'am," and walked out through the front door of the station to the police car and his partner waiting outside. Of course Bracha would remind him – as though he needed reminding! He did admittedly have the most erratic short-term memory in the civilised world and rarely remembered anything unless he wrote it down, but strangely that only seemed to apply to remembering household chores and names. When it came to his work – and now also with the advent of his gorgeous little granddaughter Re'ut – he never forgot anything. Ever. Today he would knock off at five sharp this afternoon, as soon as he completed this visit to the workshop. He'd get this young lad to drive him straight back to the station, he wouldn't bother to change out of uniform but just get straight into his own private car, a brand new small Kia Picanto that nowadays proudly and permanently carried a baby seat in the back for his granddaughter, and head straight off to pick up daughter and grandchild. He'd be there on time, no worries.

Chaim Azulay tossed the keys of the police Kia Sorrento SUV to the youngster – what was his name now, Aron, Oren, something like that? – and said "You drive. Hope you've learned to stop on red, start on green, and drive smoothly in between the two. Let's go!"

Ofer Dahan smiled but didn't say anything. Everyone in the station knew Chaim Azulay was no scarier than a stuffed teddy-bear. The veteran officer simply watched too many TV cop shows and wanted to project an image, to seem tougher and fiercer than he really was. In fact he had a well-deserved reputation as the most affable cop in Ramle police station. He'd been around a bit, seen it all, and there was very little on the job that fazed him. He was quite simply the go-to guy to ease in new recruits on the job.

And today's harvest apparently consisted of this green youngster – what was his name again? Asher, Ophir? – who was to accompany him on his last job of the day.

Chaim Azulay couldn't keep up the pretence of gruffness for long – the boy actually drove smoothly and considerately and didn't speak unless spoken to. He was definitely worth cultivating.

"So, what did you say your name was? Alon?"

Ofer Dahan replied without taking his eyes off the road. "The name's Ofer, and we're going to the Achim Rimon car repair workshop on Bezalel Street, number 37. We're going to make our presence felt but not behave heavy-handed, just have an informal look around and see if there's anything that looks like illicit dismantling of stolen cars there."

'The boy's done his homework,' thought Chaim Azulay to himself with a small smile. 'Obviously knows I need help with names.'

"Right," he said out loud. "We take it easy, shake hands all round, nothing mob-handed. They'll probably have a lot of Arab workers there too. They should," he glanced sideways at Ofer Dahan behind the wheel and continued slowly, with emphasis, "they *should* be Israeli Arabs. Which is fine. If you have any reason to suspect that anyone there is an Arab from the Palestinian Territories, just catch my eye. No heroics. If necessary we'll want to check IDs, but all low-key. We're not there on behalf of Immigration or the Border Police, we're just doing our job, which is to follow up on reports of the possible dismantling of stolen cars. That's it. Routine. Let's make sure we keep it that way."

Ofer Dahan said nothing but nodded assent. Chaim Azulay glanced at him once more and nodded to himself with satisfaction. Yes, this boy knew when to speak and, above all, when not to speak. He'd make something of himself yet.

Achim Rimon Car Workshop, Ramle, Israel

Moshe Rimon looked up from his computer in the stuffy little metal-and-glass cubicle that served as his office in a corner of the car workshop.

Back in the old days when his father and uncle – the *achim* or *brothers* Rimon – had opened the garage together, servicing cars was simple, mechanical, usually dirty but straightforward.

Today, you had to have a Master's degree in rocket science just to know when to change the oil in a modern car. For the simple reason that cars weren't mechanical gadgets any longer, they were four-wheeled boxes of electronic wizardry. They were scarcely recognisable as vehicles, more like large combinations of advanced laptop and cutting-edge mobile phone. Permanently connected via the Internet to Google and data clouds and other complicated stuff Moshe Rimon didn't even begin to understand. Who needed a mechanic these days? You no longer brought your car in to your friendly neighbourhood workshop for servicing, you took it in to a laboratory where a white-coated technician hooked it up to complicated – and costly – diagnostic apparatus to electronically monitor the state of its health.

All this cost money – and when you'd gotten to Moshe's age, 'north of fifty-five' as he liked to say – you were more interested in just coasting to retirement than in having to learn new skills, investing huge sums of money in new equipment, training new staff with expertise that he himself hadn't a hope of grasping.

Which is why the lucrative sideline of chopping stolen cars had appeared as a godsend when it was proposed by one of his creditors.

In the mixed Jewish-Arab city of Ramle on Highway 40 south of Tel Aviv, there were plenty of people whom Israel's surge into the brave new high-tech electronic world had left behind. Jews and Arabs alike. Where religion and politics divided them, the need to make a living united them.

And nowhere was it easier to make a living than in the grey zone of gently modifying the rules of possession between people with money and those less privileged.

In plain English: theft.

In Moshe Rimon's case, theft of cars.

But the electronic world had more or less put an end to the lucrative business of stealing cars and selling them on. Everything was electronically tagged nowadays. All that remained – and in fact it generated far more money – was to still steal cars, but now to immediately chop them up for spare parts. Whole cars were too easily traceable. Before Israel's security barrier separating the Jewish state from the Palestinian Territories went up, there was plenty of money to be made by Israeli Jews stealing cars in Israel and driving them over to eager Palestinian Arab buyers. Now the barrier put more or less of an end to this trade.

What remained therefore was to regroup and adapt. No more links with Palestinian Arabs in Nablus and Jenin and Ramallah; now the links were with Israeli Arabs in Lod and Ramle and Rahat.

And there were two good lines of business these days. Three, if you included the official front of honest car servicing, repairing punctures and replacing cracked windscreens.

The first was the chop-shop – stealing both high-end but also budget models and quickly breaking them down for resale as spare parts. There was a lot of money here.

The second was something that had suddenly experienced an inexplicable surge in recent months: fairly old cars, vans and pick-ups brought in to Moshe Rimon's workshop for storage. Not for chopping, not for resale, just for storage to be picked up later.

Moshe Rimon wasn't quite sure what it was all about or who was behind it. All he did know was that he got paid hard cash to store the vehicles. Five hundred shekels straight into his pocket for each vehicle stored on his premises, with the promise of another five hundred per vehicle when it was picked up. He'd be stupid to say no to a thousand smackeroos in parking fees – and he already had more than twenty vehicles dotted about both inside the large, ramshackle workshop and parked up in the walled-in yard outside.

Moshe Rimon sighed contentedly and reached for his mug of Elite instant coffee to take a sip. His three workshop assistants Mahmoud, Osama and Amin – he reflected not for the first time that he didn't even know their surnames and wasn't particularly interested in finding out what they were called – were down the far end of the garage straightening out the bent metal fender of a panel van. They were good workers who knew how to turn a blind eye to Moshe's illegal practices. Hardly surprising since they themselves were illegals, Palestinian Arabs from the Territories who had neither work permits nor residence permits for the State of Israel. They lived at the back of the workshop, sleeping on mattresses behind a pile of old tyres and showering every evening in the workshop's bathroom. It was Moshe who brought them their food every day, and it was also he and he alone who spoke to the workshop's few customers. The three Arabs just got on with whatever they were asked to do.

And the arrangement worked fine so long as it continued uninterrupted.

On this day it was interrupted.

Moshe was about to light his last cigarette of the afternoon before closing shop when he saw two uniformed police officers enter the workshop.

His heart skipped a beat.

"Hi!" said the older of the two cops, a round-bellied, middle-aged man of medium height who had a disarming smile on his face. "You the owner, or is he around somewhere?" The policeman looked around without much interest or enthusiasm.

Moshe Rimon put down his untouched coffee mug and got up.

As he walked toward the two visitors the younger one looked him up and down, scrutinising everything about his appearance without saying a word.

"That's me!" said Moshe with as much cheerfulness as he could muster. Visits from the boys in blue were never a good thing, especially not now that he was 'looking after' vehicles that were undoubtedly somewhat on the shady side of the used-car market. He wiped his hands on his trousers and held out his right hand to shake the officers' hands.

Chaim Azulay grasped the mechanic's proffered hand and pumped it vigorously, saying this was just a routine visit.

"We're calling in on all the businesses on the street to follow up on some attempted break-ins in the area over the past few weeks. Probably just some young kids bored out of their minds after school but hey, we've got to go through the motions, right?" He beamed cheerfully despite his blatant lie.

'Just a *jobnik*, a pen-pusher,' thought Moshe Rimon to himself. 'He just wants to get this over and done with and get back to his doughnut or bagel or whatever he left uneaten in his car. It's the other one that bothers me.'

He was right to be worried about Ofer Dahan. The younger officer hadn't yet spoken a word, he hadn't shaken hands, but he was taking an immense interest in the large number of vehicles parked in the workshop.

Something wasn't quite right here, Ofer Dahan thought to himself. In this day and age, even relatively small outfits like this one would be specialising either in a particular make or makes of car, or in particular types of repair work. No workshop could afford the expensive diagnostic equipment to take in such a huge variety of vehicles that he was seeing here, because each make required different diagnostic equipment.

What's more, he wasn't seeing any expensive diagnostic equipment of any description. In fact, if his eyes didn't deceive him, probably the nearest thing to electronic wizardry in the entire workshop was the laptop he could see in the small glass cubicle from which the proprietor had emerged. Well, that and the electric bulbs in the ceiling. In today's high-tech world, there simply weren't any such old-fashioned workshops still in existence that could make a living patching up such a wide, eclectic mix of models and makes. Nobody had such fixer-uppers any more – everyone in Israel seemed to be driving new or relatively new imports from the Far East or Europe.

Something was fishy here. Ofer Dahan, still not having spoken a single word, left his colleague and the workshop owner and sauntered slowly over to the vehicles parked along the sides of the big shed-like workshop.

"What's his game?" asked Moshe Rimon, more nervously and aggressively than he had intended.

Chaim Azulay smiled disarmingly and replied. "Kids, eh!" he said deprecatingly. "Always wanting to show their bosses they're keen, bloodhounds on the lookout. Never mind the boy, he'll just wander around a bit trying to look impressive and come running back to me when he discovers his hands are dirty. So, tell me, any break-ins or attempted break-ins recently, anything you perhaps haven't reported to the police?"

Chaim Azulay looked around, caught Ofer Dahan's eyes and nodded almost imperceptibly in the direction of the three workshop assistants who had been wrestling with the van's metal panel but who now stood still, looking more than a little nervous.

The police had that effect. Even law-abiding citizens who'd never even returned a library book late tended to exhibit signs of nervousness in the presence of the law. That was nothing, and Chaim was accustomed both to seeing this and also to putting people at their ease. But his sixth sense, his copper's gut feeling – and he had an ample gut – told him something was not quite right with one or more of these three. Possibly nothing more sinister than a string of unpaid parking tickets, perhaps a case of overdue alimony payments, but still worth checking out.

Ofer Dahan noted the look and the ever so slight inclination of his superior's chin in the direction of the silent trio and he made his way casually toward them.

Amin clenched his left fist around the large metal bar he'd been using to straighten the fender. Sweat beaded on his forehead. The other two started moving slowly away from him, each in opposite directions.

Ofer Dahan called out. "Hold it a minute, can I see some ID please?"

Amin lunged at him with the iron bar. The other two broke into a run and scattered in different directions, Osama slipping over some scattered tools lying on the floor of the workshop and flying headlong into the side of a blue pick-up truck.

Ofer Dahan was already tensed and ready for trouble. So much for the old man's yakking on about taking it easy and no mob-handed tactics. Ofer's right hand closed around his canister of pepper-spray and had it in his fingers when his attacker's metal rod swooped down toward his head. He twisted his body to the left and the heavy metal bar struck him a glancing blow on the right forearm, momentarily numbing it and sending the spray canister flying from his grip. Ofer grimaced in pain, dropped quickly to his haunches and straightened back up almost immediately, sticking out his right foot and sending Amin flying flat onto his face.

As Amin scrambled to get back to his feet Ofer Dahan leapt onto his back and pinned him down with the full weight of his body, digging his left knee hard into the small of the sprawling man's back.

Amin roared in pain and bucked this way and that, trying desperately to shake off the policeman. From behind, Ofer Dahan grasped the man's neck in a vice-like grip with his left hand and with his right retrieved his pistol, thumbing off the safety and pressing the muzzle deep into the right shoulder-blade of his would-be attacker.

"Keep still or I'll blow a hole in your back!" Ofer Dahan shouted. Amin stopped wriggling and the officer released the man's neck and seized his left wrist, bending his arm backward and shifting his own body to pin the man's hand flat against his back under his own body weight. Moving his gun up to the soft back of the neck he growled "Move and it'll be last thing you do!" The policeman transferred his gun to his left hand and with his right grabbed Amin's right hand and snapped it back behind him, placing it beside his left. With his right hand, Ofer Dahan reached to his belt for his handcuffs and secured the man's wrists in a single smooth, practised movement.

The policeman stood up and holstered his weapon, retrieved his can of pepper-spray and then looked first for his older colleague and the other three men.

Chaim Azulay was struggling with Moshe Rimon, who had pushed the officer onto his back and was shouting in broken Arabic to his two remaining workers to come help him. As Osama and Mahmoud emerged from their hiding places in different parts of the large workshop and started making their way towards the two struggling men, Ofer Dahan shouted to them in Hebrew to stand still and put their hands high into the air.

Neither paid him any attention, but the interruption gave Chaim Azulay enough time to bring his knee up with surprising agility into Moshe Rimon's groin, causing the latter to let go of the police officer and crumple to the floor, screaming in agony and clutching his most prized possessions.

At this the two Arab workers started running toward the older officer. Their intention was merely to slip past him and get to the main door of the workshop and out into the yard, and from there into the street to make good their escape.

Neither Chaim Azulay nor Ofer Dahan had the faintest inkling of their intentions, however. Seeing two men running straight toward his older partner and having himself just been attacked by their colleague, Ofer Dahan was certain they meant to harm the older officer, two against one. He withdrew his weapon once again and shouted to them, in Hebrew, to stop.

Osama and Mahmoud didn't stop. Whether because they did not understand a word of Hebrew, or because the adrenaline was pumping and they wouldn't have taken in anything in any language, or because they were absolutely determined to make good their escape to avoid being picked up by Israeli immigration police as illegal aliens, they continued barrelling down toward the front door, toward where Chaim Azulay was now getting to his feet and Moshe Rimon was still writhing in agony on the floor, clutching his unmentionables.

Ofer Dahan shouted once more for them to stop and, when they continued running without slowing down, heading straight for the still panting and somewhat unsteady Chaim Azulay, the younger officer fired three rounds at their legs. The first two missed completely, ricocheting off the concrete floor and burying themselves into the bodywork of an old Renault Trafic van. The third round hit the rearmost of the two fleeing fugitives, biting into the fleshy part of Osama's right calf and sending him stumbling headlong into the back of Mahmoud, who was in front. Both fell to the floor, Osama yelling in pain and clutching his right leg while Mahmoud fired off a string of curses in Arabic that neither of the two police officers fully understood but that no doubt contained a lot of piquant details about Osama's genealogy for bungling their escape.

Ofer Dahan rushed up to the two men, pistol grasped firmly in both hands. "You OK?" he shouted at Chaim Azulay.

Azulay nodded, approaching more slowly and with his gun drawn too. He looked particularly displeased over having to even touch the weapon.

"For heaven's sake!" he burst out in the Moroccan-accented Arabic he had learned from his parents. He almost spat the words at the two workshop assistants sprawled on the floor. "You idiots! Why did you have to go and attack police officers? We were here to check for stolen cars, you fools! All we wanted..."

He didn't finish the sentence as he caught some movement out the corner of his eye. "Get back on the floor and spread your arms and legs!" he snapped at Moshe Rimon who, white as a sheet from having had the favourite part of his anatomy rearranged without the benefit of anaesthetic, was starting to get to his knees.

Moshe Rimon got painfully and slowly back down to the floor. He'd discovered that any form of movement really hurt his groin. Better then to give his vital parts a rest while the coppers did what they had to do. The Arabs could fend for themselves, he didn't care about them. He'd do his time in jail for hiring illegal labour, then get others to take their place. Plenty more where they came from.

Ofer Dahan was speaking into his radio, asking for backup to secure the four people in the workshop.

Chaim Azulay surveyed the mass of human limbs stretched out on the concrete floor. He just hoped help would arrive soon to clear up this mess. Their simple task – checking for any signs of stolen cars being broken up for resale as parts – had developed into an operation with unforeseeable connections. Why the panic with these people, even to the extent of attacking police officers? Just because of a couple of stolen cars? Or was there something else that he didn't know? Money-laundering? Was the garage a front for a drugs ring? Was it an illegal immigration issue? Terrorism?

Chaim Azulay shook his head and waited for backup, putting in a call to his wife Bracha. She was going to have to sort out how best to get their daughter and granddaughter to the clinic – he was going to be stuck here for some time yet.

He sighed, scowled at Moshe Rimon, nudged him none-too-gently with his foot and asked "So. What's all this about then? Let's have some ID to begin with."

And that was how the first part of Adan Hamati's plan began to unravel before it ever got properly off the ground.

Because several of the vehicles he had planned on using were now impounded by the police as the boys in blue began the slow process of checking chassis IDs, VIN plates and registration numbers to try and match vehicles to rightful owners. Not always an easy task bearing in mind that most identifying marks had been filed away.

As yet, however, Adan Hamati knew none of this.

Nor did Aisha Naddi, Zahir Tafesh, Ghalib Ajrour or Amir Assaf.

'Deir Yassin' tunnel entrance, northern Gaza Strip

Ghalib Ajrour and Aisha Naddi sauntered as nonchalantly as they could into the greenhouse, each carrying a blue plastic crate typical of the sort used for moving plants and seedlings around the nursery.

The crates did not contain plants or seedlings, however. They each contained two small backpacks with small packets of dried plant seeds strewn on top for cover. The two youngsters walked over to the large metal potting table and placed their crates on the ground, then walked back through the large, transparent plastic-walled greenhouse to the main door and stepped out into the bright sunshine.

Ghalib led the way, with Aisha following a step or two behind. 'That's the way it's supposed to be,' thought Ghalib to himself as he reached into the back of the small beat-up Skoda pickup and lifted out another crate. 'The men lead the way, the women know their place and follow in our footsteps. Aisha will learn, I'll make sure she does. Any trouble with her and she'll feel the back of my hand before she knows what's what.'

And with that he turned around and beckoned to Aisha to take the crate he proffered.

Aisha Naddi was having none of it. She was an equal member of this team. She would lift out her own crate thank you very much, she didn't need some muscle-headed idiot to do any lifting work for her. She looked into Ghalib's face, kept her arms firmly to her sides and kept walking past him till she reached the little pick-up truck. She reached in and yanked out her own crate.

Ghalib was seething but didn't say anything. He knew he could take her with ease – in every sense of the word – but he also knew that if he started an argument with Aisha, her verbal acrobatics would leave him reeling, looking and feeling like an idiot. Nobody else managed to do this to him, only this bloody bitch of a girl. But his time would come, she would learn soon enough just how far she could go. Which as far as he was concerned wouldn't be all that far from where he chained her to his bed. Or the kitchen stove. Or the floor. Or wherever he pleased to have his way with her. He'd bang her into submission. Let her keep riling him – her punishment would simply be that much worse when it came.

He turned on his heel and carried the crate as though it were nothing more than a bunch of flowers. He knew that the slim girl would struggle with her burden. Good.

Back at the potting table, with the four crates laid out on the floor, the two looked at each other, neither wanting to be the first to break the sullen silence.

Aisha spoke first. "Check our watches one last time, OK? What time do you have? Mine says 16.37."

Making an elaborate show of keeping her waiting for an answer, Ghalib looked around the greenhouse, saw that they were alone as promised, looked at each of the crates in turn, then down at his wristwatch, and nodded. "No it's not, the time is 16.38."

"Yes, it is now!" flashed back Aisha. This knucklehead was totally brain-dead. If you waited a whole minute to answer the question out of some misguided sense of macho, then yes, it would be 16.38 by the time you looked at your watch. Aloud, however, she said none of this, merely nodded.

"We have a long time to wait till nightfall, let's make ourselves comfortable but keep out of sight as instructed." And with that she sat down on the sandy soil of the greenhouse, under the large potting table which backed onto the light grey hollow breeze-blocks from which the central wall of the fertiliser storage room was made.

Sitting there in her body-hugging black T-shirt, loose black combat trousers, black socks and boots and very little else, looking small, incredibly pretty, blood-pumpingly sexy and particularly vulnerable, the very sight of her almost caused Ghalib Ajrour to salivate.

It was all he could do to drag his conscious mind back to the task at hand.

'Later!' he muttered silently to himself. 'There'll be plenty of time for that later when we get back.'

He paused.

'If. If we get back.' He winced as he sat down in the sand beside Aisha, taking care not to sit too close to her or accidentally touch her.

They had more than an hour till it got dark, and just after dark two other people dressed just as they were would walk unobtrusively to the greenhouse, enter, ignore the two people under the potting table, make a show of switching off lights and then in full view of any Israeli spy blimp high in the sky would get into the parked Skoda pick-up and leave.

As far as anyone was concerned, the greenhouse would be as empty as it had been that morning.

Only Aisha Naddi and Ghalib Ajrour knew different.

Al Quds tunnel entrance, northern Gaza Strip

Zahir Tafesh and Amir Assaf had already spent one day and one night in the small ground-floor room of the Matrouk family home. They hadn't moved from the room except to visit the adjoining bathroom. The father of the Matrouk family, Khaled, brought them their meals with his own hands. His wife and four children had received strict instructions to ignore the two young men, not to speak to or otherwise engage with them. They would only be here for a day or so before they went south to Rafah, Khaled lied.

He knew full well where they were going. And so at least did his wife Wafa – the children, the eldest just eight, were perhaps too young to fully comprehend their parents' role in the ongoing *jihad* against the Jewish occupiers of their homeland Palestine, tantalisingly visible just beyond the electronically monitored security fence. So close you could almost touch it.

Almost, but not quite. Because even approaching to within a couple of hundred metres of the fence meant that Zionist Occupation Force soldiers on the other side would start shooting. Absurd! Even if you ignored the political aspects, that is to say the exact route of the border between the Gaza Strip and the area occupied by the Jews, the fact was that the whole of the Strip up to the border fence was Arab – even the Jews agreed on that. But Gaza Arabs were banned from approaching the last couple of hundred metres of their own territory.

"For security reasons," said the Jews. Yeah, right. According to the Zionist imperialists, Gaza Arabs were apparently a security risk even within their own territory inside Gaza. And the Jews thought this was acceptable! Any wonder the conflict was going on – and would go on for as long as there was a breath of air, a drop of blood, in the body of any right-thinking Palestinian Arab!

Khaled Matrouk had not always been an extremist. In his youth back in the early 1990s he had embraced the idea of rapprochement between Israel and Palestine, those far-distant Oslo Accords. Now finally there would be peace! But that too turned out to be a bitter disappointment. Their great leader Arafat had not succeeded in wresting Al Quds from the Jews, and without Islam's third-holiest site – which the Jews claimed was their holiest site, the idiots! – safely in Muslim hands there was obviously not going to be either reconciliation or peace. The Jewish settlements had continued, and the only reason he was living in a settlement-free area, the Gaza Strip, was because brave Arab fighters had constantly harassed the Jews and killed them until they drew the obvious conclusion that they were not wanted, and upped sticks and withdrew behind their accursed fence. This was back in 2005, and the whole of Palestine – indeed the whole of the Arab world – had erupted in a frenzy of celebration at this victory.

Well, if it worked here in Gaza, it would work in the West Bank too, and the rest of the territory occupied by the Zionists.

It really didn't take much persuasion for Khaled Matrouk to agree to allow the tunnel to be dug from inside his strategically positioned home. The beauty was that even if they had their suspicions, the Jews were always unwilling to take action against a target where children were present. And Khaled and Wafa made sure their children were always present – and visible. The Jews moaned and complained about the use of young children as "human shields"; the Gaza Arabs recognised the use of young children as just about the only tactic in their meagre arsenal that could successfully protect their fighters, their weapons stores, and their attack tunnels.

Khaled and Wafa Matrouk's kitchen was the perfect location for the opening of the attack tunnel that led under the sands into Israel. There were quite a few tunnels like this one still intact, even though the Zionists had destroyed about thirty of them in their last war waged against innocent Arabs in Gaza.

Khaled knocked on the door to the room and entered without waiting for an answer. It was his house, after all.

Zahir and Amir looked up at him as he walked in. "Have you finished eating? There'll be no more now – you'll be out of here in a few hours."

THE THREAT BENEATH *The Hart Trilogy*

The two young men smiled up at Khaled and thanked him for the meal. "Please give our thanks to your wife for her delicious cooking. And our thanks also to you for your hospitality. Hope we haven't been too much of a problem for you," said Zahir Tafesh.

"We've tidied up, and we'll fold the bedsheets and towels and leave them on the beds before we leave," Amir Assaf added.

Khaled Matrouk smiled wryly but didn't say anything. Yes they spoke Arabic, even though it was funnily accented, and yes they obviously burned with the zeal of a proud and liberated Palestine, but these kids certainly didn't have the local Arab mind-set. They were more European in their thinking than Palestinian, what with all their fancy manners and peculiar politeness. It stuck out like a sore thumb! Where did that nameless chap say they were from? Switzerland? Sweden? Swaziland? Where was Swaziland anyway? It was something foreign in any case.

"That'll be fine," he said out loud. "You're welcome. And it is we who should be thanking you. You're doing an important job. I don't know what your mission is on the other side, but I hope to see you coming back out of that hole into our kitchen sometime soon – no martyrdom for you."

After a few more words of polite well-wishes he picked up the tray with their empty dishes, turned around and headed for the door.

"I'll make sure my family is at the far end of the house once it is dark," he said over his shoulder. "You start moving when you need to go, my wife and children won't interrupt you."

And with that he pulled the door shut and was gone.

Amir glanced down at the luminous dial of his cheap black Climax analogue wristwatch. Thirteen shekels for a used watch from the flea-market in the *shuk* – and it hadn't been easy to find an analogue watch in this day and age! He looked up at Zahir and they both smiled. Wristwatches! In the electronic era when everyone and their donkey had a smartphone, who in the civilised world still used an analogue wristwatch? It just felt so old-school, so obsolete, so twentieth century!

Of course, they both understood the need for being able to tell the time without having to use a backlit electronic device in the dark.

They lounged back on their beds, each absorbed in their thoughts, and waited for nightfall.

Ramle Police Station, Israel

Chaim Azulay leaned back in his seat and looked across at his young partner Ofer Dahan.

"It's out of our hands, the civvies are dealing with the workshop owner, but what the hell are we to do with all those vehicles?" He scowled and looked out the window. The Rimon takedown had spoiled his entire evening. Chaim's wife Bracha, who was just preparing to go pick up her daughter and granddaughter when Moshe Rimon and the three Palestinian Arabs were brought in, had been forced to stay on and do their paperwork. Malcha had had to make her own way to the clinic with Re'ut. None of the local cab companies had a baby seat suitable for the little infant so she had had to go knocking on neighbours' doors until she found another young mother with a car and a suitable child seat – and that neighbour in turn had had to call her own mother-in-law to come look after her three young kids at home while she ferried Malcha and Re'ut to the clinic, and then back again afterwards.

It was a mess, start to finish. Fair enough, they'd collared three illegals – although as yet it remained to be seen if they were simply illegals working in the Jewish state, or terrorists lying low ahead of a planned attack. There were always plenty of the former in Israel; Palestinian Arabs living illegally in the country and only too happy to earn half the legally mandated Israeli minimum wage. Which was still twice what they could earn in the West Bank – always provided they could even get a job back home despite the thirty-one billion dollars the world community had donated first to Yasser Arafat and then to his successor Mahmud Abbas specifically for the purpose of job-creation and infrastructure-building in support of a civic Palestinian state. Thirty-one billion dollars just since the signing of the Oslo Accords – and still no new jobs created in West Bank population centres such as Nablus, Jenin, Ramallah or anywhere else. There were, however, plenty of shiny, new, expensive Mercedes and BMW and Lexus cars on the roads of those cities...

The presence of illegal aliens working in Israel was admittedly a constant problem, but it was more an issue for the border police, the employment protection service and the trade unions. Vastly more troubling for the security establishment was the fact that there had been countless cases over the past few years of Palestinian Arabs living and working illegally in Israel, and who out of the blue had carried out either lone-wolf or well-orchestrated terrorist attacks on buses, in restaurants, at hotels, at tram stops and railway stations. Islamist sleeper cells. The nightmare of security forces everywhere in the civilised world.

Time would tell into which category these three fell. Meantime, what of all the thousand and one vehicles in the yard and also inside the workshop? Not that there was any particular burning need to physically move them elsewhere for safekeeping – it was logistically easier and far cheaper to leave them where they were and simply lock the premises so nobody could gain access to them.

The problem was working out what they were for. Just stolen cars for resale? They were for the most part fairly old and dented vehicles. All in good working order, every single one started first time and there were no signs any of them had been prepared for taking apart – accessories, upholstery, instruments, everything was intact.

Or had they been stolen for parts? Nothing suggested this was the case. In fact, for a car repair workshop there were surprising few parts in stock, new or used.

They all had one thing in common, however. All had their vehicle IDs filed off – from chassis, engine and transmission alike. And they were all too old to have their VIN registration etched into their window glass – that was a more recent legal requirement on the Israeli market, which as with so much else was aligned with EU regulations. There was no telling anything about the origins of this large stock of vehicles. Not only that, the registration plates didn't match either – the number plates did not even match the make of vehicles on which they sat, let alone the model. Obviously swapped with other cars, either stolen vehicles or cars not reported stolen, or vehicles that had been tampered with. After all, how often did the average car owner actually check that the number plate on his car was the same when he rushed out to work in the morning as it had been when he parked it at home the night before?

Chaim Azulay banged his fist on the table in frustration and looked up at Ofer Dahan.

"Right, let's get down to it. Get that chap to give you a list of the number plates from the vehicles in the Rimon workshop, and run them against the plates of all vehicles reported stolen in the past couple of months. After that..."

He didn't get further because Ofer Dahan leaned across the desk and handed him a neat printed list of car registration numbers.

"That's them all – all the number plates from the workshop. And here," he picked up another sheet of paper and pushed it across the desk, "is a list of vehicles reported stolen over the past half year. I asked Traffic to narrow down the search parameters of stolen vehicles, limiting the list to only those makes we recovered from Rimon's garage."

Ofer Dahan looked across at his older partner and a small smile played across his face.

"Know what?" he continued. "We're dealing with what is probably the laziest auto booster in the world – all the vehicle IDs have been filed off the cars in the shop, but all the number plates have been swapped with one another in the same shop! No need to look any further – every vehicle with a filed-off ID in the garage has its genuine number plate on another vehicle in the same garage. Our friend Moshe Rimon isn't terribly bright. Either that, or he's really, *really* lazy!"

Ofer Dahan leaned back in his chair and waited for Chaim Azulay to respond.

"Well," said Chaim. "That makes things a whole lot easier for us. You've done the legwork, so you go give this to the guys questioning Rimon. Tell them the identities of the vehicles are no longer a mystery, we just need to know why he went to all this bother. Or rather," he smiled slowly, "why he didn't even bother to do the job properly."

As Ofer Dahan got up to leave, Chaim called out after him. "Don't forget to thank him for making our job easier! You can go home after that. You're not all bad for such a wet-behind-the-ears rookie."

Ofer Dahan smiled to himself as he closed the door behind him. From veteran officer Chaim Azulay, who struggled so hard to live up to his gruff and tough image, this was praise indeed!

Chaim got to his feet and reached for his mobile phone, punching the quick-dial for his wife Bracha's number. He could even hear her phone ring outside at the front desk. He smiled tiredly. With a bit of luck he wouldn't have to pull an all-nighter at the station after all. That young Ofer boy had done well.

13 metres below the sands of Gaza

Nobody had warned the four youngsters about how hot it would be so deep underground.

The Gaza tunnelers, most of them small-built, undernourished young kids whose parents sent them to their Hamas taskmasters after school every day and at weekends to eke out the family income, had done an amazing job despite the primitive conditions in which they worked.

For the most part, the tunnels were dug by hand, small young hands swinging small hand-shovels in the confined space deep underground and passing the sand back to the entrance where it was taken away to be used in the manufacture of the concrete siding panels that would later be inserted along the length of the tunnels to shore them up.

There was electricity, there was a phone line since there was no cellular phone reception so deep underground. There was even a pipe supplying drinking water.

But there was no cooling. And their damp, sweaty clothes stuck to their bodies as the two teams made their way to their separate staging points deep inside Israel.

Aisha Naddi paused for a moment to catch her breath as Ghalib Ajrour soldiered on ahead, never breaking his crouching progress. Being so much shorter than he was, Aisha could walk almost upright. And their tunnel was wide enough for them to carry their bulky backpacks without scraping against the rough concrete side walls.

She was right, the downhill gradient had definitely levelled out and in fact they were now heading gently upward. Their breakout exit wasn't as deep as the rest of the tunnel – the staging point was about nine metres below the surface and the first seven metres or so had already been dug out for them and lined with curved concrete sides for stability. They'd only have to remove the steel retaining roof panel and then dig out the remaining couple of metres or so of relatively soft sand to make the breach and breathe the air of Israel. Or rather Occupied Palestine as Adan Hamati kept insisting they call it.

Aisha hitched up the two packs she was carrying on her chest, the same size and weight as the two on her back, and trudged on.

It was finally happening!

12 metres below the sands of Gaza

Backs aching from their forced march bent at the waist, Amir Assaf and Zahir Tafesh took their final steps into the staging area twelve metres below their exit point into Israel.

Amir took off all four of his packs and dumped them unceremoniously on the trampled earth. Zahir lifted his off and placed them more carefully on the ground. He had prepared the charges with his own hands and he knew what he was doing, but it was always a good idea to treat explosives with respect, even if the detonators were not yet in them primed and ready to be discharged.

Both sat down and peered up into the gloom of the vertical stack rising high above them. Their trek down the tunnel hadn't exactly been uneventful. The lights flickered nervously the whole time, going off for several seconds at a time and plunging the whole place into darkness. Neither wanted to contemplate what would happen if the lights failed completely. They had flashlights, of course, but walking more than a kilometre at a depth greater than that of five graves, with just a small flashlight to guide them, was not a pleasant prospect.

And the water pipes, when the taps were opened so they could conserve their own water rations, turned out to produce nothing but a trickle of damp sand. Either there was a blockage somewhere, or a connection had been severed at source, but the fact remained that there was no pressure behind the trickle of wet sand. Damn, it was hot. They resorted to their fast-depleting water bottles.

Both Amir and Zahir wanted out of the tunnel as quickly as possible. But a quick look at their watches revealed they had more than an hour to wait.

Underground. Without a supply of water. At least, not in the water pipe.

Just how long did it take for an hour to pass?

Ramle Police Station, Israel

It didn't take many minutes for Moshe Rimon to reveal all.

Which, as it turned out, wasn't a whole lot. He'd received money to allow his workshop to be used for the storage of vehicles. Five hundred shekels per car up front when they arrived, another five hundred per car when they left. It was easy money. He didn't have to do anything apart from switch all the number plates around, and make sure all the cars started easily every day. His routine was to start up each car, let it idle for a minute or two to make sure the battery had enough juice to fire up the engine the next time, then switch off and move on to the next vehicle.

No, he didn't know when they would be picked up. No, he didn't know the name of the person who brought him the cars. Yes, it was always the same person. Yes, he was Israeli. No, he was not Jewish. Yes, he was an Arab. No, he didn't know where he lived.

Moshe Rimon began to breathe a bit easier. There had been no rough stuff, he hadn't been beaten up or threatened with torture or anything like that. He'd walk out of here soon enough. He had admittedly been denied access to a lawyer – this was because he was not being held for fencing stolen property – a case for the boys in blue – but under anti-terror legislation since the three people in his workshop were illegal aliens from an enemy state.

That meant the local Ramle uniformed officers were now replaced by three men sporting close-cropped hair and wearing casual clothes. Virtually identical casual clothes involving khaki cargo pants, sturdy-looking mid-brown sand-boots, white or black T-shirts, and thrown loosely over their T-shirts they sported short-sleeved lightweight safari jackets. And here is where they all showed their individuality because one was black, one beige and the third dark blue. They might just as well have worn a uniform with a badge saying "Shin Bet" on their collars.

They didn't introduce themselves, they just walked in like they owned the place, held the door open for the uniformed officers to leave, and sat down in a ring close to their interviewee.

And that's when Moshe Rimon started sweating.

He talked. He talked like he'd never talked before.

But he really didn't have much to say that they didn't already know. Because Moshe Rimon really had no idea who he had been dealing with, that much was clear.

What was equally clear was that this was a job for Shin Bet, not uniform, and that the focus was either the territories administered by the Palestinian Authority from Ramallah, or the territories administered by Hamas from Gaza City.

The three Palestinian Arabs found in the workshop were not involved in anything more sinister than trying to earn a living, albeit illegally. Caught as they were between a Palestinian Authority that refused to provide them with jobs yet banned them from working for the Zionist Occupation, on the one hand, and on the other hand an Israeli government that for security reasons severely curtailed the number and type of Palestinian Arabs it allowed to enter the Jewish state to work, it was hard not to feel sorry for people desperate enough to risk arrest just to tie down a job, even an illegal one in an enemy state. But now it was up to an Israeli court to decide what to do with them, it wasn't the Shin Bet's pigeon.

It was vital now that the details of the Moshe Rimon case were reported and input electronically, for immediate despatch to all Shin Bet units working cases that might be related.

More than twenty stolen vehicles, all required by their client to be kept in good running order.

Did this tie in with any known or potential scenario elsewhere in the embattled state of Israel?

Upstairs bedroom, no. 12 Bodenheimer Street, Ashdod, Israel

It was the first time Marita Ohlsson had ever heard Benny Hart swear. At least she assumed it was swearing, because it was all in Hebrew, which she did not speak. Of course it might have been Arabic – she'd heard somewhere that many Hebrew expletives were in fact uttered in Arabic, for some inexplicable reason that was beyond her. It certainly wasn't Swedish or English, the only two languages in which she was fluent, if one ignored the Spanish she had studied for three boring years at school. All she'd ever learned in Spanish was to say "No hands please!"

And that was not a command she had had any use for in bed with Benny Hart. Not in any language.

At the moment, however, the language coming out of Benny Hart's mouth was causing her to redden, even though she didn't understand a word of what was being said.

"Give me thirty minutes!" he yelled into the phone. "No, I'm not in a position to deal with this now." He eyed Marita Ohlsson lying back in bed, the sheets tucked up under her chin. He'd been in a totally different position just half a minute ago, and now this! Un-bloody-believable. "Make that forty-five minutes," he snapped into the phone and clicked off.

Benny Hart looked down at his Swedish liaison. They'd certainly been liaising, but now the fun was over. At least for now. "Work," he said, apologetically. "I have to go to the office. Yes, I know," he held up his hand to ward off her storm of protests. "I know its evening and I'm off work. But with us, as I'm pretty sure it is with you too, there's no real concept of being 'off work' – even when we're 'working' together," he smiled wickedly as he reached over to pull the bedsheet off Marita. "I've just bought us an extra fifteen minutes," he said as he fumbled for the switch for the bedside lamp.

"Enough!" she said, smiling at him. "Give me two minutes to shower and I'll be with you. Come on," she continued quickly as she saw him start back in surprise. "Don't tell me this has nothing to do with why I'm here in the first place. OK, let me ask you a question. Hand on heart – that's up there on your left. No, your other left," she continued as Benny placed his left hand on the right side of his chest. "Hand on heart, can you honestly say there's no link between my case and the reason you're rushing off now?"

"I don't know, and that's honest. At face value, there's absolutely no link whatsoever. It's a domestic issue, pure and simple – a whole bunch of stolen cars that the local boys think may possibly have a terrorist, not just a purely criminal, purpose. You stay here, that way you can enjoy a three minute shower instead of just two – or as long as the hot water lasts after I've finished." He bent down and kissed her tenderly on the lips. "I'll give you a call if there's any link whatsoever, however tenuous. I promise. OK?"

And without waiting for her answer he bounced out of bed and strode off to the bathroom to shower and ready himself for the quick drive to Ofakim. Damn, he wouldn't after all be needing the forty-five minutes he'd just negotiated. He would, however, definitely be needing a cold shower. There'd be plenty of hot water left over for Marita.

Marita watched the back of his muscular body as he walked away. Oh well, she'd relax in bed for a while and then see if Benny had anything in the fridge for them to eat, or if he'd only planned a long lie-in starting at 6 pm and lasting all the way through the night until it was time to head off for work the following morning. That had pretty much been their routine on their Eilat holiday the previous year.

Quite a healthy routine, when one thought about it. Dieting and exercise all in one.

Marita turned over and fell asleep. She didn't even hear the door click shut as Benny Hart left his apartment one hundred and eighteen seconds later.

Down in the car park, Benny got behind the wheel of his Hyundai i35, reached into the glove compartment and pulled out a magnetic blue flashing strobe light which he clamped onto the roof of his car. He pressed a switch in the dashboard and the roof light, a pair of rectangular red-and-blue strobe lights concealed in the grille just above the front bumper, and an identical pair of red-and-blue strobes set into the tail lamp cluster at the rear of the car added extra urgency to his progress, clearing traffic ahead and warning traffic to the rear to be aware of sudden and fast changes of direction. There was another button to activate the siren but he didn't touch that. He didn't anticipate having to do so at all on the fast trip to his office in Ofakim and the secure, encryption-protected computer in his office.

Seemed like things were afoot, but what? Benny Hart floored the accelerator and shot out of the parking lot and into the already thinning stream of after-work traffic.

Northern Negev Desert, inside Israel

Breaking through the last couple of metres of soft earth and into the fresh air had been surprisingly easy. Amir Assaf had undone the bolts holding the overhead metal retaining panel and lowered it gently to the ground. Above them was softish sand that had to be dug out with hand shovels.

That task had been remarkably simple because the sandy soil in this part of the northern Negev desert was very soft and with remarkably few stones. They certainly weren't any sweatier at the end of that task than they already had been after their long underground walk.

It was Zahir who had been the first to penetrate through the last remaining centimetres of soil. He had been concerned that recent work on construction of the new kibbutz houses might have resulted in them coming up below a paved, cemented or even concrete surface, building foundations or a walkway perhaps. But the intelligence had been good and the last bit of excavation had been easy.

Working quickly he opened up an aperture large enough for his body, climbed out and lay flat on the ground, his dull black clothes causing no reflections and catching little of the sparse moonlight.

Amir passed up the eight backpacks, two at a time, and then climbed out himself. He was careful to leave the narrow, makeshift aluminium ladder in place to permit a quick entry should they be lucky enough to make it back after completing their mission. But just as he took the last step up and over the edge, out into the open, the top of the ladder started wobbling and before he knew what to do it had tottered back and collapsed back into the dark depths of the tunnel.

'Bugger!' muttered Amir to himself. He glanced quickly up at Zahir to see if he had noticed what had just happened. He hadn't. Ah well, no point worrying him about this now, they'd solve the problem when they returned.

If they returned.

Once all their equipment was up top, they wriggled out of their dusty black overalls and dropped them down the hole, Amir taking care to relieve Zahir of his overall before his partner could get too close to the tunnel opening and perhaps notice the missing ladder. Zahir quickly pulled up some dried stalks and passed them to Amir who placed them haphazardly across the gaping hole to conceal the tunnel opening. It wasn't a fool-proof disguise but it would do, for the time being at least.

Amir and Zahir shouldered their packs, two each at the front and two more on their backs, checked that their water bottles, hand-grenades, pistol holsters and knife scabbards were still securely in place, and looked around to get their bearings.

To their left was the perimeter security fence and the sandy track used by the off-roaders that patrolled the fence, checking for breaks or other signs of penetration. To their right some metres away was the road that ran parallel to the fence for some distance before making a sharp bend and heading towards the school building.

Walking in the shadows on either side they followed this road until it branched off toward the kibbutz factory. The kibbutz produced plastic shopping bags in the factory. Lovely – a whole lot of toxic chemicals already on site. All they needed was a little catalyst in the form of the packs Amir and Zahir were carrying.

Zahir lifted off one of his small black packs and placed it on the beaten earth just where an overground six-inch pipe disappeared beneath the surface. This was the pipe that carried a cocktail of ready-mixed chemical granules from the storage silo outside to the buffer tank inside the factory, where the process of converting the raw material into plastic bags took place.

Zahir reached into his backpack and switched on its mobile phone, which would activate the primed charge, then they continued on their way, heading for the rear of the kibbutz kitchen. There, just as they had been told, was a row of cooking-gas canisters. Zahir placed another of his packs beside the left-most canister and Amir placed one of his own packs against the canister furthest to the right. They switched on the devices' mobile phones and made a quick exit toward the kibbutz perimeter fence.

Zahir had a moment of panic while he searched for his wire-cutters. "Here," said Amir and handed over the pair he carried on his belt. "We carried one pair only, remember?"

Zahir wiped the sweat from his brow and went to work on the lower part of the fence, snipping deftly up and across and then bending out an opening large enough for them to crawl through.

Without a word he passed the wire-cutters back to Amir and crawled out through the hole in the fence. Once safely out he beckoned for Amir to pass him the bags and after they had been handed through, Amir followed. Zahir then bent the cut section of the wire fence inward to make it look as though the fence had been breached from the outside, indicating that a person or persons unknown had entered the kibbutz.

Once they were satisfied that the scene did indeed look like a break-in, and not a break-out, they darted off into the darkness and headed for the road leading from the kibbutz main gate out to the main road, about a kilometre away.

Amir signalled to Zahir to take the left side of the road and he took the right, both of them clinging to the cover provided by the triple rows of sparse eucalyptus trees sprouting from the drainage ditch on either side.

It was when they got to the junction with the main road that they had their first premonition of failure.

Where there should have been a white Ford Transit van parked by the roadside, its rear end jacked up to indicate it had a punctured tyre, there was nothing.

Nothing but empty road as far as the eye could see.

It was ten past two in the morning, they were on a deserted stretch of road in the northern Negev desert inside Israel, and they had no transport waiting to take them to their meeting-point in Rahat.

What they didn't know was that their designated Ford Transit van was securely locked away in Moshe Rimon's workshop, guarded by the police.

So far, everything had worked according to plan.

Until now.

Zahir looked at Amir, who looked angry. Zahir looked away. Anger wasn't going to help them. If they were to continue they needed to channel their energies positively.

Zahir crossed the road to where Amir was standing and whispered to him to pull back behind the last row of trees and sit down on the ground, away from the blaze of any passing headlights, to discuss their predicament.

Blaze of headlights?

Zahir thought hard, not saying anything to Amir who was cursing a little too loudly in Arabic.

The first car to pass by would become their mode of transport. They had the means to ensure that.

But the clock was ticking. There weren't many hours of darkness left and they needed to be on their way away from the kibbutz when they made the phone calls that would set off the charges. They needed a few hours of darkness to enhance the sense of confusion in the kibbutz and for security forces to continue converging on the scene as they made their way away from it, travelling in precisely the opposite direction.

The success of their plan depended on it.

Amir nudged Zahir in the ribs as the headlights of a vehicle approached from the west. Now, with a bit of luck, the vehicle would slow down to turn right onto the road leading into the kibbutz – the road they had just walked along – giving Zahir Tafesh and Amir Assaf a better chance of success.

Pulling down their black knitted cotton ski masks to cover their entire faces save for their eyes and noses, Zahir and Amir reached down for their handguns and waited, one on either side of the narrow road that peeled off from the deserted rural highway.

As the car indicated right and slowed down, starting to turn into the ninety degree right-hander, Amir stepped out into the narrow roadway from the car's left, as Zahir simultaneously leaped out from the right side of the road and hammered on the passenger window with his gun barrel.

The startled driver, an elderly man of about sixty-five who was alone in the car, reacted by inadvertently slamming on the brakes to avoid hitting Amir. That was all they needed. As the car tyres screeched to a halt Amir darted out from in front of the vehicle and to the left side, grasped the driver's door handle with his left hand and tried to wrench it open. It was locked from inside. Raising his right hand he fired a single round into the driver's window, reached through the shattered glass and smashed the barrel of his handgun into the bespectacled eyes of the driver before the latter could take any action to avoid the blow. Amir then reached in and opened the driver's door from the inside, releasing all four door locks.

Zahir yanked open the front passenger door and fumbled with the driver's seat belt buckle, eventually managing to undo it as his fingers became increasingly slippery with nervous perspiration.

Amir hauled out the profusely bleeding driver and half-dragged, half-lifted him across the road to the ditch. Throwing him onto the ground he aimed his pistol at the head of the driver just as Zahir leaped at him, thrusting his gun hand down as he caught up with Amir.

"You fool!" he whispered fiercely. "We can't have more shooting at this time of the night, it'll alert anyone within hearing distance. People may ignore one shot, thinking they didn't hear right. A second shot will alert everyone within hearing distance. Just tie him up and gag him, and leave him here."

Amir looked at Zahir, a scornful smile playing across his lips. "Tie him up!" he squeaked in a mock girlie voice. "We don't tie up Zionist occupiers, we execute them!" And before Zahir could fully take in his partner's words Amir raised his right foot and with all his considerable weight jumped down on the elderly driver's neck.

The sharp crack of his neck snapping sounded like the report of a pistol in the silent night. Zahir looked with unbelieving eyes first at the dead man on the ground, his neck and head angled unnaturally to the left, and then up at Amir, who was wearing an air of determined accomplishment.

"What did you do that for, you fucking animal?" screamed Zahir, resorting to Swedish without even thinking of it. He would have continued had Amir not clamped a large, sweaty hand across his exposed nose and balaclava-covered mouth. Zahir struggled to breathe, kicking and lashing out, while Amir spoke quietly but urgently into his ear.

"Stop it! Stop! We can't afford to show false mercy. There's going to be plenty of killing on this little holiday of ours, you know that. It's just that if everything goes according to plan, we won't be sticking around to see the actual killing, we'll be safely back in Gaza. It started to look like there would be a change of schedule because someone stuffed up their side of the plan and failed to deliver our vehicle.

"But now," continued Amir, "we have a new vehicle so we're back on track and still have a chance of doing everything exactly according to plan. So stop behaving like a spoilt little bitch and let's get on with the job. This was just a minor obstacle. Now we get back to plan. We've lost less than fifteen minutes. Come on, let's move it. No more noise, OK?"

Amir waited for Zahir to collect himself and when he nodded assent Amir slowly removed his hand, ready to clamp it back should his partner flip out again.

But Zahir had regained his composure. Amir was right. This was a minor hitch and they had neatly overcome it. Time to move on.

They removed their ski-masks and pocketed them, put their packs on the rear seat and got into the car, Amir behind the wheel and Zahir in the front passenger seat.

Amir looked at the steering wheel and nodded in appreciation. "Ford Focus, and a new one too! Should have some go in it. Let's see what Israeli roads are like to drive on."

And with that he reversed the car back out of the kibbutz approach road onto the main road, turned the wheel left and headed east, past the road leading to the kibbutz and the dead man lying in the ditch. They were heading for the Israeli Bedouin town of Rahat in the Negev desert. They had an appointment with a Hyundai minivan at the Sonol petrol station at the entrance to the town.

Amir grunted. "Let's hope the next vehicle is there," he muttered under his breath.

Zahir reached into his pocket and pulled out his mobile phone. He had three calls to make to the kibbutz they were fast leaving behind.

Nobody would answer his calls, of course. But the entire kibbutz would feel the effects.

'Deir Yassin' tunnel exit, northern Negev Desert, Israel

The very instant his watch showed one a.m. Ghalib Ajrour got up from his crouched position, grabbed the screwdriver, reached overhead and started drilling out the retaining bolts securing the metal plate above him.

As the last bolt dropped to the ground, narrowly missing Aisha Naddi who was standing close to him peering up, he snapped at her. "Stand back! I'm going to remove the panel."

And without waiting for her to acknowledge his command or move out of the way, he swiftly spun the crossbar ninety degrees, releasing it from its brackets, and let the hinged metal panel fold in half under its own weight and drop to the ground. Straight onto Aisha's right foot.

She yelped in pain and dropped down to the ground, nursing her foot and screaming a string of curses at the man towering above her.

"Quiet, you little bitch!" Ghalib spat down at her. "One more sound from you and I'll kick you in the tits." He glared at her balefully. "Now shut up and learn to do as you're told. I warned you to move away. Your problem is you just don't listen. To anyone. Your problem. But you'll learn soon enough," he grinned evilly at her. "Forget Sweden, you're here now. You'll learn to do things our way. The proper way. I'll teach you to do what your menfolk tell you, and by the time I've finished with you you'll be grabbing my dick every time I walk into the room, begging for more."

And with that he nudged her roughly out of the way with his right foot, reached down, grasped a hand-shovel and began furiously attacking the thick layer of soft sand above his head, clearing their path to the open air above them inside Israel.

"You dunderheaded idiot!" Aisha blazed at him. "You're so bloody thick you can't even think and breathe at the same time! If I'm injured to satisfy your primitive macho instincts, how on earth are we to get the job done? Have you stopped long enough to work that one out? We're a team, neither of us will succeed without the other. Your problem is you think with your dick, starving your brain of oxygen. If in fact you can call that sponge in your head a brain. Bloody pig-shit for brains!" she yelled at him, breaking into Swedish in the heat of the moment.

Ghalib stopped shovelling, lowered his arm and turned to face her as she sat on the ground massaging her right foot. As he bent down toward her, Aisha released her foot and grabbed the pistol in the holster slung at an angle across her chest, nestling snugly between her breasts.

Her hands moving swiftly, she thumbed the safety, drew back the slider and put a round into the breech.

"You really sure want to try this?" she asked him quietly, deliberately, reverting to Arabic. "You really sure you want me to shoot your dick off and leave you to bleed to death down here? You'll be the first person in history to have a kilometre-long grave – but no coffin. Think about it, you pig-shit-for-brains idiot."

Ghalib stopped short. He didn't doubt for a second that Aisha would translate her words into action. Even at school in Gothenburg she'd been a fearless tomboy. Heck, she'd had more guts than most of the guys he grew up with. She wasn't butch or anything – quite the opposite; she was jaw-droppingly sexy, very feminine, incredibly appealing. But no-nonsense tough. She wasn't going to be made anyone's bitch. Not Ghalib's, not anyone else's. He'd been stupid to even try to put her in her place.

At least, in this place. This simply was the wrong place. He'd wait for the right opportunity.

"Forget it," he said. "It's just nerves. Sorry. How's your foot?" He bent down to examine it. Only to have the muzzle of her pistol thrust to within five centimetres of his left eye.

"You ever try anything like that again and I won't warn you next time," Aisha said slowly and with immense clarity, every syllable cracking through the confined space in the tunnel like a whip. "Next time, you'll wake up in an Israeli hospital – if you don't bleed out in the meantime. From now on, you stay in front of me at all times. Now get back to work. And since I still can't stand, thanks to you, that means *you* get back to work." And with a wave of her pistol she dismissed him imperiously back to his task of excavation.

Aisha waited until Ghalib turned around and picked up the shovel. She noted with a small smile that his every movement was now deliberate, slow, smooth and signalled in advance; he wasn't taking any chances and didn't want her to misinterpret any sudden movements.

'One down to the good guys,' she smiled to herself as she got up and gingerly tested her weight on her right foot.

No damage. It hurt a lot but she could scrunch up her toes inside her desert boot and was able to walk OK.

That was a near miss. She'd done what was necessary, putting the dumb-ass brute on warning. He wouldn't try anything now, leastaways not while they still had to complete their mission.

The problem would come after they returned – or in the event they didn't succeed and he'd want revenge for his injured macho pride before going out in a futile blaze of glory.

Aisha Naddi would be keeping a close watch on her comrade-in-arms, Ghalib Ajrour.

After a further ten minutes of digging Ghalib had cleared an opening and turned with exaggerated politeness to Aisha.

"Madam, you first as agreed." He bowed in the upright tunnel shaft, hitting his head against the concrete liner and leaving a visible bruise on his forehead.

Aisha suppressed a smile. What a prize idiot. He couldn't even be sarcastic without injuring himself. If this was the future of Liberated Palestine, perhaps she should ask for Israeli asylum instead...

Out loud she instead said: "Slight change of plans. I'll still go first. But you walk fifteen paces back down the tunnel and wait for me to tell you when to pass me the backpacks. Go."

Ghalib saw there was no point arguing with her, she still had her gun in her hand. He measured out fifteen paces, then another five for good measure. Let the bitch think he'd learned his lesson. He'd pay her back later. With interest.

Aisha shinned up the ladder and once she was up top, leaned down into the vertical shaft and whispered loudly. "Right, pass me the bags!"

After a few moments a black pack appeared, followed a few moments later by another. The procedure was repeated another four times until all eight packs were lying in the field, and Ghalib's head emerged."

"Get back down!" Aisha whispered fiercely. "You haven't switched off the tunnel lights! We're lit up like the Metro!"

Cursing himself for giving the *bint* yet another reason to openly disparage him, Ghalib shinned down the ladder and thumbed the switch, plunging the tunnel and vertical shaft into darkness. Guided by the faint light of the quarter-moon filtering down the shaft, Ghalib made his way back up and was greeted with a pile of dried branches.

"Cover the opening," Aisha whispered.

Ghalib wondered, not for the first time this evening, when exactly Aisha had slipped into the role of leader, issuing orders and pushing him around like he was nobody. His pulse raced as he savoured what he would do to the girl when the time was ripe. She'd learn. Oh, she'd learn all right.

Meantime, he did as he was told and covered up the opening to the vertical shaft.

Hefting their packs, two each at the front and two at the rear, they launched into an easy run away from the tunnel opening toward the short end of the field where they could see the ghostly outline of a light-coloured pick-up truck.

As they neared the vehicle they both looked around nervously. Had anyone seen them? So far, not a sound, nothing out of the ordinary save the usual sounds carried on the desert night air. Far to the right they could both hear and see the glow of a self-propelled irrigation machine making its way slowly down a field, watering the crops as it inched its way forward. Its diesel engine throbbed resolutely in the still night air and overlaid on that was the hiss of spraying water hitting the nozzles under pressure and falling as a spray of gentle rain onto the moisture-starved desert sand and the crops growing in it. Behind it trailed the ominous black snake of a flexible six-inch pipe that fed water under pressure from a connection point a hundred metres away. On top of the machine's lead tower was a revolving amber light, flashing out its staccato warning that here was a massive agricultural beast at work, an autonomous giant propelling itself on its huge tractor wheels and that anything that came in its way would be first drenched in cold water and then ground into the desert sand under its massive rubber tyres.

Aisha and Ghalib had been warned about this, but actually seeing this eerie giant with its single amber eye flashing in the dark, roaring away and belching smoke from its exhaust pipe, called up images of a demented Cyclops gone berserk. Aisha shuddered at the sight and they both turned their attention back to the pick-up truck.

It was a white four-door Mazda 4x4 crew-cab pick-up as promised, and it was parked under the eucalyptus trees as promised. They edged closer, ears and eyes keenly attuned to anything untoward.

Nothing, everything was calm. Ghalib went straight to the front of the vehicle and retrieved the ignition key from the hollow inside the front right bumper.

So far so good. Both doors were unlocked and Aisha climbed into the right rear passenger seat. Ghalib looked at her quizzically and raised one eyebrow. "Come ride up front with me," he said.

"I'd rather sit back here," responded Aisha. 'No way am I going to sit beside you, you knuckle-head,' she thought to herself. 'I'm going to sit behind you so I can blow your head off if you try any monkey business.' She tossed her bags on the seat beside her and put on her seat belt. It paid to be doubly safe whenever she was around Ghalib, she realised.

Ghalib Ajrour shrugged as though it didn't bother him, pulled off his packs and chucked them onto the floor on the passenger's side. He climbed in behind the wheel, put the key in the steering lock, twisted it and fired up the diesel engine. It started with a loud clatter but soon settled to a quiet, slightly off-beat thrum.

He eased the tall 4x4 out of the soft sand by the roadside and up onto the tarmac. After a few minutes they came to a T-junction and turned east. As they approached a second junction, Ghalib slowed down and pulled in beside a bus shelter on the main road, just past the junction leading to Kibbutz Sadot Darom. There Aisha climbed out with one of her small black packs, leaving her door open. She placed the bag behind the concrete bus shelter, kicking a pile of sand and leaves over it.

She got back into the truck, shut the door and put on her seat belt. "Drive!" she commanded. Swarthy though his complexion was, Ghalib visibly reddened upon hearing the imperious tone of her voice.

'I guess I'd better watch it,' Aisha said to herself. 'This idiot's going to explode before we're done. Calm down girl, there'll be plenty of time to deal with this dinosaur when we get back.'

She paused.

'If we get back,' she thought to herself, looking out the window at the black trees flying by in the dark night.

Out loud she said: "Ofakim, here we come. Let's get there in one piece," she added as she saw the speedometer needle hovering nervously around the hundred kilometre an hour mark. Way too fast for such a tall and heavy vehicle on treacherously unstable, knobbly off-road tyres. That fool Ghalib couldn't do anything right.

The fool Ghalib was too busy dreaming up plans that involved first bedding and then beheading the delectable Aisha to notice his speed.

That was when he lost control of the car in a fast sweeping left bend in the road and ploughed straight on, the nose of the car shooting over the edge of the blacktop and straight over the edge, down into the ditch on the right of the road. The front bumper dug deep into the soft sand, leaving the left rear wheel spinning furiously – and uselessly – in the air, clawing for grip where there was none.

In the rear seat of the crew-cab, Aisha thanked her lucky stars she'd worn her seat belt. Even so she'd come perilously close to smashing her face onto the headrest of the front passenger seat as the abrupt stop threw her forward until her seat belt locked and snapped tight, restraining her.

"You bloody idiot!" she yelled at Ghalib, who resorted to flooring the accelerator to get the truck out of the soft sand. All this did was cause the rear right wheel to spin even faster, smoking as it whined uselessly against the tarmac. The left rear wheel continued to spin uselessly in the air.

"Take your foot off the gas!" commanded Aisha. "Put the lever into four-wheel drive and engage reverse. Then press gently – and I mean *really* gently – on the gas and see if this gets us out."

As he started wrestling with the lever of the part-time four-wheel drive system, Aisha had an idea.

"Hold on a minute. Let me get out – I'll climb onto the cargo bed at the back and try to weigh down the rear of the truck so the wheel touches the road. Hold it." And with that she opened the door, jumped out of the pick-up and climbed onto the rear bumper, holding onto the upper bar of the tailgate and trying valiantly to use her body weight to tip the rear of the vehicle down.

It was no use, she simply didn't weigh enough to make the slightest difference. The rear of the vehicle still perched at a crazy angle, the left rear wheel still poised way above the road surface.

Aisha got down and walked over to the driver's side. "Straighten the front wheels," she commanded. "Are you in four-wheel drive? OK, just lightly touch the gas and see if this gets you out."

Ghalib feathered the accelerator and the truck dug even deeper into the soft soil.

"You prize idiot!" Aisha screamed at him. "You're still in first gear, you didn't put it in reverse! Now you've dug in even deeper, and with the front wheels too this time!"

Aisha Naddi took a step away from the vehicle. She felt that if she was close enough to see Ghalib Ajrour she wouldn't be able to stop herself putting a bullet into his fat head. What an unbelievably thick-headed ape of a man! Full of macho pride but unable to do a thing right. And this was the sort of male who wanted to wind the clock back and forbid females from driving in the ideal Islamic society of their choice. Without their womenfolk, knuckleheads like Ghalib Ajrour wouldn't even be able to breathe and sit down at the same time, they probably couldn't even figure out how to procreate, wouldn't know what went where. She stamped her foot in frustration and turned on her heel. She had to distance herself from the idiot before she did something she regretted.

It was as she turned to walk back to the rear of the disabled Mazda that she saw a pair of headlights in the distance approaching from the rear.

They might be able to salvage something from the situation if they played their cards right.

And provided she could keep the idiot away from anything involving buttons, switches, levers and pedals.

Better still if she could keep him away from an oxygen supply, she thought wistfully to herself.

Aisha ran back to the driver's door and issued a stream of instructions to Ghalib. She gave him no choice. They would handle this her way and try to extract themselves from their predicament.

Ofakim, Israel

Benny Hart felt frustrated. Not about having to leave the delicious Marita Ohlsson at home in his bed, but about that elusive feeling he had that he wasn't quite seeing a pattern that he felt must be staring him in the face.

He sat back, chewing on the end of a plastic pen. What did he have? He ticked off a mental list.

There were four young Swedes of Palestinian descent wanted for questioning in connection with a terrorist act in Gothenburg. Check.

There was evidence that a bank card belonging to one of the four had been used at an ATM in Gaza. Several times. Check.

This was therefore a possible, perhaps likely, indication that at least one the terrorists, possibly even all four of them, were in Gaza. Check.

If so, they had managed to get into Gaza. Definitely not from Israel. Which meant that the Gaza border with Egypt was not as hermetically sealed as Egyptian strongman President al-Sisi liked to believe.

What should have been a routine check of a car workshop in the mixed Jewish-Arab Israeli city of Ramle had turned up a horde of stolen vehicles that, surprisingly, showed absolutely no signs of being prepared for chopping but that instead showed every sign of being prepared for instant use, engines regularly started up and batteries kept charged so they could be picked up at a moment's notice. Neither uniform nor Shin Bet had any inkling what this was about.

And now information was flooding in about a penetration into a kibbutz near the seam line with Gaza. The fence had been breached and several bombs – it was unclear how many – had gone off inside the kibbutz, caused considerable damage. No information as yet about any injuries or fatalities. The army's local Givati Brigade unit was out in force going house to house in the kibbutz, and as yet the perpetrators hadn't been found.

Benny Hart did not believe in coincidences. Ever. There was a link, there had to be.

He had the uneasy feeling that it was the action-ready stolen vehicles that were the key. But what was their purpose?

As he was pondering this he received a call on his mobile phone. It was Marita.

"Hi you. What's up?" she said.

Benny groaned. His brain already hurt from wrestling with the puzzle facing him. The last thing he needed right now was distraction from the woman he found irresistibly distracting, the woman who had elevated inter-agency liaison to a whole new level. If either of their bosses found out, they'd both find themselves down at their local job-centres grateful for work as parking attendants.

Benny had to get a grip. Out loud he said: "Not sure, but something. And I reckon it may tie in with your four. Just not sure how."

There was a pause at the other end. "You want me to come down to your office? Strictly business!" she added as she heard him launch a weak protest. "We need to wrap this up as quickly as possible. Two pairs of eyes are better than one. Let's examine together what you have and see if I note anything you haven't, and vice versa. If there's a link we'll see it, one way or the other. And if there isn't, then both you and I can get on with the job of looking elsewhere."

Benny nodded to himself. It made sense. "OK," he said and gave her the address of his office in the neat little desert town of Ofakim. Marita told him she already had his office location, which caused Benny to raise an eyebrow in wonder. If SÄPO liaison Marita Ohlsson was expecting the Shin Bet operations centre to be the size of corresponding units in the West, she was in for a surprise. With a population below 25,000, the entire town of Ofakim was probably smaller than the average shopping-mall in Stockholm.

And at its heart was the centre for Shin Bet's monitoring, surveillance and planning of Gaza counter-terrorism operations. A handful of rooms on the top floor of a two-storey office building whose ground floor was shared by an estate agent, a florist, a felafel eatery, an old-fashioned hardware store whose product line didn't seem to have changed since the 1970s, and a lawyer whose legal practice seemed to consist of nothing more exciting than picking his teeth with an ivory toothpick and doing his daily shopping at the budget-price Rami Levi supermarket on the other side of the shared parking lot.

Ashdod, Israel

SÄPO agent Marita Ohlsson showered quickly, dressed casually in lightweight khaki zip-off trousers, a white T-shirt and a blue long-sleeved cotton shirt unbuttoned down the front. Choosing between sandals and lightweight canvas boots, she decided at the last moment to go with the latter, pulling on a pair of socks before lacing up her footwear.

Just before leaving Benny Hart's apartment she grabbed her small backpack with its emergency equipment: two small bottles of Ein Gedi mineral water, a small but powerful LED flashlight, a Swiss army knife that seemed to have attachments for everything but, strangely enough, no corkscrew, a pack of six Elite nutrition bars for snacking when nothing else was available, a lightweight black fleece jacket and a narrow roll of stretchy, sticky black insulating tape.

Marita Ohlsson never went anywhere without her trusty insulation tape – it was great as an emergency bandage, it held torn clothes together, worked wonders when shoelaces snapped, it had gotten her out of a difficult situation more than once when her cute little Toyota Aygo had had its front fender cover panel knocked off by careless drivers back in Stockholm – the fender cover was a flimsy plastic moulded panel held in place by just four small metal clips! Cheapo beyond belief, but she still loved her little city-car. And she'd once used her trusty insulation tape to good effect to restrain a violent drunkard involved in a street brawl outside a Stockholm bar until uniformed police arrived to cuff and arrest him. Black insulating tape was Marita's security lifeline in an increasingly insecure world.

In the parking lot she got into her metallic blue Mazda 6 rental car and belted herself into her seat. Accessing the Waze app in her mobile phone she scrolled to the address in Ofakim that Benny's sister Amira had keyed in on her arrival in Israel and set off, shifting the gear selector into Drive and easing out of the parking lot and onto the still deserted night road.

Once out of the city she let the powerful two-litre engine stretch its legs up to the speed limit, eating up the kilometres as she sped south-east toward Ofakim and Benny Hart's office.

As the car surged onward along the deserted rural road, she saw seemingly endless fields stretching off to her left, with the occasional turnoff to a *kibbutz* or *moshav* breaking away to the right. As the car drove steadily east and she saw in the distance what at first looked like the tail lights of a tall vehicle, perhaps a tractor, by the side of the road. Odd, at this time of the night.

As she drew near she saw that it wasn't a tractor but a pick-up truck which had driven off the road in a fast sweeping bed, its hindquarters perched at a crazy angle up in the air as its nose dug deep into the ditch on the right.

In two minds whether to drive on or ask if anyone needed help, she had her mind made up for her when a dishevelled young girl of perhaps twenty or so staggered into the roadway from in front of the disabled vehicle, holding out her hand in a plea for the driver to stop.

Marita slowed down as she drove past the stricken vehicle and the girl, and pulled over to the side of the road. As she started to get out of the car the young girl reached into the pocket of her jacket and pulled out a pistol, gleaming dully and evilly in her surprisingly steady hands.

"Stop!" shouted the girl in English just as a shadowy male figure emerged from the ditch and leapt toward the still idling Mazda's driver's door. All Marita had time to reflect on was that he was as huge as the girl was small. Marita even had a first inkling that something seemed vaguely familiar before the man caught up level with the door, yanked it fully open and swung his fist at her head.

Then everything went black and Marita neither saw nor heard anything more.

She awoke with a terrible headache and a sickeningly dry taste in her mouth. She could see nothing, there was a bag or blanket over her face, but she could feel that she was moving. Rhythmically, smoothly. So she was in a vehicle of some sort. She tried moving her body but her head hurt even more and in any case she was wedged on either side by something long and immovable.

She licked her lips. They were covered in caked blood. Then she remembered. She'd been the victim of a classic vehicular mugging – broken-down vehicle by the roadside, helpless-looking girl appealing for assistance, and then her own car hijacked after she was beaten senseless by a hidden accomplice.

She didn't bother worrying about any of it because even thinking hurt her brain. It wasn't until she heard two voices above and in front of her talking in Arabic that she started worrying. A female and a male. The same two who had hijacked her? Or had she been passed on to others while she was unconscious?

Marita tried to focus her thoughts, difficult though the effort was for her. She had been close to the Gaza seam line when she was hijacked. Her hijackers were speaking Arabic. They hadn't spoken to her apart from the girl's command, in English, to stop as she started getting out of her car. She could only draw the conclusion that she was in the hands of Palestinian terrorists, probably Hamas, who were operating from the nearby Gaza Strip and that she was being kidnapped in the belief that she was an Israeli, to be ransomed against the freedom of hundreds of Palestinian security prisoners held in Israeli jails.

Marita screwed up her eyes in the enforced darkness and tried to remember the statistics from the last such kidnapping-inspired exchange. To the best of her recollection, after five long years in captivity, Hamas had finally released a young kidnapped Israeli teenager in exchange for more than a thousand Palestinians. But it had taken five years for Israel to release those prisoners. What did Sweden have to offer? Sweden didn't hold any Palestinian prisoners.

She was still trying to work out whether it would be best to try and engage her kidnappers in dialogue when her mind was made up for her.

What sounded like a bitter quarrel between the man and woman in the front of the car – and Marita was almost certain this was her own rental car and that she was on the floor in front of the rear seat – suddenly lapsed into curses in Swedish.

Swedish! Why would an Arab woman be cursing an Arab man in Swedish, in Israel? It was all Marita could do to keep her mouth shut.

The woman had broken into a flawless, Gothenburg-accented tirade of abuse against the man, who responded in Arabic with a few choice swear-words in Swedish directed back at the woman. The woman apparently didn't quite rate the man's intellectual capacity as much higher than that of a cucumber, to which the man replied that if he had a cucumber he'd insert it into an intimate part of her body and finally give her what she was longing for. From there the conversation deteriorated to an even more biological level, but Marita was no longer paying attention to the piquant details.

Because two things were now abundantly clear. Firstly, huge though the man was and small though the woman was, there was little doubt that it was the female who had the upper hand. Marita could hear it in the way she spoke to him and about him. She lacerated him with scathing, razor-sharp sarcasm, he responded with brute crudeness – but apparently did not dare attack her physically. Part of that could be because it was obvious from the direction of their voices that it was he who was driving, with the woman in the front passenger seat, just above and in front of Marita's head as she lay trussed on the floor.

And secondly – and here Marita's head throbbed even more – she now knew why there was something fleetingly familiar in the moments before her lights had been punched out. These were two of the Swedish suspects wanted for questioning in relation to the terrorist action in Gothenburg.

Marita groaned inwardly as she recalled how close she had come to blowing her cover by speaking to her captors, just moments ago. Her passport was in her left trouser pocket, she could feel its hard outline still zipped up safely in place, together with her wallet in which she carried her Swedish driver's licence and SÄPO ID card. They evidently hadn't searched her belongings.

So both Swedish and Israeli intelligence had been wrong. The suspects – at least two of them – were in the area, but they weren't in Gaza. They were in Israel!

How on earth...

Marita blacked out again for a few moments, waking up as the rhythm of the car tyres on the asphalt changed. Gone was the regular thrumming of rubber on smooth blacktop as the car cruised on into the night, now she could sense that the car had slowed down, it was twisting this way and that, the underlying surface was bumpier.

City streets!

Marita heard the two discussing something quietly in Arabic. She didn't understand a word. Apart from "OK". Well, that was pretty much universal and meant the same in just about every language.

What next?

She had her answer as the car slowed to a crawl, lurched over something – a speed bump perhaps – turned abruptly right and then immediately right again before coming to a stop.

The front doors opened but didn't shut. There was a sound of something scraping off the floor of the front passenger compartment. Fairly heavy, thought Marita. Then the driver's door slammed shut and the whole car shuddered.

"Din fanskapsidiot!" Marita heard the girl whisper fiercely through the still-open front passenger door. Once again the woman was swearing at the man in Swedish. Just two words, but with so much invective injected into the words. They meant 'You bloody prize idiot'. It seemed that their lingua franca was Arabic, but when the time came to express just how much they hated each other both resorted to their native Swedish. And still Swedes complained that the country's immigrants didn't learn Swedish and didn't integrate! Rubbish – it seemed Swedish was the only language they really felt comfortable in, at least when it came to expressing their mutual animosity. Something to be said for the success of the Swedish education system after all...

Marita felt her mind was wandering.

"Why'd you have to slam the door like that? It's the middle of the night, you'll wake everyone up! Idiot!" Again the woman spat out the words in Swedish.

The man muttered something in Arabic and Marita both heard and felt the left rear passenger door open and the man reach for her feet.

In a panic Marita realised they were going to take her away from the relative safety of the car. It could only be to kill her. They were in a city – the sound of the streets and the girl's admonishment made that clear. They were going to take her somewhere to finish off the job.

Just as she tensed her tied-up legs to kick out at the man in what would undoubtedly be a futile gesture, she heard the girl shut the front passenger door quietly and walk round to the left rear passenger door. An argument ensued. In Arabic. Why couldn't they stick to something she could understand? They'd been so helpful so far, without realising it.

Apparently the girl won the toss – which didn't surprise Marita but really relieved her – and she felt the rear passenger door shut quietly.

Then silence.

Marita tried to calm her nerves. Was this a trick? Were they waiting for her to do something? She had no idea.

Marita started to count. She'd lie perfectly still and count up to five minutes, and after that she'd try to do something about her situation.

'One thousand and one, one thousand and two, one thousand and three...' Marita counted silently, in her head. She would neither move a muscle nor make a sound until she had counted to five minutes.

She was saved the tedium of counting all the way to the end by the sound of her mobile phone, the second of the two burners she had purchased the day before. The one in the compartment in front of the gear lever she used only for Waze navigation, this was the one in her shirt pocket that she used for calls. But there was no way she could reach it.

Wriggling desperately as she tried to shrug off whatever was covering her face, Marita tried pulling her hands apart where they were bound behind her. Nothing – she couldn't move at all.

Ofakim, Israel

Glancing down at the time display in the bottom right corner of his twenty-seven inch computer flatscreen, Benny Hart wrinkled his nose and wondered, not for the first time, what was keeping Marita Ohlsson. It didn't take that long to cover the distance from Ashdod to Ofakim – even to someone unfamiliar with the roads. She had Waze, after all.

Benny got out of the chair, stretched his stiff body and grabbed his mobile phone from the desk. He hit Marita's number as he walked out of his office and down the corridor to the lunch room and its refrigerator stocked with bottles of cold water and – his favourite – orange juice.

As he strode down the corridor he glanced out the window and something in the car park below caught his eye.

A metallic blue Mazda 6. With an Avis rental sticker on the front door. Unless this was one of those coincidences Benny didn't believe in, Marita was here. But why wasn't she answering her phone? And where was she? The distance from the parked car to the main door of the building was no more than twenty metres, and it didn't take many seconds to walk up the stairs to the second storey. There she was supposed to call him and he would come to the front door and let her in.

No answer. He didn't like this.

Benny Hart burst out the door of the top-floor suite of Shin Bet offices and leapt down the stairs to the ground floor, taking them three steps at a time.

Once out of the building he bolted straight to the parked car and grabbed the front passenger door, seeing if it would give. It opened wide. He peered in. The key was in the ignition. And there was that small black backpack Marita always carried with her! This was definitely her car.

Just as he was about to slam the door shut he heard a muffled sound from the rear, behind the front seats.

Wrenching open the rear door he saw what looked like a body. Dead or alive? Benny reached instinctively for his gun, his left hand ready to pull back the slide and insert a round into the breech.

"Who's this?" he barked in Hebrew.

Hearing a voice so familiar yet so totally unexpected, Marita let out a surprised yelp. "Benny?" she screamed. "Is that you? Get me out of here. Please! Now!" There was no mistaking the urgency, bordering on hysteria, that edged her voice. Benny knew Marita well enough to know it wasn't hysteria born of fright but rather of the flood of adrenaline released now that a dangerous situation was on the cusp of receding.

Holstering his weapon and grabbing hold of the cloth covering her head, Benny removed a black fleece jacket that was covering her face and threw it onto the rear seat.

He didn't waste time asking questions, just turned her further onto the right side, eliciting a groan of pain from her as her trussed-up body was ground into the ridges and bumps of the car's thinly carpeted steel floor. Reaching into his side pocket Benny pulled out his key-ring and using the serrated edge of his front door key, he hacked and sawed at the bands of black insulating tape that had been used to secure Marita's wrists and then moved around the back of the car to do the same with her bound ankles.

When Marita saw what had been used to secure her, her cracked and bruised lips twisted into a rueful smile.

"The buggers!" she said. "That was my own tape. They rifled through my bag. First time I've had a taste of my own medicine."

As she crawled stiffly out of the rear of the car, Benny helping her to her feet, she took stock of her situation.

No bones broken, but her bruised face and cracked lip caked in dried blood meant she probably wouldn't be winning the Miss Sweden competition any time soon.

Before answering any of Benny's questions, she took a quick, experienced look at her rental car. No dents, no obvious damage, nothing even stolen. Her phone was still there in the front, and glancing through the window she could see that even her small black backpack was there on the floor in front of the passenger seat. Open, but intact.

Bending slowly and painfully after being cooped up rigidly for so long, she reached down to the rear floor of the car, grabbed her black fleece jacket – she hadn't even recognised the smell of her own clothing that had been shoved over her head, she reflected ruefully – walked around to the front, pulled out the ignition key, shut the driver's door and then walked around to the front passenger door. Opening it, she reached down and pulled up her black backpack, hoisting it painfully onto her stiff right shoulder. It felt a bit odd but that was hardly surprising – she'd been lying awkwardly, partly on her back, partly on her side, on the hard floor of a car for … for how long? No matter. She'd sort it out later. Bag on her right shoulder, fleece jacket draped across her left shoulder, she shut the door, blipped the remote control and the central locking did its work. Benny fell into step beside her as she headed slowly toward what she assumed was his office building.

She filled him in briefly, concisely and without elaborating on unnecessary details as they walked up the stairs and entered the office suite.

Benny didn't interrupt her until they were both seated in the lunch-room of his workplace, a glass of cold orange juice in front of each of them which Marita gulped down thirstily and which he replenished twice more before she pointed to the coffee machine and asked him to do the needful.

Bedouin town of Rahat, northern Negev Desert in Israel

Amir Assaf and Zahir Tafesh pulled slowly into the Sonol filling station on the outskirts of Rahat.

They were supposed to ditch their vehicle here and switch to a blue Hyundai minivan.

That was the original plan, in case anyone had seen the white Transit van they used to escape from the kibbutz.

But there had been no Transit van waiting for them, white or otherwise, and they had improvised. Which is why they were currently in a Ford Focus, whose dead owner was rotting in a ditch about an hour's drive back.

And now there was no blue Hyundai minivan waiting for them.

This was the second glitch in their plan. What was going on here? And were Ghalib and Aisha also having similar problems?

Zahir bit his lower lip. He needed to think. "Pull in between the big bus and the wall over there, let me work out where we go from here," he said quietly.

Amir eased the car into place, reversing in so they could get out in a hurry if it became necessary.

Zahir, ever the cool, objective planner, considered their options.

First, send Amir out to check all over the gas station to make sure their Hyundai van wasn't parked out of sight somewhere.

Amir returned less than a minute later, shaking his head. Nothing.

'OK, now's when it got interesting,' thought Zahir to himself. He reckoned he knew what their next step should be, but he thought he'd better ask Amir for his opinion. Both because two heads were better than one, but more importantly because he had seen that Aisha was setting herself up for some serious trouble with Amir's cousin Ghalib by taking decisions over his head and treating him like the numbskull he undoubtedly was. Zahir had no intentions of making the same mistake with the equally knuckle-dragging Amir.

"What do you say," he asked Amir, praying his partner wouldn't go for the wrong option and necessitate a time-wasting argument, which in any case may end up with them adopting the wrong plan.

"The way I see it, we have two options," continued Zahir, "and we need to decide which to take. First, we can continue on in this car. We already have it, it still has almost three-quarters of a tank of fuel, we're ready to go so no time is lost – we just drive out. But," he went on, holding up his hand, "who's to tell when the loss of this car may be reported to the police, or perhaps even if someone finds the dead owner. Which leaves us with the second choice: find a new set of wheels. The upside if we do that is that it will take that much longer for anyone to find us, the downside is it will take us that much longer to find another car. What do you say?"

Zahir held his breath and could almost hear the cogs turning in Amir's sluggish brain as his partner turned his attention to the problem. Zahir could see that Amir hadn't even given this issue any thought until now.

"Don't want to waste time looking for a new vehicle, but the longer we drive around in this one, the greater the chances of us being picked up. I say dump it and get another."

Zahir almost exploded with relief. He wouldn't have a fight on his hands to try and steer his partner away from an unnecessary risk.

Now came the next question: how to get another vehicle? They'd have to be really lucky to have another car come their way like this.

They were.

Getting out of the car to stretch their legs for a minute while debating their next move, they saw a smart red 8-seater Chevrolet Traverse SUV with blacked-out rear and side windows pull up at a self-service fuel pump. A woman in her late thirties or perhaps early forties, wearing a long ankle-length skirt and long-sleeved top, got out and inserted her credit card into the machine, punched in her PIN code, retrieved her card and started filling her tank. While she waited her hands moved up self-consciously to her head, where she tucked a stray strand of hair neatly into her head covering.

Zahir looked at Amir, who looked back and smiled. He knew the type. Definitely Jewish. Religious and therefore very modest. This was not only going to be easy, it was going to be a real pleasure. He nodded at Zahir and they both made their way the few short steps back to their stolen car. Amir started the engine, made sure their headlights were off, and inched forward until they could peer beyond the back of the bus and keep the woman and her car under close observation.

When she finished filling her car, the woman waited for the machine to spit out her receipt, which she tucked into her purse with annoying slowness, then turned back to the driver's side and got in. Slowly, gently, checking her rear-view mirror, she buckled up and started the engine, switched on her headlights and edged away from the fuel pump. Stopping at the forecourt exit, she looked long and with exaggerated thoroughness at the empty, dark road in both directions before easing her big soft-roader out onto the blacktop and gradually picking up speed to a sedate cruise of exactly seventy-five kilometres an hour.

Amir and Zahir followed. As soon as they could safely do so, they overtook her on a straight stretch of road and sped on ahead. At the first bend in the unlit rural road Amir slewed the Ford across the carriageway, effectively blocking both eastbound lanes. The central divide would prevent the Chevrolet from moving into the lanes for the oncoming traffic, and on the right side there was a steep ditch. The woman would either have to ram their car or stop.

Esther Harel looked once more in the rear-view mirror to check everything was OK and turned her eyes back to the road.

Just in time to see what appeared to be a traffic accident up ahead. It looked like a speeding car had hit the central safety barrier and bounced back into the middle of the road, blocking her path.

Esther Harel was not a fool. She knew better than to stop on a deserted stretch of road in the middle of the night far away from civilisation. But what choice did she have?

After hesitating a few moments, she slowed down and made up her mind. She'd pull up, engage reverse gear and back up a safe distance down the deserted road, stopping a good distance away to call the police.

Unfortunately, Amir Assaf had predicted that very move. He was nowhere near the stalled Ford Focus. In fact, he was already behind the Chevrolet before Esther Harel made up her mind to stop. When he saw her brake lights flicker on he started running up to the car from behind, his feet pounding the blacktop and his pistol in his right hand. He drew level with the front passenger door just as he heard the transmission clunk out of Drive as Esther prepared to move the lever into Reverse.

Amir pointed his gun straight at the female driver's head and ordered her in English to unlock her door. Seeing the abject terror in her eyes he knew she would comply. As soon as he heard the click of the central locking Amir wrenched open the door just as Esther's hand slipped off the gear selector in shock at the unexpected interruption that had exploded out of the black night. Out of the corner of her eye she saw another man, shorter and slimmer, run out from behind the stalled car in front, shouting and waving a gun in her direction.

Esther Harel froze, her mind numb and her limbs momentarily paralysed with fear. As she started recovering from the initial shock she suddenly twisted her torso to the left, toward Amir but still securely belted into the driver's seat. Before she had time to open her mouth Amir panicked at her sudden movement and fired two rounds into her half-turned abdomen. She didn't feel anything at first, then waves of nausea and the most indescribable pain hit her. Her last conscious thought was of her three children.

Zahir ran as fast as he could but was too late to do anything about the point-blank execution. No point berating the idiot Amir over yet another needless death and the even more needless worry of having to dispose of another dead body before someone drove by. He snapped open the driver's door as Amir holstered his weapon, and dragged the woman out. He pulled her lifeless body all the way to the nearside ditch and dropped her in it, hearing her skull crack against a rock or a drainage pipe – it was too dark to see what.

By the time he got back to the Chevrolet Amir had driven the Ford to the side of the road and abandoned it there. He was already behind the wheel when Zahir made it to the SUV and climbed into the passenger seat.

It was as they drove off that they heard the young children crying from the dark, cavernous interior of the car.

Amir stamped on the brake pedal and Zahir, who had not yet put on his seat belt, flew into the dashboard with a mighty thump. He felt a rib crack with the impact. Recovering quickly, he looked round as Amir reached instinctively for his pistol.

Three sleepy faces looked up at him, dazed, confused and definitely very, very scared. These people were definitely not their mother Esther. It was the youngest, a boy of perhaps two or three years old, who looked intently at Amir's face and let out another mighty scream. Amir was so taken by surprise that his finger instinctively squeezed the trigger of his gun. The report was deafening in the enclosed passenger compartment. The bullet hit not the infant but his nine-year-old brother still strapped into his seat beside the baby. He died without making a single sound. The eight-year-old girl sitting all by herself in the third row of seats struggled to undo her seat belt. It was pointless – she was hemmed in by the middle row of seats in front of her, occupied by her screaming baby brother and her now dead older brother.

Zahir put out his hand to restrain Amir's gun hand but to no avail. Amir kept shooting until his magazine was empty and the gun clicked empty several times. Only then did Amir register the blood pooled on the chest of the dead older boy and the blood seeping out of the bodies of the still – barely – breathing baby and his sister.

Zahir grabbed hold of Amir's gun and wrenched it out of his grasp.

"Enough!" he screamed. "Stop! No more! You're a killing machine! What's the point? We could have just taken them out of the car and left them by the roadside, someone would have found them. They're kids – they couldn't have told the police anything useful even if they wanted to. What was the point of that?"

A strange look of rapture glazing his eyes, Amir looked contemptuously at Zahir and snatched back his gun. Slowly, deliberately, he ejected the spent magazine, inserted a fresh one, checked the safety and holstered the gun.

"After what the Jews do to our children in Palestine, this is fine by me. Stop talking and help me get rid of the swine. At least that bitch," he jerked his thumb nonchalantly in the direction of the girl, "won't be bringing any new Zionist dogs into the world."

And with that he got out of the car and opened the rear door.

Amir didn't seem to notice it, let alone care, but Zahir saw that the two younger children were still alive. Only just. But alive. He let Amir throw the older boy's body in the ditch – nothing to be gained from being overly cautious with an already dead corpse, and certainly nothing to be gained from further antagonising the butcher – but for his part Zahir laid the body of the baby gently by the roadside and ran back to the car to make sure it was he who retrieved the girl.

Amir gave him a look of contempt and retook his place behind the steering wheel while Zahir struggled with the tangle of seat belts to get the girl out of the rear of the car and laid her down beside her little brother. Part of him prayed nobody would see the two, just the empty Ford and assume it was an abandoned breakdown.

But part of him hoped someone came along soon for the sake of the two injured children. Even though that meant the hunt would probably be on for them – at least some of the bullets from Amir's gun and gone clean through the young bodies and punched neat holes in the car's right rear panels as they exited. A bullet-riddled new car was bound to attract attention.

Zahir felt a sinking sensation in his gut. What had he gotten himself into? Not because of the killing – there was going to be plenty of that if their plan worked out. But because of the unnecessary killing.

Children. In cold blood.

Zahir Tafesh shook his head silently and didn't say a word. Amir glanced sideways at him and didn't say a word either.

But both thought precisely the same thing.

'I'll ditch this idiot first chance I get.'

Al Quds tunnel, Gaza Strip

Adan Hamati was in his element. He had despatched his four protégés, he'd heard no gunfire, seen no bright lights suddenly snapping on over on the other side of the Jews' accursed fence. True, he'd heard a couple of helicopters in the distance, separated by about half an hour, but that was par for the course – choppers could be heard day and night as the Israeli military flew within their own air space, safely out of reach of the RPGs that were always waiting to be fired from inside Gaza.

Nothing. All was quiet.

Time then for Adan Hamati to play his own part.

The four youngsters were the diversion, the warm-up act. Adan was the main act.

And what he had in store was going to put both him and Palestine firmly on the world stage. Once and for all. No messing around, no room for diplomatic niceties. The people in suits and ties could argue about the results for decades and centuries to come. Adan was a man given to few words.

He believed in action.

Action forced on him by the Zionist Occupiers of Palestine.

But not for much longer.

Adan slipped down the vertical shaft of the Al Quds tunnel and made his way at a calm, steady pace until he arrived at the vertical shaft leading him up into what the Jews unknowingly still thought of as their state. Let them sleep comfortably tonight with that thought. Many of them wouldn't wake up from their sleep.

He paused at the end of the tunnel, under the vertical stack leading out into the open inside Occupied Palestine. The ladder seemed to have been dislodged and was lying on the floor of the tunnel. Struggling for several minutes he managed to get the ladder back into place and started climbing up cautiously, hoping it would hold.

It did.

As Adan Hamati emerged cautiously from the tunnel opening inside Israel, pushing aside the branches and loose brush that had been left by Zahir and Amir to cover the hole, the other half of his end-of-days plan was playing out deep inside Israel.

More precisely, in Israeli towns and cities with a large Arab population. Such as Nazareth, Akko, Lod, Rahat.

And Ramle.

In all these cities and others too, cars, vans and pick-ups were emerging from dingy workshops, people's backyards, off-street car parks.

All the vehicles had one thing in common.

They were stolen.

There was also something else they all shared. They were all being driven by Israeli Arabs.

People who either through religious fervour, or political conviction, or good old-fashioned blackmail with the threat of dire physical consequences for their loved ones at home, had either willingly or through coercion accepted a mission.

To some, a sacred mission, a part of their holy *jihad*. To others a military operation without firearms, but still no less a part of their personal *jihad*. And to still others, a high-risk task with only one certain outcome: their own injury or death at the hands of the Israeli police or military – but it was still preferable to the horrific scenario that had been spelled out for their family members back home if they didn't play their assigned roles.

And so the invisible convoy rolled out.

Invisible because it wasn't a noticeable stream of vehicles all heading in the same direction. But a convoy nonetheless because the driver of every single one of those vehicles was part of a carefully orchestrated joint mission.

A mission to bring the country to a standstill.

Gridlock. Terminal transport chaos. Steel boxes standing bumper to bumper on strategically selected roads throughout the country.

With one exception.

It started innocuously enough. An old white Nissan pickup stopped in the slow lane on Route 4 leading south between Haifa and Hadera. As traffic sped by in the overtaking lane and a tailback of cars started building up behind the stricken vehicle, a dented and beaten-up Peugeot van pulled up alongside in the overtaking lane and nudged the rear of the stranded vehicle, its rear wheels slewing across the overtaking lane and coming to a complete stop almost transversely across the roadway.

Both lanes were now blocked. And the traffic built up, horns blaring and engines revving uselessly.

An old Nissan pickup truck that had pulled in somewhat ahead of the first stricken vehicle started reversing back down the by now empty dual carriageway and swung across the hard shoulder, effectively blocking the route for any emergency vehicles that might possibly make their way up through the rapidly building logjam of private cars, commercial trucks, Egged commuter buses and the ubiquitous scooters that kept much of Israel moving.

The drivers of the three vehicles used in the barricade held their breath and waited. If a single two-wheeled scooter made it through and past the massive gridlock expanding exponentially by the minute, that would be a sign they hadn't been entirely successful.

Nothing moved.

At all.

The three drivers each pulled out a jerry-can of petrol, sloshed the contents inside their vehicles, taking particular care to soak the soft upholstery and the rubber tyres, struck a match and left. Looking back one last time as they made their way into the drainage culvert that led directly to the Arab-Israeli village of Khirbat Zureik, they smiled as they saw the conflagration take a firm hold of their vehicles and spread back down the locked mass of vehicles behind them, leaping from one to the other as shiny plastic fender covers were gratefully slicked by flames looking eagerly for new fuel.

The three men disappeared into the dry water culvert leading under the highway and into the village.

This was just the start of the Israel Traffic Police's troubles. Because identical scenarios were being played out at two other locations further south on the same southbound stretch of road. And also on the northbound carriageway of the same road. In fact, identical barricades of stolen, burnt cars and vans and trucks were popping up along all the country's main arteries: the coastal Highway 2 that linked Haifa with Tel Aviv, Route 5 in both directions, Route 1 leading between Tel Aviv and Jerusalem. To name but a few.

Always the same MO. Not one barricade of burning and exploding vehicles, but two, three and sometimes even four such barricades on each stretch of major highway, in each direction, effectively shutting down all vehicular traffic in both directions of each route. Including Israel's much-vaunted Highway 6, the high-speed toll road that prided itself on keeping the country moving – for those who could afford to pay the fee on this beautiful piece of engineering.

Israel's main highways and motorways were grinding to a halt.

And on the lesser roads the situation wasn't much better. If anything, it was worse.

Because suddenly, the popular Waze navigation app that everyone and their uncle used in Israel started registering broken-down vehicles on roads large and small. Everywhere. All it took was for someone driving that route to ditch their stolen vehicle by the roadside, click on the icon for 'breakdown', and the system automatically tagged it as an obstacle. When several drivers – all driving through carefully selected junctions, crossroads and interchanges – all logged breakdowns *en masse*, the Waze software equally automatically rerouted traffic to other smaller roads.

And that is where all those stolen vehicles driven by unarmed *jihadis* were being dumped. Right in the middle of the road or by the roadside, usually in groups of two and three and then set alight before their drivers made their way on foot.

Nobody gave them a second glance. Why should they? By now whole families had abandoned their vehicles and were making their way on foot to nearby friends, relatives, colleagues, even closed-down shopping malls and all-night fast-food eateries. Anywhere just to get away from the increasingly dangerous chaos that was enveloping the road system.

Waze, that marvellous and highly intelligent interactive navigation system so beloved by drivers all over Israel, had been used as one of the most potent weapons against the Jewish state.

And there was more to come.

Israel's immensely effective motorcycle-borne first-responders – paramedics, police officers, anti-terror squads – were all caught up in the mayhem.

Now the air corridors started getting busy. It was the only way to get emergency crews to the relevant sites to try and bring some order into the fiery chaos.

But it wasn't possible to airlift heavy firefighting equipment to the points of conflagration.

So the fires raged on, leaping from row to row of gridlocked vehicles as hundreds, then thousands, then tens of thousands, of people abandoned their vehicles and ran to safety, watching in disbelief as they saw the eerie glow of fires north, south, east and west.

Wherever there was a road, there seemed to be fire.

And there were also people watching the flames, with a sense of growing helplessness and increasing rage. Because by now it was becoming abundantly clear that this was not a case of a traffic accident gone bad but of deliberate terrorism. On a massive scale.

While some Israeli Arabs cheered as they watched the news on TV, most other Israeli Arabs sat in stunned silence and physically felt the fear that was inexorably enveloping them, clutching at their throats and almost certainly preparing to reap a harvest of young Arab lives. Because if there was terrorism afoot, guess who would be blamed irrespective of whether or not they were involved, guess who would pay the price with their lives? Or, more specifically, guess whose children would pay the price?

The State of Israel was in turmoil. Its infrastructure paralysed, its electronic communications grossly overburdened as thousands upon thousands of people all jammed the airwaves at the same time. And all the time with thousands upon thousands of people trudging along the sides of highways, motorways and minor roads, all desperately looking for a way to get home and let the authorities deal with the mayhem, which seemed to be fast reaching a crescendo.

But it wasn't reaching a crescendo. Not yet.

That would come later, if everything went according to Adan Hamati's plan.

Ofakim, Israel

After leaving the kidnapped woman in the back of her car, Ghalib looked around the car park for their next scheduled ride.

It was Aisha who located their white Peugeot panel van. Its ignition key was on the floor under the driver's rubber floor mat. She got in behind the wheel and Ghalib, looking daggers at her but saying nothing, climbed into the passenger side of the front bench seat.

Ghalib punched in their destination in Waze. They were heading south, on the final leg of their mission. Hopefully it wouldn't be their last journey, because they both hoped to make it back. But only Allah could decide that.

Aisha gunned the engine and they set off, less than thirty seconds before Benny Hart burst through the front door of his office building onto the car park. As their navigation system guided them through the streets of Ofakim, Aisha and Ghalib breathed a sigh of relief. Aisha looked sideways at her partner. Noticing her head movement, he looked at her and a small smile played across his lips.

"So far so good," he said, "despite the occasional hitch in the plans. Let's see if we can't get the rest done without coming up against any obstacles."

Aisha looked at him appraisingly, then turned back to concentrate on the road. That's all she wanted – to get this done without coming up against any obstacles.

The biggest one of which, by her reckoning, was the man sitting beside her.

Ghalib Ajrour would have to be ditched first chance she got. Whatever that took, in whatever way was necessary.

Sitting hunched up against the passenger door with the extra seat between them gaping empty, Ghalib Ajrour was thinking exactly the same about Aisha Naddi.

He'd have to ditch her first chance he got. But before he did that, he had some plans involving himself sans trousers and her sans all clothing. He smiled to himself and looked out the side window.

"Put your foot down!" he said to Aisha, still looking out his window. "We have to finish this before sunup."

Aisha didn't reply, except to put her foot down. The diesel engine hummed smoothly as they sped on south, deeper into the sparsely populated Negev Desert.

Kiryat Malachi, Israel

From Akko up north on the Mediterranean coast east to Nazareth in the Galilee, and from both down through the rich agricultural and industrial heartland of Israel through the Jezreel Valley and the plains of Sharon and Dan, all the way south through the vibrant commercial and financial hub of Tel Aviv and then even further south through to Ashkelon on the coast just north of the Gaza Strip, traffic was at a standstill.

The same modus operandi had been repeated everywhere. Cars blocking the roads, then set alight. Blocking all traffic in both directions. And Waze adding to the confusion after being expertly manipulated to do what it did best – provide information about blocked roads and redirect traffic. Unfortunately, the system now redirected traffic onto even more severely blocked roads.

Because there wasn't just one barricade per road – that would have been a relatively easy obstacle to clear. The problem was that the pattern, the burning barricades, had been replicated several times on each stretch of main road, hindering all efforts at clearing the burning wreckage as the flames eagerly engulfed the stacked-up cars and trucks and buses blocked behind them. And when emergency services did manage to smash a path through such a barricade, they only made modest progress before they were stopped a short distance later by an identical barricade.

With the motorways at a flaming standstill and Waze manipulated by both genuine and hoax reports of blockages on minor roads, gridlock was total.

The only way of getting anywhere was by air.

And aerial monitoring of the chaos down below revealed that it seemed to have ceased abruptly at the Kiryat Malachi junction south of Ramle on route 40, some 60 kilometres north of Beer Sheva. South of Kiryat Malachi everything seemed to be flowing perfectly normally.

That was a relief.

Or was it an indication of something else?

That was precisely what Benny Hart was wondering as he looked at the digital images flitting across the second flatscreen he had stolen from a colleague's desk and rigged up at his own workplace. It showed Traffic's graphic of what was happening up north.

Why the north? Why not the south, where he was?

Not for the first time this evening, Benny smoothed down his trusty paper map from Eldan Car Rentals and pored over it. He tapped at a particular point in the desert, a small town with one main road leading to it and the same road continuing south-east out of it leading to Highway 90 and further south to Eilat.

Dimona.

A small town known mostly in the press for the fact that since the late 1960s it had been home to a sect known as the Black Hebrews, a community of African Americans who claimed they were of the Jewish faith and who had made their home down south in what was then the extremely remote little hamlet of Dimona. Today the Black Hebrews were a thriving community, many of their children even did the obligatory army service for Israeli citizens – equally a sign of goodwill on their part and acceptance on the part of the State of Israel.

But that's pretty much all there was in Dimona. Next stop was Eilat – and that was 220 kilometres further south, a punishing two and a half hour journey by car on Highway 25 and then Route 90.

There was precious little else in Dimona.

Apart from Israel's much-vaunted but officially non-existent nuclear centre. To the extent that it was even officially acknowledged it was referred to as a scientific research facility. To everyone else it was the Jewish state's production hub for the manufacture of nuclear weapons.

Perhaps.

Or maybe not.

Few people knew for certain what went on there. If anything.

Benny Hart tapped his forefinger on the spot marking Dimona. It's what he'd thought all along. He still had no proof, but the indications were all there. He'd go with his hunch.

Benny reached for his phone. One quick call to Amira to tell her to alert her boss Calev Mizrachi that there was every reason to suspect that there was a strong link between the spate of vehicle thefts, the deliberately staged traffic chaos, the evidence that the four Swedish terrorist suspects were or had been in Gaza, the terrorist infiltration from Gaza, and the attempted abduction of Marita Ohlsson.

And the fact that roads south leading to Dimona were unaffected.

Because the way Benny Hart saw it, what was important here was not what was happening, but what was not. More specifically, the real focus should not be on where things were happening, but on where they weren't.

The Swedish aspect was Amira Hart's pigeon together with her boss Calev Mizrachi and her liaison Marita Ohlsson, even though the action was taking place on domestic territory in Israel and was therefore a Shin Bet, not a Mossad, concern. Shin Bet would as always be working closely with the Israel Defense Force or IDF. And the police, both Traffic and anti-terror squads, would be needed to play their vital roles in keeping a lid on things.

It was a bureaucratic mess and, with so many roads out of commission, a logistical nightmare.

Just the sort of problem Benny Hart detested.

Even before Benny cut the call to his sister and scrolled the menu to call his supervisor, Amira Hart was already on her feet, darting to her front door, car keys in hand.

She slammed the door shut and ran out to her green Kia Rio. She was halfway there before she remembered that in her haste she hadn't even locked the front door. She didn't bother turning back – this was a national emergency beyond anything the State of Israel had ever experienced before. If they didn't manage to avert what she was now convinced was in the offing, having her home burglarised was going to be the least of her problems.

If indeed her home was still standing twenty-four hours from now.

Route 25, south of Beer Sheva

By the time Benny Hart had put two and two together and come up with a possible, potential, likely, probable – whatever – target, the situation had changed completely.

He was now in his car speeding south.

Zahir Tafesh and Amir Assaf in their hijacked Chevrolet Traverse SUV and Aisha Naddi and Ghalib Ajrour in their Peugeot van were already past the largely sleeping city of Beer Sheva, whose centre they skirted on the beautiful, newly constructed urban bypass.

They kept heading south.

But as Amir and Aisha left Beer Sheva in their rear-view mirrors, their passengers Zahir and Ghalib each made one phone call.

To the same number.

It was only after the second of these calls came through to the recipient that he in turn placed one call.

After that, all the roads leading west, east and north out of Beer Sheva were blocked by swarms of stolen cars, vans and pick-up trucks leaving lock-ups, garages, backyards and small backstreet workshops.

Once again the MO was exactly the same, although the effect this far south of the country's main population centres was not quite as devastating – there simply weren't as many vehicles on the roads down here, especially not at this time of night.

But the roads going north were well and truly blocked by barricades of burning vehicles, backed up a couple of kilometres away by the same again. And again. And again.

The traffic chaos had spread south deep into the Negev Desert.

But not all the way south.

Highway 25 from Beer Sheva to Dimona was still open. And so was Highway 40.

With continuous reports streaming in via his in-car communication radio, Benny Hart, with Marita Ohlsson in the passenger seat beside him, began to sweat profusely.

It was all becoming abundantly clear.

The police and army were moving, and so was the air force. He hoped they'd get there in time.

But what would they be looking for? And would they recognise it if and when they saw it?

And what could they do? You could hardly expect the Israeli air force to shoot any and every vehicle travelling on a public road. The police could block the roads – provided they could use the roads to get to where they needed to set up their roadblocks…

It would be down to the army. Tracked vehicles could get anywhere, on-road or off-road.

Meantime, Benny Hart had a snap decision to make: Highway 40 or Highway 25? The latter was shorter and faster, but something told him that was too easy.

As the junction between the two highways approached, he made a split-second decision and wrenched the wheel right.

The longer Highway 40 it would be. From there straight south onto the 224 – there should be no traffic on that small road at this time of night – and then snap left and north-east onto the 204.

The army could use the trails criss-crossing the desert – their slower tracked vehicles would probably take about the same time to get to Dimona as he would to cover the longer distance in his faster and lighter passenger car.

He floored the accelerator and the car leapt forward, its bi-Xenon headlights carving a swathe of bright, almost blue-white light through the inky black night.

Route 204 north of Yeroham

So far it was working out pretty much as Adan Hamati had envisioned.

In his powerful but cosmetically beat-up Toyota Hilux he had made good time. He didn't understand more than the odd word of Hebrew but judging by the fact that all the radio stations he had tuned to seemed to be giving endless news bulletins and there was not a single Hebrew-language radio station playing music, he assumed that thus far the chaos he had envisioned was panning out perfectly.

For him.

His four-wheel drive Toyota Hilux pickup had been waiting for him, and the Jewish Waze system had guided him effortlessly – in Arabic, no less, thank you very much! – all the way through to highway 40, from where he continued south on the 224 to the small dusty town of Yeroham, and from there he took the little-used, for the most part forgotten, 204 dogleg back up north-east to his target.

Dimona.

He could almost smell his target.

The one flaw in his plan was that he had no reliable intelligence on the layout of his ultimate target. For obvious reasons. But with a vehicle packed with explosives, and four accomplices approaching from a different direction to cause the necessary diversion, he reckoned he'd figure it all out as he went.

And he still had one more ace up his sleeve.

That is to say, one ace but playing in two locations. His last line of defence. Or, to put it more accurately, offensive defence.

The media loved a good story. And he'd lined up the media, with a story ready to photograph, film and tell.

In less than an hour it would all come together. He glanced at the clock in the dashboard. He'd better slow down, he didn't want to get there ahead of time.

He'd know when it was time for him to act.

He'd hear the signal. And so far, all had been serenely quiet.

South of Beer Sheva

Two vehicles sped purposefully south, heading toward Dimona. Aisha looked in her rear-view mirror and saw the headlights of a single vehicle far distant in her rear-view mirror, sometimes disappearing as she took a bend or crested a hill, then reappearing in the distance as the road evened out for a while before the next curve.

Road signs warning of camel crossings and the dangers of flash-flooding in usually dry *wadis* hurtled past, in and out of her field of vision.

"Slow down," said Ghalib. She could almost physically feel the tension in his voice. They were so close now.

The question was: was this the right time to risk the one – and only – phone call they were allowed? Each team had been given a second burner phone to use for making just one call, after which the battery and SIM card had to be removed and the phone destroyed, never to be reused.

"What do you reckon," Aisha asked Ghalib. "Should we call them now? That may be their car behind us. But what if it isn't? Shall we wait?"

Her mind was made up for her as a smart red Chevrolet Traverse SUV pulled into view behind them and slowed down, flashing its right indicator and coming to a standstill at a safe distance behind them.

Aisha also slowed down and stopped.

Nobody moved.

The driver's door of the Chevrolet opened cautiously and a figure got out slowly. A biggish man with an unmistakeable gait.

Amir! Ghalib, who had pulled down the passenger sun-visor and was looking rearward in its vanity mirror, broke out into a huge smile of relief and shoved open his door, running out to greet his cousin.

"Good to see you!" they both said simultaneously. "Everything OK?" asked Amir at the same time as Ghalib exclaimed "Now the end begins!"

They both spent a minute talking in low voices before each returned to their vehicles, engines still idling.

The pensive smiles on the two cousins' faces reflected both relief and nervousness. Relief at having made it so far, and nervousness at what lay ahead. Because everything that had happened up to now was just the preamble, the precursor to what was to come. Their actual mission.

Both passengers made their one call each, then immediately took their phones apart, removing the SIM cards and batteries and digging the heels of their boots into the phones to crush them.

Those phone calls were the starting signal for the only help they would get from here on in.

What Adan Hamati referred to as his line of offensive defence.

Offensive because it would document for the world how pathetically incapable the much-vaunted Zionist occupying army really was. The Zionists really had no way of adequately dealing with documentation of their criminal actions.

And defence because it would shield their final act.

If all went to plan.

As they covered the last few kilometres towards the sleeping town of Dimona and the nuclear facility just beyond it Amir, following at a safe distance behind Aisha who was still in the lead, looked in his rear-view mirror and let out an involuntary snort.

"What?" asked Zahir, alarmed at the sudden noise. Amir nodded his head to the rear, focusing firmly on his driving. He didn't want to lose concentration now when they were so close.

Zahir twisted in his seat. The vision playing out behind him brought a delighted smile to his face.

There were people huddled behind a bend in the road that at the apex of the curve cut through some fairly tall dunes of rock and hard sand.

Out of sight for anyone approaching from the south, until they were past the bend in the road, were people armed and waiting.

Armed with rocks, boulders, Molotov cocktails. And cameras – mobile phones as well as semi-professional video cameras. It was a lesson learned from the Palestinian Arabs of Gaza and the West Bank: entrapment, attack, plenty of photo-documentation, stills and film alike, which would be judiciously edited to provide just the right angle and predetermined effect. Custom-tailored, impeccably edited 'spontaneous' news footage…

The cameras were set, the roles had been allocated, all that was needed was for the unwitting actors to turn up.

Pallywood had come to Dimona.

Aisha Naddi, Ghalib Ajrour, Zahir Tafesh and Amir Assaf were now set for their final scene, and in his explosives-packed Toyota Hilux, Adan Hamati was hovering in the wings ready to lower the curtain on Israel's prize military asset.

Ahead of the four Swedish Palestinians lay the Dimona nuclear facility.

Behind them lay their line of offensive defence, Molotov cocktails, rocks and cameras at the ready.

Behind that line, Adan Hamati was fast approaching.

And behind him, Benny Hart and Marita Ohlsson were speeding at breakneck speed, having made it through the Route 40 bypass around Beer Sheva mere minutes before all hell broke loose north of that point, bringing all routes between Beer Sheva and the centre of Israel to a standstill.

Somewhere further back but safely just through the expanding road blocks of stricken, burning cars spreading north from Beer Sheva, was Amira Hart, speaking to her Swedish liaison Marita Ohlsson via her Bluetooth headset, coordinating their time of arrival and, more importantly, the directions from which they would arrive.

Both cars, it turned out, would be using the same road. The southern approach to Dimona.

Route 204.

Unmarked approach road to Dimona Nuclear Facility

As first Aisha's vehicle, then Amir's, passed the unmarked exit leading to the road that in turn led to the road that led to the road that led to Israel's Dimona nuclear facility, their movement automatically triggered cameras mounted high up on the roadside lamppost. The cameras detected the vehicles and equally automatically passed on the licence plate details via an encrypted channel to a battery of computers that carried out an instantaneous check of their identities.

That check revealed both vehicles were stolen, and both were unfamiliar in the Dimona area.

Which in turn triggered a Grade Two state of emergency, the second-lowest for the facility. If the two vehicles were photographically captured a second time on any of the approach roads leading to the high-security facility within the next 14 days, this would initiate proactive steps to detain their drivers and question them.

It didn't take 14 days for either of the vehicles to reappear. Both were captured by CCTV at exactly the same junction just three minutes later, but now approaching from the direction in which they had first driven.

In any other circumstances, in any other location, this may have been a simple case of somebody driving on an unfamiliar stretch of road getting lost and doubling back.

But a convoy of two vehicles travelling slowly, both reported stolen further north, and both trailing each other a second time past a sensitive military location, was not a coincidence.

And in any case, the security system at Dimona had no room for coincidences.

As the two vehicles cruised slowly past the entry to the nuclear facility, multiple proactive teams were despatched from both the facility's compound and from three other stations located out of sight on either side of the main road. It was a pincer movement, with several mobile security units approaching the two suspect vehicles from either side.

As the short convoy of two stolen vehicles crawled to a stop at the roadside so the four young terrorists could prime their explosive backpacks and get to work, two dark blue BMW F850GS off-road motorcycles burst onto the tarmac behind them, one from each side of the road. With eardrum-splitting bullhorn sirens screaming and headlights on high beam, and with immensely powerful forward-facing blue and red strobe lights flashing an irregular beat that was highly disruptive to the senses, the four youngsters stopped dead in their tracks, completely disoriented, frozen in place by the unexpected interruption.

The pillion passenger on each bike, sitting somewhat higher than the rider, held a lethal-looking firearm whose muzzle was pointed straight at the group of four suspects.

As first Aisha Naddi and then Ghalib Ajrour drew back in shock, Amir Assaf and Zahir Tafesh both dived back into their van to make good their escape.

They had nowhere to go.

Approaching from the other side of the road was a grey short-wheelbase Land Rover Defender, driver at the wheel and three black-clad SWAT-type figures hanging onto grab-rails with one hand and directing evil-looking Tavor automatic rifles at the four suspects. From the left roaring across the rocky desert floor came an open-topped skeletal four-wheel-drive vehicle looking like something spawned in an illicit romance between an escapee from the 'Mad Max' movie set and NASA's moon buggy programme.

It too carried a driver and three heavily armed men.

As commands in Hebrew were yelled at the four suspects to stop and raise their hands, it was Amir who was first to regain his wits.

He emerged from halfway into his van, holding his hands up high over his head and screaming in English "My name is Amir Assaf! I'm a Swedish Jew, both my parents are Israelis! I was kidnapped by these people! I've no idea who they are! Please get me out of here!"

And with that he dropped onto his knees in the roadway, beside the open door of the Chevrolet.

The other three looked at him in amazement, not quite knowing what to do. It was Aisha who was the first to understand what Amir was doing. His name was not only Arabic, it was also Hebrew.

Driving home his temporary advantage, Amir continued yelling. "Look! Here's my ID card. Please, just get me out of here!" and with that he moved his right hand to his back pocket to pull out his wallet which would quite rightly show that he was a Swede with the extremely Israeli Jewish-sounding name of Amir Assaf.

Had circumstances been different, had they been dealing with regular uniformed police rather than an anti-terror squad whose sole aim was to prevent even the hint of a suggestion of an attack on what was potentially Israel's most prized military target, the ruse might have worked.

It didn't.

As Amir dropped his hand towards his back pocket to pull out his wallet, he was peppered by a hail of bullets.

As the first round spat from the muzzle of the nearest motorcycle pillion rider, Zahir moved at lightning speed to snatch one of the backpacks that lay so tantalisingly close just inside the open door of the van. They all featured impact detonators; if he could just throw at least one bag into the air, it would explode upon contact with the ground – the explosion would be unavoidable.

His left hand got to within ten short centimetres of the nearest bag before he too was hit by four rounds, two to his upper chest, one in his throat and one in his forehead. He was dead before he slumped against the side of the van in a grotesque half-sitting, half standing position.

Ghalib meantime moved with surprising agility toward the motorcycle that was nearest him. There was no time for the pillion passenger, the marksman of the two-wheeled team, to bring his weapon to bear on the fast-approaching suspect. The rider slipped the clutch and simply rammed the huge terrorist. The knobbly front tyre of the off-roader hit Ghalib squarely in the genitals. With a combined weight of bike, rider and passenger thrusting almost 350 kilograms into the forward momentum of the knobbly front tyre, Ghalib Ajrour never stood a chance. He screamed in anguish at the impact. As he collapsed to the ground, grasping what was left of his tattered genitalia, his last conscious thought as he passed out was that he would likely never have the opportunity to put his plans for Aisha into action.

Aisha stood as still as a statue, not having moved a single muscle of her body. Her eyes, however, took in the two dead bodies and the tiniest smile of satisfaction played fleetingly across her lips as she saw the wet patch – urine? blood? – spreading across the crotch of Ghalib's trousers. At least her nemesis was now quiet. She wasn't sure if he had fainted or died, but she knew which she preferred.

She also knew that she preferred not to be taken alive.

But she also preferred to make sure Ghalib Ajrour, that sexist, primitive monster who had plagued her for longer than she cared to remember, was well and truly dead.

So Aisha spoke in English, still without moving.

"He's got a bomb under his shirt," she lied. "I want to live, I can defuse it but you won't know how to do it because it's got a fail-safe."

And without waiting even a second she darted straight onto Ghalib's prone body. Aisha Naddi knew she was going to die, but she was going to make sure enough bullets also hit Ghalib, and the only way was to make sure she was with him.

Ghalib Ajrour never knew it, but finally his innermost wish had come true: he was on his back with Aisha straddling him. He even had his penis – what was left of it – in his hands.

It was a shame he never had the chance to savour the irony of fulfilling his wish before his heart stopped beating, penetrated by at least three bullets. Aisha died on top of him.

Route 204 south-west of Dimona

Adan Hamati drove gently past the bend in the road that concealed his line of offensive defence. There was another one just like it north, on route 40, which would deal with anyone approaching Dimona from that direction.

As he drove past the invisible cordon, he briefly flashed his emergency hazard warning lights to acknowledge that his was the last car to be allowed through.

Now it was all up to the people manning the rock and camera barricade to ensure that nobody came up behind him while he pursued the final stage of his plan.

Adan Hamati drove on, unhurried and calm. He looked once again at the dashboard clock. He had plenty of time.

He cruised gently on the deserted blacktop until he saw a faint track that headed off to the right and disappeared behind a rocky outcrop. That was perfect. He'd hide up out of sight until he saw the signal in the night sky that would tell him to launch his part of the mission.

The final countdown was on.

From where he was parked up, he'd be able to both hear and see his signal on such a still night. He'd trained his four youngsters well. All they had to do was follow their instructions.

What Adan didn't know was that his four youngsters were unable to follow their instructions, now or ever.

They were lying dead in the middle of a road barely a kilometre away.

Less than a minute after Adan Hamati pulled in behind his temporary shelter, Benny Hart and Marita Ohlsson came roaring up towards the hidden attackers in Benny's white Hyundai i35, police strobe lights flashing their urgent message to clear away any traffic he might encounter on the deserted road. And less than a minute behind him, Amira Hart was speeding in his wake, her police light also flashing its message to anyone and everyone to get out of her way.

It was the flashing lights that galvanised the people manning the barricade.

As Benny rounded the bend at speed, his car was struck by a hail of rocks from both sides and three Molotov cocktails were hurled in his direction, two from the left and one from the right. In the briefest of split-seconds Benny saw several more lights on either side of the road – it all happened in such a blur he wasn't sure if they were more fire-bombs being lit prior to being thrown at him, or whether there were some sort of electronic light source – camera flashes perhaps? He pressed the accelerator and screamed through, the tyres bumping over several large stones strewn across the road where they had bounced off the metalwork and catapulted ahead. His first instinct had been to brake, but instead he buried the gas pedal in the floor and the car surged ahead, with fires burning in the roadway where two fire-bombs had missed their target. One had hit the car but was burning fairly harmlessly on the rear part of the roof and dripping flaming petrol down the rear glass windscreen. The petrol would run off onto the road before it could do much damage other than blister the paint and burn through the rubber seals surrounding the glass. But it wouldn't be serious.

They were through. Nothing but darkness ahead. Until they rounded another bend and saw what looked like several vehicles strewn all across the roadway and several alongside the road, with flashing blue and red lights on many of them.

As the anti-lock brakes on Benny Hart's car bit into the discs, he saw that he had run out of roadway and was heading straight into the back of a grey Land Rover stopped in the middle of the road, blue and red lights flashing. Benny heaved the steering wheel to the right and the nose of his car dipped, jacking up the rear bodywork as the car plunged off the tarmac onto the rocky hard shoulder and finally into a patch of soft sand off the hard shoulder, finally coming to rest beside a strange-looking off-road buggy that looked like a skeletal web of tubes welded together with an engine in the front and four individual seats bolted to the floor. It too had flashing blue and red lights mounted front, rear, and to the sides.

As Benny got out of his car, Marita Ohlsson was speaking urgently to Amira Hart, warning her of what was in store for her.

Too late.

Speeding along at the wheel of her green Kia Rio, Amira Hart saw some flashes up ahead where the road disappeared round a bend but couldn't make out what they were. When Marita's call came through Amira was already at the bend in the road and witnessed a scene that looked like it had come straight out of hell.

Rocks strewn across the roadway, fires burning on the road surface, black-clad people in hoods and masks carrying rocks, petrol bombs, and on either side, the eerie glow of mobile-phone cameras and video-camera display screens lit up the faces of their operators.

Amira understood immediately what she was up against. She had personally experienced it before on a deserted night road south of Nablus a couple of years ago, and many Israeli civilians living in Judea and Samaria – the West Bank – experienced it on an almost daily basis on their way to and from work and home.

Attacks on civilian motorists by gangs of Arabs wielding rocks, Molotov cocktails, iron rods, powerful catapults made of metal tubing.

Amira was alone in the car, and the road was already littered with stones, some as large as footballs.

Her training kicking in instinctively, Amira Hart responded with the two main actions drilled into her during her defensive driving training.

Firstly, always keep moving, and move fast. Never slow down, never stop. Move fast both to get away, to reduce the length of time you are exposed to this mortal danger and also in order to cut down the time available for your attackers to rearm – whether with rocks, petrol bombs, new missiles to be loaded into catapults, whatever.

And secondly, always try to keep your front windscreen between you and your attackers. In most passenger cars apart from top-of-the-range luxury models and of course armoured cars, the side glass and rear windscreen were the points most vulnerable to penetration by sharp, heavy, and/or high-velocity objects such as rocks or other 'cold' non-firearm missiles launched at high speed, such as rocks from a catapult or slingshot. The metal body panels such as the doors and roof offered better protection, but surprisingly the front glass windscreen offered probably the best protection. This was because for reasons of cost and weight, the side and rear glass was simply tempered, which meant that in an impact it would shatter, sending a shower of broken glass particles flying around inside the passenger compartment. The front windscreen, on the other hand, was by law required to be laminated, made of a sandwich construction that would allow the glass to crack if hit by stones kicked up by a vehicle in front, for instance, but not splinter. The glass, even if broken, would be held firmly in place by the laminate, the sandwiched layer of clear bonded plastic holding the shattered mosaic of glass in place.

So Amira Hart floored the accelerator and the automatic transmission kicked down from fifth to third and then second, thrusting the car ahead with ferocious speed. At the same time she took deliberate aim at the attackers standing in the roadway. There was nothing she could do about attacks from the side – she put her faith in her speed to minimise the risk from the sides. But the point was to proactively reduce the risk from the front, thus shielding herself behind her windscreen – the least vulnerable point of potential penetration by rocks – while at the same time using the momentum of her car to intimidate would-be attackers to get out of the way.

Or, if necessary, to run them down if they didn't move.

Three of Amira Hart's attackers didn't move. They stood their ground. The human instinct is to avoid running over another human being.

But the three teenage attackers, huge rocks in hand, hadn't counted on coming head-on against a driver who had been trained for just this kind of eventuality.

Two went down like skittles and the third leapt to one side at the very last micro-second. Amira's car lurched momentarily to the side as first the front wheels and then the rear crunched over the broken bodies mown down below the knees.

Amira almost lost control when the car was thrown dangerously off course by the force of the impact but she kept her foot planted to the floor as the car made it past the bend and the road straightened out ahead of her.

She could hear the thunderstorm of rocks and see the explosions of fire-bombs uselessly peppering the road behind her as the scene faded away in her rear-view mirror.

Amira hit the speed dial in her dashboard-mounted mobile phone and Marita Ohlsson answered almost immediately.

"What happened?" spoke Marita breathlessly. "We got cut off! Can you see the barrier across the road? Benny says you should turn back!" The words tumbled out of Marita as fast as she could think them.

"Stop!" said Amira, to no avail. "Marita! Shut up!" There was a stunned silence at the other end.

"I'm through, it's OK. Where are you? OK, hold it, I can see a bunch of flashing lights up ahead. Is that you?"

Before Marita could reply Amira's Kia Rio drew up and screamed to a halt behind the grey Land Rover.

Amira got out as her brother Benny strode up to her and her Swedish opposite number Marita Ohlsson came around from the other side of the Land Rover.

"You OK, Amira? Are you hurt?" Benny blurted out.

'How cute,' thought Marita. 'He's worried about his sister, even though he's just been through a near-death experience himself.'

'How pathetic,' thought Amira. 'He's still playing the macho I'm-the-man-let-me-protect-you role when I've been able to whip his ass from before kindergarten all the way to today.'

Out loud, however, she said: "I'm fine. What's the status here?"

By way of response Marita Ohlsson took her Israeli liaison by the arm and walked her to the scene of death at the front of the gathering of vehicles.

Four dead bodies. "My four Swedes," said Marita Ohlsson, simply and without a hint of emotion. "They were four young kids. Still teenagers. Now we'll never be able to question their role in the attack in Gothenburg. It's a mess."

Amira decided not to respond. She wasn't sure whether she was detecting a hint of reproach in her Swedish counterpart's tone of voice, or whether she was merely expressing regret that the case on the Gothenburg attack would have to be closed without conclusive evidence of the part played by the four dead suspects.

Amira dug out her ID and presented it to a plain-clothes man who was evidently running the cleaning-up operation.

"What's the situation here?" she asked in Hebrew. "I have no jurisdiction here at all," she jerked her head back in the direction of Marita, "but I'm the liaison officer for that woman over there, who is from the Swedish security services. We've been hunting these four for a while now. I suppose they're all dead, they didn't reveal anything before dying?" she asked with a tiny trace of hope in her voice.

The security officer shook his head. "Nope, nothing. That one," he pointed to the body of the dead Amir Assaf, "ranted on about having been abducted by the other three, but that blond guy," he continued, jutting his chin in Benny's direction, "says that's rubbish, they were all part of the same thing. What that thing is, we're not quite sure. Except that they drove past the on-ramp to the nuclear facility, and then repeated the move. Their vehicles are reported as stolen – and the plates don't match the vehicles. When we stopped them, they initiated an attack. Uniformed police are on their way now, but they're having to send cops up from Eilat and Mitzpe Ramon because everything is blocked solid from here north."

Amira nodded. Nothing for her to do. Or for Benny, for that matter. Which meant nothing for Marita either, except to wrap up and go home with a neat report confirming that all four suspects in the killing of two Swedish Jews, a Swedish pensioner and two police officers, as well as the attempted murder of the Israeli ambassador to Sweden and her husband, had themselves met their death in the Negev Desert. It would be up to her boss Calev Mizrachi to work out with the men in suits at the Prime Minister's office how this would be presented to the public – and to the government of Sweden, of which the four suspected terrorists were citizens.

She chatted another few moments with the security officer, informing him about the ambush further back and requesting police or military help in clearing them away, then called over Benny and Marita to coordinate exactly when and where they would all meet with the Dimona security department for debriefing and to provide their written and verbal reports.

And that was the precise moment when all hell broke loose.

Rocky outcrop just outside Dimona Nuclear Facility, Israel

Twenty minutes had gone by.

Without the signal he was waiting for.

There was plenty else to see, however.

To his right he could see what looked like a fairground of bright lights and flashing blue and red strobes sparkling through the night sky.

That had to spell trouble.

Adan Hamati's mind raced. Those were obviously police cars up to the right – the direction he needed to take.

Back down to the left, the direction from which he'd come, was the barrier he had signalled into place. If he turned back there, his people probably wouldn't recognise his vehicle in the darkness of the night – they certainly wouldn't be expecting him to approach from the wrong direction – and would pelt him with the missiles they'd prepared, following his very own instructions. With his vehicle packed with high-explosives, this was not an end Adan relished. He certainly didn't mind dying, he just didn't want to die killing his own people, and above all not without taking as many of the Zionist enemy as possible.

That left just one option. Press on. Continue on to the right, toward Dimona. Just as he was about to slip the gear lever into first gear and inch his way forward in the dark, Adan saw the night sky to the left light up with flashes of flame and he saw the headlights of a car approach the barricade at high speed.

Adan watched in dismay as the car made it through the barricade, slowing down only momentarily before it ploughed on through. It sped on into the desert at breakneck speed, heading straight for the police vehicles up ahead. Adan noticed that this too was an unmarked police vehicle – it had a flashing blue light perched on the roof and blue and red strobes up front and rear.

Not good.

Adan thought for a minute, then made up his mind. He'd go ahead with his plan, come what may. At least he'd take a few of the bastards with him.

Just as he was about to move off, another car approached the barrier from the same direction, barrelling on at high speed and breaking through it without slowing down. In fact, it even accelerated, judging by the sound of the engine that was carried on the still night air. With his window down Adan could even hear distant screams of pain – or rage – as this second car, also boasting the flashing blue light of the police, continued onward at even higher speed than the previous one.

Adan didn't have much time to lose. Up to now, he'd been a bit ahead of schedule. Now, he had no time to lose. He shifted the gear lever resolutely into first gear and drove carefully out from behind his makeshift hideaway and bumped up onto the tarmac.

Years ago he'd seen that American movie, what was it called? Two unpronounceable names, women's names. The film was about two middle-aged women who were being chased by half the police force of the United States for something Adan never quite understood. Typical Hollywood rubbish. The two women were driving a beautiful old American convertible and when they reckoned they had nowhere to flee and nothing more to lose, with the police closing in behind them, they floored the accelerator and flew straight off the edge of a cliff, their speeding car sending them to their deaths at the bottom of the ravine far below.

Very romantic, very Hollywood, very idiotic.

Adan Hamati had no intention of speeding uselessly to his death.

He wasn't going anywhere alone. A whole lot of other people were going to be sent to their deaths with him.

If he had his way.

Looking up into the night sky one last time for the light that would signal the start of his mission, Adan Hamati strained his ears for the sound that would indicate he should be on his way.

Still nothing.

He paused, engaged four-wheel drive for the rocky stretch ahead of him, and bumped his way back up onto the tarmac, slipping back into two-wheel drive and continuing slowly in the direction of Dimona.

Up ahead of him the fairground of coloured lights – white, red and blue – was still pulsating on and off with a bright irregular beat.

Adan Hamati paused by the roadside, headlights still off. He looked at the scene ahead and from the elevated seating position in his Toyota Hilux, he could see a couple of civilian police cars, one of them seemed to have driven off the road. These must be the ones that had broken through his barricade, he thought, because their bodywork and at least the rear glass too was smashed. In the middle of the road was a grey Land Rover, and on either side of the road and up ahead on the tarmac there was an assortment of official vehicles with flashing blue and red lights, motorcycles as well as off-roaders.

And in between them, with a sinking heart, at least one vehicle he recognised from his carefully laid plans. A white Peugeot van. Near it was another car he didn't recognise, a new-looking red SUV.

But even from where he was and through the people milling around the brightly lit scene, he recognised a number of faces.

First of all, the four people on the ground in various grotesque poses. He could only assume they were dead because they didn't move and everybody ignored them.

Then there was that small black woman. He'd seen her in Gothenburg just a year ago! What was this all about, how on earth could she be so close to him? Again! Who was she, anyway?

But above all, it was the sight of the tall fair-haired giant of a man that made up Adan Hamati's mind.

His nemesis from Gothenburg – and once again from across the sand dunes and security barrier in Gaza. The one whom he'd last seen standing atop a dusty Land Rover looking in his direction through a pair of binoculars!

Him again! Blondie!

Adan smiled to himself, a mirthless grin of savagery. His upper lip curled, revealing a row of perfect white teeth. He wanted to sink those teeth into that bastard's jugular.

No matter, the whole lot of them would go up in one glorious bonfire.

Adan's mind was made up. So near yet so far! He could almost touch the perimeter fence of the Dimona nuclear facility! To be stopped here! This was too much.

Blondie would pay. So would the rest of them. Adan had nothing to lose.

Engine still idling, he opened the driver's door quietly and got out. Stepping back to the rear offside, he reached into the cargo bed and quickly located what he knew was there, waiting for him. There was just once single control for arming the whole vehicle. For safety's sake it required a simultaneous two-handed operation, a kind of primitive dead-man's grip. Adan smiled at the irony of the expression. Pulling the two wire-fed controls into the front via the open driver's window, he got back behind the wheel, said a prayer for Palestine, engaged first gear, pressed the control in his left hand while grasping the steering wheel with the same hand, then picked up the remaining control in his right hand.

He looked at it thoughtfully. Not pensively – he was resigned to his fate, it was what he desired. He just wished he could be around to see the effect of his action. What a pity he'd miss the after-effects. Dismissing the thought with a shrug of nonchalance, the fingers of his right hand grasped, then pressed, the control into the palm of his hand. It was now armed.

There was only one way for this to end.

It could only end with the pressure being released in either his left or his right hand.

Either action would have the same effect.

The Toyota would blow a crater the size of a football stadium in the Negev Desert. If it was not to be near the Dimona Nuclear Facility, it would be among a group of Zionist security forces.

Allah would welcome him.

And dance on the remains of the Jews.

Adan Hamati floored the accelerator and the off-roader leapt forward on the tarmac, speeding towards the pool of light in the otherwise dark desert night.

Near Dimona, Israel

It was Marita Ohlsson who raised the alarm.

She was standing apart from the others, speaking in Swedish on the phone to her superiors in Stockholm.

Because she was outside the ring where all the action was taking place, where all the bright lights blinded them to what was happening beyond the illuminated circle and where all the noise obliterated the sounds of anything approaching from outside the crime scene, nobody apart from Marita saw or heard a thing.

It was Marita who saw a large dark shape barrelling down toward them at speed, no headlights on but diesel engine growling powerfully.

Without thinking she yelled a warning, but it was in Swedish, which the Israeli security officers would not have understood.

But Amira and Benny Hart were there, and they were both native Swedish speakers. Bilingual, at any rate.

Amira yelled in Hebrew for everyone to get off the road, while Benny swivelled around behind the grey Land Rover and pulled out his gun in one fluid motion. As his right hand unholstered the Glock and started bringing it up to firing height, his left hand pulled the slider back and instinctively grasped the grip to steady it further. No bothering with the button safety – experienced operators relied on the second built-in safety, the duplicate trigger that also had to be pressed to fire the weapon. Precious micro-seconds could be saved in an emergency.

Like now. Even as the muzzle was on its way up it was already spitting bullets into the oncoming pick-up. As the sound of Benny Hart's gun crackled through the night, the advancing Toyota, now no more than about three hundred metres away, was met with a hail of bullets from the Tavors, M4s and Glocks of the other security officers, who had all plunged off the roadway and were standing well away from the tarmac, feet planted firmly on the ground as they pumped round after round into the approaching blacked-out off-roader. Only Marita stood unable to help, unarmed as she was on foreign soil. She did the only thing she felt might help – she wrenched open the door of the still-idling Land Rover and, still standing on the road, reached in and released the handbrake, engaged reverse in the automatic transmission and let the off-roader rumble backward, driverless, into the path of the oncoming pick-up.

As the two vehicles approached one another, one going full speed ahead and the other plodding along in reverse at a rather agricultural gait, the shooting stopped because nobody wanted to hit the driver of the Land Rover.

Only there wasn't a driver in it.

Adan Hamati didn't know that. He yelled "Allahu Akhbar!" and consigned his soul to his god and his people as the force of the impact wrenched his left hand off the steering wheel and released his grip on the bomb remote control.

The shock-wave was massive. The noise was ear-shattering and the force of the explosion sent the sturdy Land Rover hurtling vertically several metres into the air before it came crashing down in large chunks, landing squarely on the bodies of the four dead terrorists.

As it exploded in a ball of flame, the back of the Toyota curved into the shape of a banana from the sheer force of the energy suddenly released. The entire rear of the vehicle flew in small pieces into the air and blasted an area several metres behind the vehicle. Anyone in its vicinity would have been shredded to pieces. But there was nobody behind the Toyota pick-up. And in front of it, the sturdy Land Rover had taken the brunt of the force.

As the last pieces of wreckage floated slowly to earth and the assembled group of motley security officers – Dimona Nuclear Security, Shin Bet, Mossad and SÄPO – surveyed the scene, it slowly dawned on Benny that he had witnessed a miracle.

Not only had nobody apart from the person driving the approaching vehicle been injured or killed.

There was one sound, near at hand, that was eclipsing everything else.

The front half of the Toyota was still more or less intact. It wasn't connected to the back of the car. In fact, the back of the vehicle didn't even exist except as piles of assorted metal bits and pieces strewn over a wide area to the rear.

The front half, which consisted of just the front wheels and the engine compartment, with the vestige of the windscreen's metal frame still more or less intact but glassless and twisted out of shape, was lying forlornly in the road.

And the engine was still running sweetly.

Holstering his weapon as he approached the wreckage, Benny Hart surveyed the scene and burst out laughing.

The others looked at him, wondering if the Shin Bet agent had gone mad.

"Toyota quality!" spluttered Benny weakly between giggles. "The bloody thing just blew up, taking half the Negev Desert with it, but the engine is still running!"

Holding his sides as laughter racked his body, Benny peered at the surprisingly intact grille in the front of the wrecked Japanese pick-up.

"But of course!" he lapsed into a new bout of helpless laughter. "Toyota Hilux! Don't you people watch TV at all? Seems BBC motoring programme Top Gear was right after all, you simply can't destroy a Toyota Hilux!" And with that he was off once again into peals of uncontrollable laughter.

After a few moments he calmed down and regained his composure. There was a whole lot of work to be getting on with. Dead bodies – now unfortunately crushed almost beyond recognition by exploding cars.

At least one dead body in the Toyota Hilux – his mouth twitched involuntarily as he once again recalled the BBC TV motoring programme episode in which the three journalists had spent an entire week to trying to kill one of these vehicles, setting fire to it, blowing up an entire building under it, drowning it, attacking it with a wrecking-ball, only to see it survive all that maltreatment and more besides.

'C'mon, get serious!' he muttered to himself. 'There's work to be done here, lots of it.' Starting with forensic identification of the person at the wheel of the Toyota.

Surveying the scene of mayhem and destruction, Benny Hart realised that it could all have ended up much worse. Very much worse.

For the moment, at least, he thought with a sigh of relief, the Apocalypse Scenario could be put back into its restraints.

Today, at least, there was no need to unleash it.

But it had been a very close thing. Very close indeed.

Swedish Foreign Office, Stockholm

Israeli Ambassador to Sweden Ronit Gottlieb smiled sweetly but said nothing.

The Swedish Foreign Minister was almost apoplectic with frustration, spittle flying from the corners of her beautifully painted lips.

"I want you to know that we are taking this very seriously, very seriously indeed. Four Swedish citizens executed in cold blood by your security forces! No civilised nation in the world would be expected to condone this kind of appalling behaviour. We will be recalling our ambassador from Tel Aviv for consultations!" She spat out the words, shaking visibly with rage.

"Indeed, Madam Minister," replied Ronit Gottlieb, crossing one immaculately trousered leg over the other and leaning back in her chair, making herself even more comfortable. "It is regrettable that your office is taking this stance. "You will recall – no, please do *NOT* interrupt me!" she smiled dangerously at the Swedish Foreign Minister. "I repeat, do not interrupt me, I haven't finished speaking and I have absolutely no intention of abiding by your bizarre interpretation of diplomatic protocol."

The Foreign Minister looked like her heart was about to explode but she was so taken aback at being baited in her own lair that she slumped back into her seat, beads of perspiration forming on her forehead just below her neatly brushed blonde hairline.

Israel's ambassador to Stockholm Ronit Gottlieb continued, speaking quietly but with the disdain apparent in her voice. "You will recall that your four Swedish citizens killed two of your own police officers. You may not take that seriously, but in my country, we take a very dim view of police officers being murdered in the line of duty. Secondly, they killed two Swedish civilians. I understand," she held up her hand in warning as the Foreign Minister showed signs of spluttering a response. "I understand that you may not take that very seriously either – they were after all just Jews. But again, in my country, we treat all people alike. Oh I know you prefer not to believe that, spouting your usual trite nonsense about 'Israeli apartheid'. But that merely shows your own woeful ignorance – you seem not to be aware that many of the judges in our high court are Arab, some Muslim and others Christian, and that in the entire Middle East, the only country where Christianity is actually growing is in Israel. And that's before we even begin to mention that the only nation in the world with a net increase in Shia Muslim followers is – you guessed it – Israel."

Ambassador Ronit Gottlieb leaned forward in her chair and fixed the Foreign Minister with a hard stare.

"Don't forget," she went on, "that an elderly Swedish pensioner was also killed in the attack carried out on your home territory by the four Swedish citizens for whom you suddenly seem to have developed an amazing affection after they failed to kill thousands of my people in Israel – Jews, Christians and Muslims alike. You may think nothing of the welfare of your own pensioners, but, once again, in our society, we pride ourselves on treating everyone with equal consideration, especially the aged, the very people who helped build our society. It would appear," continued the Israeli ambassador, "that there really isn't very much you and I have in common, at least not when it comes to the sanctity of human life."

"And that brings me to the third issue, the third thing that your four Swedish citizens did – on Swedish soil – that appears not to worry you overly. The attempt on my life and that of my husband. Understand one thing: were it not for our excellent Swedish SÄPO bodyguards, who extracted us from that life-threatening situation at great personal risk to themselves, you would have had an international incident on your hands."

Ronit Gottlieb leaned back once again, making a great show of examining her immaculate fingernails.

She looked up again. "Of course," she continued slowly, "if it's an international incident you want, we're perfectly happy to oblige you with one. You are of course totally at liberty to recall your ambassador 'for consultations' as you so loftily put it. And we are equally at liberty to direct that upon your ambassador's return to our shores, the Swedish Embassy in Israel be moved to Sderot. That's just across the border from

Gaza – you know Sderot, the town that your Hamas buddies use for target practice every time you send them more Swedish money with which they can build even more rockets."

She paused. The Foreign Minister hadn't said a word, but looked as though she was about to have a heart attack. Was she really hearing this? In her own office, besides?

She was.

"Because we will, you know," continued the Israeli ambassador. "And we'll say we're relocating you specifically for your protection. Because with the high level of Hamas attacks against our state – tacitly and sometimes even overtly financed by the current Swedish government – we reckon that the safest place for your embassy is Sderot because that is where we have the best coverage from missile attacks thanks to our Iron Dome anti-missile system.

"Of course," she went on, a small smile playing on her lips, "Iron Dome is very expensive to run, so it may not be operational all the time...

"And with all those tunnels dug into Israel by the Hamas government you so strongly support, there's always the chance that your embassy staff driving to and from your new embassy in Sderot may unfortunately be the target of Hamas terrorists – sorry, I mean 'freedom-fighters' to use your preferred vocabulary – who make their way into Israel. Why, only the other day there was a tunnel collapse caused by a leaking water pipe in one of the tunnels your friends had dug a long time ago. If not just water but also information were somehow to leak in the opposite direction, to certain key people in Gaza," the ambassador smiled pleasantly, "to the effect that your official embassy cars are actually disguised Shin Bet vehicles, and details were somehow provided of your planned car journeys, who knows what might happen?" She paused and gazed innocently at the stunned Foreign Minister.

"And don't forget," she added, hammering home the final nail in the coffin, the one that meant the most to the soft-bellied Western diplomatic corps based in Tel Aviv that just loved that coastal city with its bustling café life, extensive cultural activities, pristine beaches and endless rounds of Embassy socialising, "don't forget that down in Sderot, your embassy will have none of the wonderful facilities to which they've become so accustomed in Tel Aviv…"

She let the sentence drift away unfinished, looking interestedly out of the large panorama window of the Foreign Minister's office and taking in the vibrant scene outside in Sweden's beautiful capital city of Stockholm.

The Swedish Foreign Minister looked as though she'd been punched in the midriff by a particularly hefty boxer.

Israeli Ambassador Ronit Gottlieb smiled sweetly and got to her feet. "Well, if there's nothing more, Madam Minister, I'll take my leave. No, please don't bother to get up, I won't be shaking your hand."

And with that the ambassador turned on her heel and sauntered slowly out of the grand office, shutting the door gently behind her and smiling angelically at the Foreign Minister's personal assistant hovering nervously beside his desk in the anteroom.

Aftermath: Israel-Gaza border

It was the sudden collapse of a long, narrow stretch of open field that trigged the most brutal war yet between the Jewish state and the Islamist rulers of Gaza.

Day after day, week after week, the steady seeping of water from the faulty water pipe in what had been the 'Al Quds' tunnel used by Amir Assaf and Zahir Tafesh had undermined the sandy foundations of the tunnel. True, this tunnel like all the others was lined with arched concrete panels for added strength. The problem was that the concrete panels themselves had to rest on something.

Sand.

And that sand was being gradually, inexorably, eroded away by the steady flow of water from the leaking pipe.

A three hundred metre long stretch of Hamas attack tunnel leading from Gaza into Israel collapsed one Friday morning in spectacular style. The *kibbutznik* ploughing the field with his heavy John Deere tractor got the shock of his life when the small front wheels wobbled for no apparent reason as they drove over a perfectly normal-looking stretch of open field, followed moments later by the massive rear wheels and heavy rear-mounted plough plunging vertically down as the soft surface collapsed.

Hardly daring to move in his air-conditioned tractor cab for fear of further unsettling the stricken green behemoth, farmer Ari Leibowitz called his kibbutz on the in-cab com-radio and informed them that he had likely ploughed through a Hamas tunnel opening.

That call was relayed to the military command centre at nearby Ze'ilim army base which despatched local forces at high speed to secure the area.

When the first IDF Humvee pulled up alongside the tractor, whose engine was still running, its large front tyres bit down through the soft surface as it lurched to a halt and the heavy front of the vehicle, with its massive 6.5-litre diesel engine still throbbing, disappeared into a void that suddenly opened up beneath it.

The driver and his two heavily armed colleagues only just managed to scramble to safety before the rest of the lumbering vehicle lurched crazily and then slipped slowly, majestically, into the gaping underground cavern that seemed to be opening up along a neat east-west ribbon. The whole process was slow, almost ultra-slow, like in a cartoon.

But there was nothing cartoon-like about the frantic response it elicited.

As the first Israel Air Force helicopter arrived, hovering above the scene of ever-expanding carnage and confusion below, from her position in the cockpit pilot Karni Avnery saw how the line of collapse snaked west under Israel's security barrier and the three hundred metre wide no-go zone of the Gaza Strip.

And from the Gaza Strip the missiles started flying in response as confused Hamas and Islamic Jihad warriors interpreted the action – and the collapsing snake of sand clawing its way into their territory – as an attack by the Zionists.

The fury of the initial missile barrage from Gaza was followed up immediately by hurried calls to Hamas and Islamic Jihad martyrs to rush to their predetermined attack tunnels to carry out suicide bombing missions via the relatively few remaining concealed tunnel openings deep inside Israeli territory.

Israel meanwhile unleashed a veritable wall of artillery fire against predetermined command and control targets in the Gaza Strip, taking out military targets wherever they were to be found.

And because the Gaza Strip was ruled by Hamas, that meant military targets deliberately and cynically embedded within civilian population centres – under hospitals, in schools, inside the many UN facilities that consistently turned a blind eye to terrorist operations within their internationally funded domain.

After its energy-sapping war with Hamas in summer 2014, Israel had finally decided that 'never again' actually meant just that: the Jewish state would never again allow itself to be fought to a standstill for weeks and months on end by Islamists hell-bent on terrorising the country's civilian population. Israel's problem was not, and never had been, the military might or fighting prowess of its adversaries; it was the fact that the Jewish state was compelled by the rest of the world community to fight a slow war with one hand tied behind its back. While Islamist foes flying the flags of Hezbollah, Fatah, Islamic Jihad, Hamas and countless other groups used their own civilians for cover and targeted Israeli civilians, the world community remained silent. But when Israel took steps to counter these attacks, even taking the unprecedented step of warning civilians in enemy territory of forthcoming assaults so they could leave the target area, the world community roundly condemned the Jewish state for any and every death in the clearly defined target zone.

The relatively new Israeli government of Prime Minister Tal Nahum had decided after summer 2014 that 'never again' really would be 'never again'. If Israel were to be unfairly blamed, ostracised, sanctioned and penalised for waging a defensive war even in the most moral way possible, castigated and abused by a world forum kowtowing to Arab and wider Islamist sensitivities, then Israel might as well, for the first time ever, actually earn that criticism.

Israel would get the job done, once and for all. The Jewish state, its back to the Mediterranean Sea, could hardly be treated any worse than it already was. It might as well do what it was constantly being accused of doing. What difference could it possibly make?

And so the Apocalypse Scenario played out in Gaza.

It had been designed to be deployed against Iran and by default against Iran's brutal Shia proxy, Hezbollah.

Now it was instead wreaking wholesale havoc, death and destruction on the already embattled Gaza Strip.

A Gaza Strip whose terrified civilian population was sandwiched between their hated Islamist Hamas rulers on the inside, the utterly detested Egyptian army to the south, the Israeli navy keeping guard in the blue waters of the Mediterranean to the west.

And now also the veritable wall of iron and lead pulverising their already shattered economy, lives and territory from the east, from artillery positions in Israel's Negev desert and from the air.

Benny Hart had done his utmost to keep the Apocalypse Scenario safely on a leash.

But snap judgements, human error, a leaking water pipe and the loose sands of Gaza determined otherwise.

The threat beneath had become an apocalyptic scenario. And everyone's worst nightmare had become reality.

In Tehran, the Iranian President put down his phone, sat back in his comfortably upholstered chair and smiled gently.

In Stockholm, Sweden's Islamist Prime Minister Mahmud Sadeghi snapped shut his encrypted mobile phone, placed it gently on his desk, got up from his seat and walked over to the large windows giving a panoramic view across the rooftops of the beautiful capital of Sweden.

He rubbed his hands in suppressed excitement.

What was it his imam in the Stockholm suburb of Rinkeby had taught him, all those years ago, about the 'end of days'?

Ashdod, Israel

"This isn't going to work."

Benny Hart glowered at his pint-sized sister Amira. "I said we'd be at home all weekend and didn't want to be disturbed." He sat back, quietly fuming as Marita Ohlsson, draped in one of his outsize shirts and precious little else, beat a diplomatic retreat to the upstairs bathroom for a shower. Let the brother and sister sort things out themselves.

"And I said I'd be home all weekend – and would be having company of my own!" Amira Hart retorted. "Check your phone sometime. Although I suppose you were too *busy* (she emphasised the word) to come up for air."

Benny Hart leaned against the kitchen counter and looked quizzically at his older sister. He'd never seen her like this before. Sure, she was feisty. Large and massively strong though he was, he had always been in awe of her mental agility – he'd never yet won an argument against her – and of the tongue-lashings she was prone to launch into if things didn't work out as intended.

But this – THIS – he'd never seen before. My goodness, the pint-sized *bint* was actually blushing! Under her ebony-black skin, Amira Hart was blushing red hot – even the roots of her glossy black hair seemed to be flaming red.

A slow, wicked smile spread across his face.

"What's his name and how much are you prepared to pay?" he asked innocently. "I mean, Marita and I can drive up to Netanya for the rest of the weekend, the Park Hotel has good weekend deals, but not until I get a name."

Amira opened her mouth to fire off a suitably chastising response when they both distinctly heard the sound of a car pull up by the front door, followed by the dull thud of a car door shutting. A moment later the doorbell rang.

Before Amira had the presence of mind to either reply to Benny or move toward the door, Benny strode over and yanked it open.

His eyes took in a massive bouquet of flowers, and somewhere above and behind them was the puzzled face of Calev Mizrachi. Amira Hart's boss, he of the famously few words. Apparently, what he didn't put into words, he put into floral tributes. The bouquet he was proffering must have been the equivalent of at least half the annual harvest of Israel's Sharon-area greenhouses.

Benny Hart's surprise was matched by that of the visitor. The last thing Calev had expected to see was a large blond man. And just to make matters worse, walking down the stairs in a crisp white T-shirt, skimpy white shorts and hair glistening wet from a recent shower was a girl.

But not the girl Calev Mizrachi had come to see. This one was blonde, fair-skinned, blue-eyed and very pretty.

The girl he had come to see was raven-haired, dark-skinned, black-eyed and extraordinarily beautiful. As far as Calev Mizrachi was concerned, this blonde couldn't even stand in the same room as Amira without looking like something on which you hung your coat and hat.

Out of the shadow behind the huge fair-haired man filling the door opening stepped the girl he had come to see.

Amira Hart smiled hesitantly and dug the fingers her left hand deep into the small of her brother's back, squeezing tight and causing him to wince in pain.

As Calev Mizrachi's frown deepened Benny smiled through his pain, stretched out his right hand and took the flowers from a somewhat taken-aback Calev.

"How beautiful! Thank you so much! But look, I'm already spoken for – let me introduce you to Marita Ohlsson. She's on a visit here from Sweden. But do you know my sister Amira? She works for the Mossad. What's your name, what do you do for a living and how much money does your father have in the bank?"

And before either Calev or Amira had time to recover their wits Benny turned around, thrust the flowers into Amira's face, grabbed Marita by the hand and strode out of the house.

He was grinning broadly and chuckling to himself.

His miniature big sister was finally growing up!

Marita Ohlsson glanced sideways at Benny as they walked to her Mazda rental. She shook her head in mock despair and wondered, not for the first time: how on earth would the Jewish state ever resolve the issue of sovereignty over Jerusalem, when even brother and sister couldn't agree on sovereignty over a modest family home in Ashdod.

END

Author's note

How much of *"The Threat Beneath"* is fiction, how close is the reality?

Can navigation aid "Waze" really be manipulated to create such havoc on a national scale?

Are the Gaza attack tunnels really such an existential threat to the Jewish state?

Is it true that Gaza's Hamas rulers really do hate the Egyptian president as much as this book suggests, which would mean that Hamas detests Egypt almost as much as it detests rival Palestinian faction Fatah?

Is it really true that the animosity Hamas feels toward Egypt and Fatah matches the hatred the Gaza-based terrorists feel toward Israel?

And perhaps most important of all: does Israel have a plan along the lines of the book's 'Apocalypse Scenario'?

As always in a thriller, the believable has to be interwoven with verifiable fact and a healthy dose of fiction – fabrications and lies inserted into a narrative to deliberately muddy the waters. It's the way worrying scenarios can take on a distinct sheen of reality. Otherwise the reader would be left with either a documentary or pure fantasy.

So if the reader worries about these and other issues after reading the book, that's good.

It's this author's way of (not) answering all the above questions.

Apart from the last one – the question of whether or not Israel has something akin to the book's 'Apocalypse Scenario'.

Only those in the know can answer that question.

But won't, for obvious reasons.

If it exists, what is likely to trigger it? And what form might such a response take?

Germany has to date supplied the Jewish state with 5 Dolphin-class submarines, and another one is possibly in the pipeline at the time of writing (spring 2015).

This is early 2015 and Iran is drawing ever closer to the threshold beyond which it will gain nuclear weapons capability – if indeed it has not already passed that red line, as some analysts suggest.

Hamas has ever-increasing capacity to fire rockets, mortars and other missiles into Israeli population centres. Both from within Gaza population centres such as hospitals, mosques, private homes and schools, and also via the myriad tunnels the terrorist organisation has dug deep into Israeli territory. These rockets are usually not guided. Not for lack of technical ability to integrate guidance systems into the missiles, but deliberately so as to ensure the sheer unpredictability of the attacks and the randomness of their targets. That, after all, is the very essence of terrorism: random, unexpected violence for political gain.

Lebanon's Hezbollah has ably demonstrated its capacity for bringing the Jewish state to a standstill by targeting huge swathes of the country – its civilian heartland and commercial and industrial lifeline – with rockets.

And today Islamic State/Daesh is on the very borders of the embattled Jewish state, from Syria in the north via Jordan in the east to Sinai in the south.

All the above are the immediate, physical, tangible threats facing Israel. They create a scenario that Israelis have learned to deal with over the decades.

But all of this is relatively minor, they are obstacles that are relatively easily to overcome. By far the bigger existential threat to Israel is posed by Western nations with a pathological inability to view Israel with anything approaching objectivity. For various reasons: voter demographics, political correctness, abject fear of Islamist retribution, over-dependence on fossil fuels, the sudden realisation that the inexorable interdependence of Western economies and the blinkered focus on short-term financial gain have over the years resulted in several key industries, including basic infrastructure, falling into the ownership of wealthy Middle East nations, rendering the West increasingly vulnerable.

Thrown somewhere into the mix is the sometimes not-so-dormant animus towards Jews: anti-Semitism. All these parameters and more play a role in the uniquely anti-Israel stance of many countries in the West.

Sweden is perhaps one of the foremost proponents of this drive against the Jewish state.

Not the people of Sweden. Certainly not those in uniform, whether military, security services, police, fire service and ambulance first-responders, nurses and doctors. But a politically indoctrinated elite among the nation's politicians, journalists and religious leaders.

"*The Threat Beneath*" has its base in the massive, deliberate and virtually uncontrolled drive by Sweden's political masters to conduct what is probably the largest social experiment in modern history: a demographic transformation – some might say outright demographic exchange – whereby a hundred thousand Muslims are being brought into the country and given Swedish citizenship. Every single year. This means that in just one decade, Sweden's population will grow by one-tenth, by a million people.

But it is an elusive "growth". Because this move is already being mirrored by a trickling – and growing – exodus of native Swedes who no longer feel at home in their own home country.

So what Sweden is experiencing is not growth but an unequal exchange of populations. An exchange that boosts segregation and throws already stark social differences into even greater relief.

It does not bode well for Sweden's future.

"*The Threat Beneath*" is not about Sweden's future, it is very much about the country's present. The troubling predicament created by the nation's politicians with a naiveté bordering on self-destruction. This naiveté has prompted Sweden's media, political elite and religious leaders to adopt a skewed focus against the Jewish state while at the same time ignoring the looming threat of global Islamism.

"*Bridges Going Nowhere*" (2014) was the first of this trilogy of thrillers — narratives with a clear socio-political content whose backdrop is the Middle East conflict. It dealt with past events in and around Israel and the way those events impacted Sweden's often partisan relationship with the Jewish state.

"*The Threat Beneath*" is the second book in the trilogy. It deals with the present situation as the complexities of an unravelling Middle East impact domestic politics in what ought to be a faraway country in Scandinavia with no apparent axe to grind, but which nevertheless insists on trying to play a robust role. Almost always with dire results for itself and for the various parties involved — the Israelis, the Palestinians, the Islamists spreading their poison throughout the world, and the innocent people fleeing the spread of their death cult.

The third book in the trilogy will deal with Sweden's future as seen from its unique, complex and often unexpectedly symbiotic present-day relationship with Israel.

The two nations have a lot more in common than meets the eye — despite the animosity of Sweden's intractable mainstream media, its politicians and religious leaders headed by the heavily politicised Church of Sweden.

The last book in the trilogy will be published in 2016.

Ilya Meyer, April 2015

Acknowledgements

As before I owe a huge debt of gratitude to my wife Rachel for her unflagging support, encouragement and objectivity while this, the second book in *The Hart Trilogy*, took shape during the autumn and winter of 2014.

While I was writing *The Threat Beneath*, reality overtook the fiction of the story not once but twice, necessitating major rewrites of the storyline; following the attacks on Charlie Hebdo and a kosher supermarket in Paris, I felt compelled to rewrite my already completed chapters detailing an Islamist attack on a newspaper in Gothenburg, and a scene where terrorists attacked a supermarket in Gothenburg leaving several people dead. Those scenes – and everything leading up to them and following from them – had to be rewritten from the ground up. I rather suspect that Swedish Security Service SÄPO by now wants to either indict me for planning terrorist activities, or possibly hire me to write simulated scenarios for their training…

The bitter reality that is a backdrop to *The Hart Trilogy* is just that – reality. Fiction in action, characters and venues, but against an increasingly depressing and very tangible reality.

I owe particular thanks to my son Nadav for his untiring patience in assisting with a wide variety of operational and publication technicalities, and to my nephew Noah for his wonderful artwork for the cover of this book and the second edition of its precursor, *Bridges Going Nowhere*.

Made in the USA
Charleston, SC
10 May 2015